NO COOPERATION
FROM THE CAT

NO COOPERATION FROM THE CAT

A Mystery

Marion Babson

WINDSOR
PARAGON

First published 2012
by St. Martin's Press
This Large Print edition published 2012
by AudioGO Ltd
by arrangement with
the Author

Hardcover   ISBN: 978 1 4713 1303 5
Softcover   ISBN: 978 1 4713 1304 2

COMM.
RES
11/12

British Library Cataloguing in Publication Data available

Printed and bound in Great Britain by
MPG Books Group Limited

There's more than one way to
skin a cat
But, no matter which way you try it,
You can be sure of one thing: you ain't
a-gonna get no co-operation
from the cat.

— *Anon*

CHAPTER ONE

Life is full of little embarrassments. Especially when Evangeline is around.

Dame Cecile Savoy had made a perfectly reasonable request: a gin and tonic. The last time I had seen the gin bottle, it had been nearly a quarter full. Now it was empty.

"Evangeline —" I called. "Have you been cleaning your diamonds again?"

"I'm cleaning yours, too." She appeared in the doorway, holding a glass jug with a tangle of jewellery immersed in a once-clear liquid. "We can't appear at the BAFTA Awards wearing grubby gems — and yours are absolutely filthy. It's all that Play-Doh from your games with the children."

"It's not Play-Doh," I said. "It's the real thing. Martha let us have the leftover pastry scraps for pastries and tarts. They were delicious. But Dame Cecile wants a gin and tonic."

"She would." Evangeline sniffed, swished

the gin around, and offered, "I could pour some off for you. There'll still be enough left to finish cleaning."

"Don't bother!" Dame Cecile looked at the sludge on offer and shuddered. "I'll just have some of your brandy instead."

"Fresh out." Evangeline smirked. "We need more. I was going to remind you, Trixie."

"You can't remind me of something you never told me in the first place," I said coldly. I hate being caught with my hospitality down.

"Well, what *do* you have?" Dame Cecile was losing patience.

"There's rum —"

"No, there isn't," Evangeline said. "Martha is soaking the sultanas in the last of it for her spice cakes."

"Whisky —"

"Martha made that Scottish dessert that's all whisky and oatmeal yesterday. We need more oatmeal, too."

"There's vodka —" I belatedly recalled that the last time I had seen the glass jug Evangeline was holding, it had been filled to the brim with Bloody Marys for Sunday brunch — and replenished at least twice. "No, perhaps not."

"Definitely not," Evangeline said.

"Perhaps a liqueur . . . ?" I waited. It came.

"The cherry brandy went into the cherry cobbler, the Grand Marnier into the whipped cream for the profiteroles, and the last of the crème de menthe into the peppermint creams. I tell you, Martha is cooking us out of house and home!"

Dame Cecile began tapping her foot.

"The cookbook will be finished soon," I promised. "Then Martha and Jocasta will vacate our kitchen and life will get back to normal."

"Normal?" Dame Cecile gave a sardonic laugh. "You two don't know the meaning of the word!"

"Look who's talking!" Evangeline glared at her. "I can remember when —"

The doorbell cut across this promising opening. No one else moved, so I went to answer it.

"Trixie." My son-in-law brushed my cheek with his lips and straightened up, inhaling deeply.

"Martha's spice cakes." He identified the aroma. "Splendid! Just what I could use with a cup of tea right now."

"We have lemon squares, too, and raspberry tartlets. Martha and Jocasta have been cooking up a storm."

"Better and better." He started down the

hallway, impeded slightly by Cho-Cho-San and Frou-Frou, who came frolicking to greet him.

"How are you, girls?" He stopped to pat the little powder puff a Japanese Bobtail has for a tail and to roughhouse lightly with Dame Cecile's French toy poodle puppy. He didn't linger, he was too anxious to get to Martha. I followed him.

"Darling," I said, when they had unwound themselves. "It's time for another trip to the supermarket. Is there anything we can get for you while we're there?"

"Oh, yes, please, Mother. We're running out of a lot of things. I'll make a list."

"Butter," Jocasta said. "Butter and margarine. I found a quaint little book with over thirty recipes for savoury butter — and we want to try them with margarine, too. So many people use that these days."

"Margarine needs all the help it can get." Evangeline had joined us. "I tried some once — and I haven't had a taste like that in my mouth since the time I fell in the swamp when we were filming *Mad Beast of the Bayou*. And then," she brooded, "the director wouldn't let anyone pull me out for half an hour — and he kept the cameras turning all the while. I was deathly ill for a week afterwards."

"Directors don't care if they kill you," Dame Cecile agreed, "especially if they've got most of the film in the can first. But wasn't that the role that won you the Karloff-Lorre Award for Best Beleaguered Heroine of the Year? How we all laughed over here when we heard that."

"When do you want to go shopping?" Martha intervened hastily, before the nasty glint that appeared in Evangeline's eye could resolve itself into action.

"As soon as possible," I said. "We'll just ring Eddie and have him collect us."

"No need for that," Hugh said. "My car is downstairs. Benson will drive you anywhere you care to go."

"Marvellous, Hugh! I'll just change my shoes —" There was no hurry. Martha and Jocasta had their heads together, earnestly debating the present and future ingredients they might need. Their list was growing longer by the minute.

"I'll come along, too," Dame Cecile said. "There are always bits and pieces one wishes to pick up. And I can leave Frou-Frou here and not have to worry about her being tied to railings outside a shop. She's so tiny someone could pop her into a shopping bag — and so friendly it wouldn't occur to her to object."

11

"Fine, fine," Hugh said absently, far more interested in the lemon square he was shoving into his mouth. "We'll take good care of her."

"I'm sure we need more than this." Martha frowned at her list. "I'll just check the larder." She disappeared into the storage space at the back of the kitchen. Evangeline met my eyes accusingly. From the sound of it, we weren't going to get our kitchen back as soon as I had rashly foretold.

Jocasta was still frowning over the incomplete shopping list and no one else seemed inclined to move when the doorbell rang again.

"I'll get it," Hugh said. "It's probably for me, anyway. I left my cell phone in the car and Benson will know enough to bring it to me if there's an urgent call." He carefully selected a raspberry tartlet from the array of delights on the cooling trays and ambled towards the door.

Before he could reach it, the doorbell rang again — and kept ringing insistently, demandingly, and arrogantly. It was reinforced by what was obviously a fist thumping on the door for good measure.

We looked at each other, except for Jocasta, who went on studying her list.

"Either World War Three has just broken

out," Evangeline said, "or that isn't Benson."

We heard the door open. "All right, all right," Hugh said irritably. "Take it easy." There was another thump, as though the door had been pushed so hard and so fast that it had bounced against the wall.

"Where is she?" a voice bellowed. "Where is she? Where is my beautiful bride?"

"I beg your pardon?" we heard Hugh reply.

"Oh, God — it's Banquo!" The colour drained from Jocasta's face. I thought she was going to faint.

"Oh, no! No!" Dame Cecile and Evangeline didn't look so well themselves.

"She said it!" Evangeline gasped. "She actually said it!"

"How dare you!" Dame Cecile rounded on Jocasta. "You wretched, wretched child! Now you've done it!"

"Quick!" Evangeline snatched at Jocasta's arm. "You must go outside, shut the door behind you, then turn around three times and —"

"No, no, no!" Dame Cecile said. "That's for whistling in the dressing room. She has to use profanity to drive the evil spirits away. Just start saying all the obscene words you know?" She looked at Jocasta doubtfully.

13

"You *do* know —"

"I thought that was for a hat on the bed," Evangeline said. "How about — ?"

I knew the superstition they were on about, only "Oh, God — it's Banquo!" didn't sound very Shakespearean to me. But what do I know? A few seasons on the Straw Hat Circuit playing Bianca in *Kiss Me, Kate* was as close to Shakespeare as I ever got.

"I've remembered!" Dame Cecile declared triumphantly. "She has to say, 'Fair thoughts and happy hours attend on you' from *The Merchant of Venice*. And then there's reciting 'Angels and Ministers of Grace defend us.' That's supposed to ward off the bad luck, too. She'd better do both of them, to be on the safe side. And never, never, never" — she glared at poor Jocasta — "quote from That Play again!"

"I wasn't quoting anything," Jocasta protested. "Banquo is his name. And he's here! And he wants — He's looking for —"

"Someone actually named a poor defenceless child Banquo?" Dame Cecile marvelled.

"Some people will do anything," Evangeline said.

"Where's my wife?" Banquo was beginning to sound truculent. "I know she's here. I can smell her — her cooking, that is. She's creating a magnificent cookbook for the

Lady Lemmings."

"I beg your pardon," Hugh said icily. "But it's *my* wife who is creating that cookbook and — Oooof!" There was the sound of a scuffle. "Come back here!"

"You never saw me!" Jocasta clutched my arm desperately. "You don't know where I am! You never heard of me!" She dashed into the bathroom and bolted the door behind her.

"That girl" — Evangeline looked at the closed door — "has been acting very oddly ever since we got back from Brighton."

"Woman," Dame Cecile corrected. "They all want to be called women these days. But have you noticed? The more they insist on being called women, the less like real women they behave."

"Where is she?" A tall wiry man with an unkempt beard shouldered his way into the room and took up a belligerent stance.

"Melisande —" he called. "Melisande — your Banquo has returned! I have dreamed of you through all those Arctic nights — and now I am back triumphant to claim my bride! Where are you? Where is the best little cook in the world?"

"Oh, Hugh!" Martha came out of the larder laughing. "That is the worst imitation of a male chauvinist pig I have ever —"

Banquo moved forward to block her path. They looked at each other with growing incredulity.

"Who" — they demanded simultaneously — "are you?"

"Martha is my wife!" Hugh pushed past Banquo to stand at Martha's side and put a protective — and proprietary — arm across her shoulders. "As I keep telling you. *She* is the compiler and creator of the Lady Lemmings' cookbook."

"She can't be," Banquo said. "Melisande is. Where is Melisande? What have you done with her?"

"*Who* is Melisande?" Martha moved closer to Hugh. "I've never heard of her."

"Melisande is *my* wife, the perfect cook, the perfect woman. I want to see her. I want her now."

"Are you sure —" Evangeline asked delicately. "Are you quite sure you don't mean Jocasta?"

"Jocasta?" He was astonished — and affronted. "Why would I want to see *her?*"

There was a muffled sob from the bathroom. I frowned Evangeline to silence. Occasionally, she can take a cue.

"See here!" Hugh had had enough. "You barge your way in here, shout and bully your way around — and you haven't even had the decency to introduce yourself. Who the hell are you?"

"I —" He all but took a bow. "I am Banquo Fitzfothergill!" He seemed annoyed when none of us reacted to the announcement.

"The media," he prompted, "call me the last of the gentlemen adventurers."

Evangeline and I looked at him and then at each other. Errol Flynn he was not.

"Ah, yes, I remember," Dame Cecile said. "It was a few years back," she explained to us. "He pushed a peanut with his nose — unshelled, of course, for better purchase —" She made it sound vaguely unsporting. "Actually, several peanuts, as they wore out, from Tasmania to the steps of his club in Pall Mall. And when he had to take a ship to cross the seas, he pushed it around the deck all day, on all fours, of course, all the way and —"

"No, no, no!" Banquo spluttered indignantly. "That wasn't me! That was Hubert von Wagnerhoff — you can't call *him* an adventurer." The implication was clear that you couldn't call him a gentleman, either.

"Oh, sorry," Dame Cecile said distantly. "Er, what *do* you do?"

"I," he announced grandly, "am a circumnavigator."

17

"A what?" Evangeline looked to Dame Cecile for a translation. Cecile shrugged her shoulders.

"I circle the world," he said. "I have done it by sailing craft — backwards, against all known tides. I have challenged the Bermuda Triangle — and won! I have just returned from a solo mission to the North Pole to personally monitor the retreat of the glaciers, the melting of the ice floes and —"

"Yes, yes, that's all very well," Hugh said impatiently. "But, whatever you're trying to prove here, you can forget about it. We know nothing about this — er —"

"Melisande," Martha supplied, an increasingly thoughtful look growing in her eyes.

"Yes, well, whatever her name is," Hugh said. "She isn't here — and we know nothing about her. I suggest you go and look for her elsewhere." He began moving forward, looking menacing. "Now!"

Banquo looked uncertain for a moment. Then Evangeline moved forward to stand beside Hugh. That did it. Hugh was menacing enough, but reinforced by Evangeline, he was too formidable to argue with.

"I'll go —" Banquo blustered. "But I'll be back! I'll find her if I have to take this town apart!"

"You do that," Evangeline said. She and

Hugh herded him down the hallway and we all waited silently until we heard the door slam behind him and their footsteps returning.

"Right!" I went over and banged on the bathroom door. "You can come out now, Jocasta," I called. "He's gone."

CHAPTER TWO

After a long moment, the door edged open cautiously and Jocasta peeked out. "You're sure? He's really gone? He won't come back?"

"Not immediately," Hugh said grimly.

"Who — ?" Evangeline went straight to the heart of the matter. "Who is this Melisande? And what have you done with her?"

"Melisande —" Jocasta's face crumpled. "I can't be the one to tell him. He'd hate me forever!" She began to sob. "I can't!"

"There, there, you don't have to," I soothed. "He's gone."

"For the moment," Evangeline said.

"I can't!" Jocasta's sobs increased. She was almost incoherent, but an occasional phrase blubbered through. "Someone else . . . tell him . . . I can't! . . . I can't!"

"Pull yourself together, girl!" Dame Cecile snapped. "They don't shoot the messenger anymore. If the man was fool enough to

20

abandon his bride and hare off on some imbecile expedition, it serves him right if she eloped with someone else while he was gone."

"Not shoot but . . . He'll hate me! . . . Never want to speak to me . . . to see me . . . again! . . . I can't! I can't! . . . I can't —"

"We've established that," Evangeline said. "But why should he hate you? Were you the one who introduced her to — ?"

"Just a minute —" Martha interrupted. "He kept saying this woman was writing *my* cookbook! Is that true? Am I second choice? And what kind of contract does she have? Is she going to come back when all the work is done and insist that *her* name is credited for all *my* work?"

"No . . . no . . ." Jocasta wailed. "You don't understand . . . She'll never come back . . . She's dead!"

"Dead?" Dame Cecile was incredulous. "But she must have been a young woman. Don't tell me" — her voice hardened — "she was terminally ill and that revolting idiot went off and left her!"

"He's *not* revolting," Jocasta choked. "And there was nothing wrong with her. Not that anyone knew about. He couldn't have had any idea that —" The great gulping sobs reclaimed her.

"What happened to her then?" Dame Cecile demanded. She and Evangeline exchanged an exasperated look. "Was it an automobile accident?"

"A terrorist attack?" Trust Evangeline to go for the melodramatic option.

"Sudden Adult Death Syndrome?" Dame Cecile was right behind her.

"Hugh — a glass of water!" Martha ordered. He rushed to get it.

"Thank you." Martha appropriated it before he could offer it to Jocasta. I stepped forward hastily, but was too late to prevent Martha from hurling it into Jocasta's face.

"Martha!"

"She's hysterical, Mother." Martha returned the glass to Hugh, who absently refilled it.

"Easy, Jocasta, easy." I put an arm around her shoulders and sacrificed one of my favourite scarves towards mopping her up. "Just tell us."

"It wasn't my fault," she sobbed. "I had nothing to do with it. I wasn't even in the room at the time."

"Of course you weren't," I soothed. "What room? Where? And when? What happened?"

"She collapsed," Jocasta said. "It was so fast. There wasn't anything anyone could do to help her. She died — right at the end of her cooking demonstration at an evening class."

"Why?" Evangeline leaped in with the question we all wanted to ask.

"It —" Jocasta's hysteria hadn't abated, it had just changed form. She began to giggle wildly. "It was something she ate!"

Splash!

"Martha!" This time I had been included in the sudden deluge.

"Oops! Sorry, Mother. But you can see — she's off again."

"That's no reason to drown her. Or me."

"I said I was sorry, Mother." But she wasn't really, I could tell.

"Martha . . . dearest . . ." She was making Hugh nervous, too. This time he ignored the empty glass she thrust at him.

"So this other woman — this Melisande —" Martha glared at Jocasta. "Is it true that *she* was the original choice for *my* cookbook?"

"Y-e-e-s . . ." Jocasta shrank back. "Yes, that's how we started out . . . it was all tied together. But she . . . she died . . . and . . . and . . ."

"And the show must go on!" Martha was working herself into a fury. "And I was *second choice!*"

Oh, dear! Oh, my poor darling Martha. I

hadn't realised that it had rankled so. At the back of my mind, Fanny Brice's rendition of "Second-Hand Rose" began to play:

Even . . . the boy I adore
had the noive to tell me
He'd been married before . . .

Martha was Hugh's second wife and, no matter that he and the first one had been divorced before he met Martha and the unfortunate woman subsequently murdered, it seemed that it had secretly bothered Martha. And now she found out she was second choice for the cookbook, too.

"Martha —" Hugh hadn't realised it, either. "Darling —" He stepped forward and tried to embrace her, but she moved away.

"You might have told me!" she accused him.

"How was I to know?" The injustice clearly stung. "You can't imagine I'd be able to keep up with every piece of fringe activity in the business."

Uh oh — wrong again, Hugh. But when Martha gets into this mood, there's no way any of us can say the right thing.

"Naturally, we kept it as quiet as we could." Indignation was doing a better job of drying Jocasta's tears than sympathy.

24

"The book was still in the early stages, so it was only known about in-house. Publicity hadn't started yet, so the media couldn't latch onto any story about the editor of a cookbook being killed by one of her own recipes. Naturally, her name will never appear on the book now."

"Recipes!" Martha wasn't letting Jocasta off the hook. "Yes, I noticed that we had some recipes already tested, but I was fool enough to assume that you had been doing some preliminary work on the easiest ones."

"I was . . . I am . . ." Jocasta's nerve was beginning to fail again. "And we all really wanted you. Everyone was so enthusiastic when your name was mentioned."

"And you kept it so quiet . . ." That was all we needed, Evangeline sticking her oar in. "So quiet that you didn't even notify her husband — her bridegroom — that his wife had died."

"We couldn't!" Jocasta wailed. "He was out of reach. Incommunicado! There was no way we could get through to him."

"Out there on the frozen tundra!" Evangeline jeered. "Hasn't anyone told you that we have satellite communication these days?"

"Only if the other party is carrying the right equipment. Banquo was trying to re-create the conditions the original Arctic explorers faced. He didn't have a cell phone or anything like that."

"Not even in case of an emergency?" Evangeline was disbelieving. Having seen Banquo, it struck me as hard to swallow, too.

"He wanted to face problems on his own. Without all the technology available nowadays —" A glint of hero worship appeared in her eyes. "He's so brave."

"Foolhardy, I'd say!"

For once, I was in total agreement with Evangeline. The man was careless idiot enough to be a film director.

"And I suppose —" Hugh had been assessing the situation from a different angle. "I suppose your company had a contract with Fitzfothergill for the book of the expedition?"

"Well . . . yes . . ." Jocasta looked away.

"All else aside," Dame Cecile said. "One can quite see why no one would wish to tell such tragic news to a man in his position. It would be much kinder to wait until he returned home and have someone break the news to him then."

"Not me!" Jocasta gave a convulsive shudder. "I can't! I can't! I *won't!*"

Oh, dear. She was off again. She was not only crying, but she seemed unable to stop the shuddering. Or was it shivering? I looked at her more closely.

"You're drenched." Martha had done a thorough job with her glasses of water. "You've got to change out of that wet blouse, you'll catch your death —" I broke off abruptly.

"Come along." I tried again, putting my arm around her. "You can borrow one of my tops. I need to change, too. We'll get into some dry clothes, then we can drop you off at your home on our way to the supermarket."

"No! No!" She pulled away. "I can't go home! Banquo will come looking for me. He knows where I live. I can't go back there!"

She had a point, but . . .

"Then where should we drop you?" Evangeline asked the pertinent question. "At a relative's? A friend's?"

"No, please, no!" Jocasta shrank back. "All my relatives are in Cornwall. My colleagues are my friends and he knows who they are. He'll look for me there next."

Another good point, but . . .

"Which hotel then?" Dame Cecile asked.

"I can't afford a hotel," Jocasta said sadly.

We all looked at each other with that fated feeling about what was coming.

"You have so much room here —" Jocasta said quickly. "And you've already sent him packing. He won't be back soon. I wouldn't be any trouble — and I already have to work here most of the day, anyway, with Martha. I could be your — your housekeeper. I'll cook for you . . . and clean . . . and do anything that needs doing. And you wouldn't have to pay me anything. Oh, please, please."

"Well . . ." Evangeline was already sold on the idea. It was the thought of all that free work that got her.

And I must admit that the idea of someone else doing all the housekeeping was getting through to me. Our cleaning service only came once a week and there was plenty to do in between their visits.

"Mother, do you really think — ?" Only Martha was holding back.

"Please . . ." Jocasta whispered brokenly.

"Prrrr?" Cho-Cho-San and Frou-Frou had been watching with interest from the side-lines. Now Cho-Cho, obviously sensing distress and someone in desperate need of comfort, moved forward to twine around Jocasta's ankles.

"Ooooh!" Jocasta stopped to pick her up and buried her face in the soft fur. Cho-Cho stretched her neck to rub her cheek

28

against Jocasta's.

That made the vote three of us who lived here against one, who only showed up to use our kitchen to test her recipes.

"Just for a couple of days while we see how the situation develops," I told Martha. "What harm can it do?"

Sometimes I wonder if I'll ever learn to keep my big mouth shut.

I must admit that it did feel luxurious in the morning to be awakened by the rich scents of frying bacon and perking coffee. I found Evangeline already seated at the kitchen table with her first cup of coffee.

"Good morning, Evangeline," I said cheerfully enough to annoy her. She gave me a nasty look, continuing to shuffle through a pile of what was obviously junk mail.

Jocasta sent me a harassed smile while flipping over rashers of bacon with the cooking tongs. They slipped — whether accidentally or deliberately, I couldn't say — and a rasher of bacon fell to the floor where Cho-Cho pounced on it with a triumphant cry. Too hot! She backed off, then returned and crouched over it, waiting for it to cool enough to devour. That was a happy cat.

"Good morning, Jocasta, Cho-Cho," I greeted.

"Good morning, Trixie," Jocasta returned automatically.

Cho-Cho looked up and chirped a greeting, then returned to her vigil. I don't think that little cat is ever going to get over her enchantment at discovering that a kitchen is a place where honest-to-Bast food is produced. Before this, her only knowledge of the process involved a tin can and a tin opener, or perhaps a ring pull, or a foil carton. A whole new world had opened to her when I adopted her and I think I can safely say she was in seventh heaven.

"Oh, good!" Evangeline had discovered a real letter amongst the junk. She tore it open and reported: "It's from Jem. He's coming up to town and would like to take us to a matinee and dinner at the Harpo."

"Sounds good to me." I settled opposite her at the table. "Any other news?"

"We'll have a good gossip then, he promises. And he says Garrick sends his best regards to Madame Cho-Cho-San."

"And she'll send hers to Garrick when we meet on Wednesday." Garrick was the theatre cat at the Royal Empire, Brighton, where Jem, who had been a child star in one of Evangeline's early plays in the West End, was now stage manager, power behind

30

the scenes — and Garrick's preferred companion.

"One egg or two?" Jocasta asked me. I glanced down to see bright trusting eyes gazing up at me.

"Two," I answered. One and a half would be quite enough for me and Cho-Cho did like a bit of egg with her breakfast bacon.

Because I was more than halfway listening for it, I caught the scrape of the key in the lock of our door at the far end of the hallway and braced myself.

Jocasta was caught unawares when the door slammed violently. She jumped and another rasher of bacon dropped from her tongs to the floor.

Cho-Cho's possessive paw stretched over it immediately and she gave a loud purr of appreciation.

Sharp staccato footsteps charged down the hallway, about to storm the castle and take no prisoners. Oh dear. Martha was still in a foul mood from yesterday. I had been afraid of that.

"Oh!" Jocasta gasped with relief as Martha appeared in the doorway. "It's only you."

Martha's eyes narrowed dangerously. That "only" had been a mistake.

"I mean —" Jocasta apparently realised this and tried to retrieve her blunder. "I was afraid it was Banquo."

"Why should it be? I thought we saw him off yesterday."

Leave it to Evangeline to stick her oar in and muddy the waters even more.

"Why should we ever see him again?"

We all looked at her incredulously. Surely she couldn't really believe we'd seen the last of him. That would be too good to be true. The best we could hope for was a long respite.

"Because it's the weekend," Jocasta explained.

"What's that got to do with anything?" Martha was as puzzled as the rest of us.

"Don't you see? Banquo won't be able to reach anyone else. The publishing offices are closed. He's come back here because Martha has taken over Melisande's cookbook —"

There was an explosive indignant snort from Martha.

"I mean, I mean —" Jocasta temporised swiftly. "That's the way he'll see it. It's Martha's book now, of course. We're hardly even using any of Melisande's reci—"

"I think we'll leave it there." It was not like Evangeline to act as peacemaker, but Martha's expression was obviously unnerving her.

"Darling." It was terrifying me. "Darling, be calm. I know this has come as a shock to you. To all of us but —"

"But Banquo doesn't know what's happened to his wife. He'll be back because he thinks *she*" — Martha sent a venomous look at Jocasta — "knows where Melisande is."

"Ridiculous!" Evangeline said. "Doesn't the creature have any relatives or friends he can go to for information?"

"He's not a creature!" Jocasta flared. "He's a brilliant inventive courageous adventurer who risks his life to — to —" She floundered for a moment, then recovered. "To bring knowledge to the world!"

Oh, dear. Why do some of the sweetest young girls fall for the cads and poseurs?

"I didn't ask for a character reference!" Evangeline snapped. "I asked whether he had any family. Or friends." She sounded insultingly doubtful about the latter.

"Of course he has!" Jocasta was on the defensive. "Lots of them! Too many. Banquo's Baggage, we called them around the office."

"The other part of the question was," Evangeline went on relentlessly, "why can't *they* break the news to him?"

"Well . . ." Jocasta considered the question. "Tom and Mick, his old school friends, don't know any more than he does. They were on the expedition with him."

"Really?" I could feel my eyebrows moving up to meet my hairline. "I had the distinct impression that he said he was on a solo expedition."

"Well, yes, of course he was." Jocasta tried to stand her ground. "But there's solo — and solo. I mean everyone needs a backup team. Both on-the-spot backup and . . . and back-at-home-base backup, here in London. Tom and Mick helped with the dog sledges with supplies and all that. And there had to be a photographer, that's Tom, for the illustrations for the book. But Banquo was always in the lead — at least half a mile in front of them. So, you see, he was solo really."

"Mmm . . ." Evangeline was no more convinced than I was. "So they didn't know anything had happened to Melisande. But what about those back at the London base?"

"Oh, those are his three cousins: Edytha, Isolde, and Valeria." Jocasta was racked by an involuntary shudder and closed her eyes briefly. "They're very protective of him, possessive, even. Melisande used to say it was like having three mothers-in-law, all hostile. She swore they'd have found some way of stopping Banquo from marrying her, if she hadn't had all that money."

"Money?" Evangeline snapped to attention. "All *what* money?"

The doorbell pealed suddenly and Jocasta's look changed to one of sheer terror.

"I'm not here!" She bolted for the bathroom. "You don't know where I am. You don't even know me!"

CHAPTER THREE

"You can come out now," Martha called
with barely veiled exasperation. "It's only
Nigel."

"Oh . . ." The door opened slowly and Jocasta emerged. "Hello, Nigel."

"Hello, hello, hello," he said affably, turning to include all of us in his greeting.

With a happy chirrup, Cho-Cho pranced
forward to hurl herself at his ankles. For
some reason best known to herself, Nigel
had become one of her favourite people.

"And hello to you, too." He scooped her
into his arms and they had themselves a
nuzzling session.

All right, Nigel might be a pain in the neck
at times, but his heart and instincts were in
the right places.

I noticed that, even as he fussed over Cho-
Cho, his eyes brightened hopefully when
Jocasta returned to the cooker and tossed a
few more rashers under the grill. His nostrils

flared and he swallowed convulsively. I wondered when he had had his last meal.

"Sit down, Nigel." I couldn't help myself. "You're just in time to join us for brunch."

"Oh, no, no. Really? You're sure it's no trouble?" Even as he demurred politely, he swung out a chair and stumbled into it eagerly. Cho-Cho touched her nose to his, then swept her cheek across his, both assuring him that he was welcome and marking him with her little scent glands as one of her belongings.

"It's nothing special, I'm afraid." Jocasta did her own demurring. "Just the usual full English."

I noticed that she had produced, from seemingly nowhere, halves of tomatoes and mushrooms, which she popped under the grill, then trimmed the crusts off slices of white bread to fry with more eggs.

"We'll be doing something more interesting later," she apologised. "We haven't decided what we're testing today."

"Oh, this is fine, great, wonderful!" Nigel was salivating, he swallowed again. "Couldn't ask for better!"

Cho-Cho met my eyes with an intense, meaningful look, then began dotting kisses all over Nigel's face. I got the feeling that she understood his situation better than we did. Nigel needed all the love and support we could give him. Was he in some sort of trouble? Again?

"Actually —" He pulled himself away from Cho-Cho's ministrations and beamed at Evangeline. "I dropped by to tell you that I think there may be some very good news on the way."

"You've managed to unload those ghastly ostriches!" Evangeline's face lit up. "I knew you would . . . eventually."

"Er, no." Nigel winced. "Not yet. I'm still working on that. It's looking hopeful, but . . ."

But he couldn't find another sucker. Not like Evangeline. Perhaps everybody else had a better idea of what they would be getting into.

"Oh." Evangeline's face fell. "I'm not 'investing' any more money," she warned.

"No, no, nothing like that. Ah, thank you —" Jocasta had placed a laden plate in front of him. He plunged towards it so eagerly that Cho-Cho was briefly squeezed between his chest and the table. She mewed a lady-like protest and squirmed free, dropping to the floor.

"Sorry, love," Nigel said perfunctorily as he snatched up his knife and fork and concentrated on the food.

"Tea — or coffee?" Martha was drawn into the circle of his need. Mouth full, he waved a hand, which we all interpreted as *anything will do.* When had the poor boy last had a decent meal? Perhaps not since he had been one of our guests when we were staying in Brighton.

I cast an anxious glance towards Evangeline and saw by her frown that she was taking the measure of the situation, too. We had all done our time in the hinterlands of near-starvation.

Jocasta was looking gratified as she watched Nigel devouring the food she had cooked. Then the telephone rang abruptly and she gave a small shriek of terror and dropped the fork she was holding.

Unfortunately, there had been a small sausage impaled on the tines and Cho-Cho dived for it. Anything that hit the floor around here was hers and — oh, joy! — the cooks were butter-fingered and careless.

"You don't need that!" I scooped her up and she struggled, protesting loudly.

"You aren't hungry," I assured her. "It's sheer hunting instinct, that's all."

The phone went on ringing. Jocasta stared at it, uttering incoherent little sounds of distress.

"Oh, for heaven's sake!" Evangeline was

39

nearest the phone and she snatched it up, demanding, "Now, what?" She listened a moment, then said, "No, no, Cecile. Just the usual madhouse."

"Oh! It's just Dame Cecile." Jocasta was just beginning to relax when the doorbell rang again. She shrieked.

"Pull yourself together!" It was Martha who spoke, although she sounded exactly like Evangeline in that moment. I hoped rogue genes weren't coming through. "You can't carry on like this. We have work to do!"

"Yes, yes, I know. I'm sorry." Jocasta apologised automatically, but I could feel her watching me nervously as I went down the hall to answer the door.

I was still trying to decide whether I should slam the door in his face when I realised that it wasn't Banquo who stood there looking down at me as though uncertain of his welcome.

"Teddy!" I said, loudly enough to reassure Jocasta. "I thought you were in Brighton."

"I was, I am, but —" He smiled imploringly. "You did *say* I could have visiting privileges."

"Oh yes, of course. Come in." I stepped back and he rushed in so quickly that I looked beyond him to see if he was being

40

pursued. I wouldn't put it past that awful wife of his.

"Where is she?" He looked around eagerly. "Where's my little darling?"

I told myself that that pang in my heart wasn't jealousy as Cho-Cho surged forward with a chirrup of delight to be swept up into his arms.

Cho-Cho was simply an exceptionally loving and friendly little cat, I lectured myself further. Naturally, she was happy to see Teddy again — he was her former owner.

But he had given her to me. He couldn't change his mind, could he?

No, no, of course not. His wife still hated the cat and would always hate her. Nothing would change that. It wasn't safe for Cho-Cho to be anywhere near Frella ever again.

Surely Teddy would never forget Frella's deadly hatred — that was why he had let Cho-Cho go. Besides, I *had* given him visiting privileges. Wouldn't that be enough for him? Or . . . ?

Evangeline's poisonous glare made me aware that I was wringing my hands as I followed Teddy and Cho-Cho into the kitchen.

"Teddy, old man!" Nigel greeted him as a friend and, possibly, ally. Was Nigel feeling a bit outnumbered being the only male

41

amongst all these females?

"Teddy!" Jocasta smiled wanly, but welcomingly. "Have you had breakfast?"

"Some," Teddy admitted, sniffing the fragrant air. "Rather a long time ago. Before I caught the early train from Brighton."

"Sit down," I urged. "There's plenty for everyone." It wasn't a bribe, but I did want to keep on his good side.

"Coffee." Martha sighed resignedly, pouring out a cup. "Perhaps toast. Since you've already had something, perhaps you won't mind waiting a bit for more. We're going to test a kedgeree recipe. I thought it would do all of us for lunch."

"Splendid, splendid!" Teddy agreed, settling himself next to Nigel, who had raised his head alertly.

"Perhaps Nigel would join the testing panel, too —" Jocasta had noticed. "If he isn't too full —"

"I'll force myself." Nigel beamed. "Anything to be of help."

Evangeline snorted as she replaced the phone. "Cecile will be joining us for lunch, brunch, whatever," she reported. "Throw another potato into the pot."

"It's rice, actually," Martha said coldly, as Jocasta scurried to unearth a chunk of smoked haddock from the freezer and ac-

42

cess the rice canister.

I knew the eggs were already waiting. Martha was incapable of getting her hands on a dozen eggs without immediately hard-boiling at least half a dozen of them to stand ready for future use in salads, dressing, or, in this case, it seemed, kedgeree.

Teddy was devoting most of his attention to Cho-Cho, but the aroma of the haddock gently defrosting and poaching was beginning to perfume the air and she stirred restively in his arms. She still loved him. Of course she did. But he didn't loom as large in her life as he once had. She loved us, too, now. And, oh, how she loved the glorious realm of the kitchen! Something new and delicious was being magically produced every time she turned around. She had never had smoked haddock before; she couldn't wait to get at it.

With an apologetic chirrup, she twisted away from Teddy and slid to the floor, racing over to the stove where she hurled herself impartially against Jocasta's ankles and then Martha's. They were both queens of the cuisine on offer. Teddy couldn't compete against them.

"Perhaps I should have brought her a little something," Teddy recognised with a rueful shrug.

43

"Nonsense!" Martha said briskly. "She has everything she could ever want right here."

"Yes." Teddy flinched, but recovered. "Yes, I daresay she has." With his wife, he was accustomed to female snubs.

"That reminds me —" Nigel was as easily diverted by food as Cho-Cho, possibly with better reason. The first pangs of hunger assuaged, he was reviving. He fished in his jacket pocket, triumphantly retrieving a small grey blob which he swung enticingly in Cho-Cho's direction. "Come and see what Uncle Nigel has found for you."

Cho-Cho swayed back and forth as the scent of catnip warred with the haddock for her attention. The catnip was closer and won.

"Very kind of you," Teddy said grudgingly, obviously wishing he had thought of it.

"Not at all." Nigel laughed, allowing Cho-Cho to capture the catnip mouse. "My pleasure."

And Cho-Cho's. She tumbled across the room in mock battle with her prize.

Even Evangeline smiled with the rest of us. Only Teddy seemed a bit put out.

"More coffee?" Jocasta refilled Nigel's cup approvingly. We were all so relaxed that no one turned a hair when the doorbell rang again.

"That will be Cecile," Evangeline said.

"I'll go." Martha sauntered down the hall. We heard the familiar voices greeting each other and the footsteps coming towards us.

Jocasta set another cup and saucer on the table, smiled a welcome at the doorway — and screamed.

Teddy dropped his cup. It crashed to the floor, the dark brown liquid spreading out from it.

"I'm so sorry —" Teddy leaped to his feet, cringing. "I can explain —" He broke off as he discovered the woman entering behind Dame Cecile was not the woman he feared. He owed this one no explanations. He had never seen her before. None of us had, except —

"Edytha!" Jocasta choked. "What are you doing here?"

"Edytha is in Ibiza," the woman said coldly. "I am Isolde."

"Yes, yes, of course. I'm so sorry!" Jocasta burbled. "It's just that you both look so much alike. And it's been a while since I've seen you — either of you."

My mind divided into two reactions. One said: you mean there can be two of them? The other said: Edytha's in Ibiza? Beatrice Lillie or Joyce Grenfell could have done something clever with that.

"I thought she was with you," Martha said accusingly to Dame Cecile.

"We came up together in the lift," Dame Cecile defended herself. "I thought you were expecting her."

I took a deep breath while Teddy reseated himself and guiltily ran one foot through the brown puddle on the floor, as though by spreading it he could make it disappear.

Jocasta had backed into a corner and obviously wanted to disappear herself. Eyes wide, she stared at Isolde as though waiting for a fatal blow to fall.

"Banquo is back!" Isolde's gaze skewered poor Jocasta. "Early!"

"Y-yes, I know." Jocasta's voice was barely audible. "He came here . . . looking for her . . ."

"What did you tell him?"

"N-nothing. I . . . I hid."

"Very wise." Isolde nodded. "Fortunately, I always screen my incoming calls. When I heard his voice, I didn't pick up the phone."

"Then you haven't told him, either? He still doesn't know?"

"Just let me get this straight —" Martha interrupted. She had begun hyperventilating. "Do you mean to say that you have known for months that this woman had died

46

— and you didn't even bother to inform her husband?"

"Banquo was fully occupied in crossing the frozen tundra." Isolde turned and raked Martha with an icy gaze that lowered the entire room's temperature by about twenty degrees. "There was nothing he could have done about it — and we didn't want him distracted from his quest. The poor darling had quite enough to contend with braving the elements of nature as it was."

And possibly they were afraid to break the news because his whole project and the prospective book deal would be jeopardised if he rushed home before he had attained his goal. More than possible. Cold-blooded calculation was written all over the woman.

If Isolde was anything like the rest of his family, no wonder the Arctic wastes held no terror for Banquo — they must seem just like home to him.

"Quite understandable." Teddy had decided to agree, even though he had no idea what he was talking about. It was obviously a reflex action of long standing, prompted by his association with the difficult woman he had married. Always agree, temporise, pour oil on troubled waters . . . anything for a quiet life.

His contribution was greeted by a barrage

47

of cold-eyed stares. He quailed visibly, but it was no more than he was accustomed to.

"I mean —" He tried to retrieve the situation. "I only —"

"And *who* — ?" Isolde demanded icily. "Are you?" *And what business is it of yours* hung in the air.

Meanwhile, all culinary activity had halted. Cho-Cho looked around at us and chirruped questioningly.

There was an answering *"Yip!"* from Dame Cecile's direction and a minor convulsion in her capacious handbag, from which a small bundle of black fur erupted and her toy poodle tumbled to the floor to be greeted rapturously by her buddy Cho-Cho. They touched noses then, chirruping and yipping, suddenly went into a wild game of chasing each other up and down the hallway.

"Aren't they cute?" Teddy looked after them, his previous train of thought easily derailed. "Wouldn't it be great if everyone could be as carefree as they are? So sweet and innocent."

"I don't like useless animals," Isolde stated, quite as though anyone had asked her opinion. "Guide dogs, guard dogs, huskies trained to pull a sledge are all right — they have some purpose. The rest shouldn't be given the space they waste.

48

And cats! Cats are utterly useless!"

"Cats catch mice," I defended.

"Oh, yes?" She looked at me with cold disdain. "And how many mice do you get up here in a penthouse?"

"Rats *are* more usual." Evangeline joined the fray. "Especially two-legged ones." The look she gave Isolde was pointed enough to pierce metal armour.

"Frou-Frou is *not* useless!" Dame Cecile had been marshalling her arguments. "She is a valued friend, a delightful companion. She amuses me, comforts me, cheers me —"

"Stop it! Stop it! All of you!" Martha's precarious composure snapped. She rounded on Jocasta. "Who is this awful woman? How dare she force her way in here and begin insulting everyone? She's your friend — make her go away! We have our work to do!"

"Martha . . ." I reproved gently.

"She's *not* my friend!" Jocasta cried. "I hardly even know her. She's Banquo's cousin —"

"I don't care if she's Banquo's ghost! Send her away!"

CHAPTER FOUR

"Er, perhaps I ought to leave, too." Preternaturally sensitive to an atmosphere, Teddy took every complaint and rebuff personally, not least the one from his former cat. "Cho-Cho doesn't seem to have time for me right now. I can come back tomorrow."

"That might be best," I agreed, a split second before Evangeline's elbow connected with my ribs and I realised I had just given tacit permission for him to return almost immediately.

"Perhaps I should come back at another time, as well."

"She didn't mean you, Cecile," Evangeline said quickly.

Nigel's plate was empty and, as it was obvious that the promised kedgeree was not going to materialise at any time in the very near future, he was already sliding towards the door without a word.

The only one impervious to hints, insults,

and direct orders was, of course, Isolde. I had the impression that it would take a stick of dynamite to shift her. Maybe several sticks.

Teddy followed Nigel, more slowly, as though hoping someone would change their mind and call him back. No one did. There was silence as he and Nigel walked to the door, their footsteps quickening as escape came closer.

Then there was an explosion of sound: a startled bray of female laughter, the ever-ready apologies from Teddy, and a discreet murmur from Nigel. The female laugh brayed out again, with words that were noisy, but not quite distinct.

Cho-Cho flicked her ears irritably; she hated loud noises. I didn't blame her; I did, too. Especially from a female voice that sounded like that of an overbearing first-class troublemaker.

"Aaah!" Only Isolde seemed pleased to hear the disturbance. "Here's Valeria now."

"Valeria?" Jocasta seemed to shrivel. "What's she doing here?"

"I told her to meet me here. We need to have a serious consultation and decide what we're going to do." Isolde frowned. "It's a shame Edytha couldn't get back from Ibiza in time for it."

"I-sol-de . . . ?" The bray turned into a yodel.

"In here, Valeria," Isolde called.

Heavy footsteps charged down the hallway towards us and a sudden rush of air seemed to gust through the doorway, the way it does when you're standing on the Tube platform and the oncoming train pushes a blast of stale air ahead of it just before it comes into view and slows to a stop.

Jocasta swayed visibly, as though struggling to stand upright in the path of a hurricane. She shrank back, staring with trepidation at the doorway. When a figure abruptly filled it, she could not choke back a whimper. She might have been facing King Kong come to carry her away.

Yet Valeria wasn't that big. Isolde was bigger. It was the force field surrounding her that trumpeted that Valeria was a force to be reckoned with. That and the deep commanding voice that now announced:

"You've found her! What's she doing here?"

Jocasta couldn't back away any farther; she was up against the fridge. She looked so desperate that I wondered for a minute whether she was going to open the door and try to crawl inside. But that would have meant that she'd have to turn her back on the two Furies. I wouldn't want to do that, either.

"I suppose —" The newcomer swept Jocasta with a scathing glance. "I suppose she's wimped out!"

"We knew she would," Isolde said.

"It's not good enough! She's *got* to!"

"She will," Isolde said. "That's why we're here. To talk to her and make her see reason."

Jocasta whimpered: the prisoner listening to the torturers discussing the best instruments to use on her. She looked from Isolde to Valeria and back again, her face a mask of anguish.

But it was Martha I was really worried about. My darling had huddled into herself, only her lower lip protruding mutinously, the way it did when, as a child, she had been about to fly into a tantrum.

"Easy, darling." I moved over to stand beside her and put an arm around her waist, as much to try to hold her back as to comfort her.

"It's all right, Mother," she said tensely. "Don't worry. I really want to hear what they've got to say."

So did I — and I wasn't the only one. Evangeline was grinding her teeth together and making an obvious effort to keep a low profile.

Dame Cecile wasn't quite sure what was going on — but she was all agog. The emotional temperature was rising into the stratosphere and I suspected she was taking mental notes for future roles.

"You — !" Valeria accused. "We've been trying to get in touch with you for weeks — but you've been avoiding us!"

"No, no, not really." Jocasta gasped. "It's just . . . I've been so busy . . ."

"Doing what?" Isolde challenged. "Your job was to assist Melisande. Without her, you had nothing to do!"

"That isn't true!" Jocasta began to show signs of fight and I mentally cheered her on. "My job is with the Glorious Gourmand Press branch of Perfection Publications. They're publishing *One for the Road* and it's been my project ever since the Lady Lemmings approached us with the idea. I was there before Melisande and —"

If Cho-Cho or Frou-Frou had been unmannerly enough to utter such a sound, I'd have called it a snarl. As it uncontrovertibly issued from my darling daughter, I groped for another word that might give her the benefit of the doubt.

I wasn't the only one lost for words. It

54

stopped Jocasta cold. Startled, she looked down at the floor, only to see Cho-Cho and Frou-Frou looking back at her with placid interest. Another menacing growl snapped her head up and turned it in the direction of the sound.

"No one ever mentioned Melisande to *me!*" Martha gritted out between clenched teeth.

"Why should we?" Jocasta defended. "She has nothing to do with the cookbook anymore."

The hiss came from another quarter.

"How dare you!" Isolde blazed. "That book was Melisande's creation — her baby! The one she'll never give birth to now. The child Banquo will never have." She paused to consider this and added, "At least, not with her."

"Was she pregnant?" Dame Cecile was trying to make sense of all the rhetoric being tossed around, but it was a losing battle.

"Not physically, not yet," Valeria said. "But it was only a matter of time, once Banquo got back from his expedition."

"Oh, stop!" Jocasta gave a muffled sob. "This is —"

"The book was her surrogate child!" Isolde declared. "She shall not be denied it. No one else's name must be on the book."

"It's *my* book now!" Martha snapped. "I've put in weeks of work pulling it all together and testing recipes. There was practically nothing to it when I took over."

"That's right." Jocasta backed her up. "Melisande talked about it a lot, but she hadn't got round to going through the hundreds of recipes the Lady Lemmings had sent in. I did all the preliminary work, winnowing out the ones that would be practical and have ingredients you could find easily. Melisande hadn't a clue. She was a typical spoiled little rich girl. She had no idea of life in the real world, what it's like for people who have to earn a living."

Isolde and Valeria each took a step forward, prepared to battle to the death. Jocasta's death, that is. Sensing it, she looked around wildly for help.

TAA-Tat-Ta-Ta-TAH! A trumpet fanfare rang through the kitchen. The sort that announces the arrival of the U.S. Marine Corps with John Wayne leading the charge. Only they use bugles, don't they? This sounded more like the arrival of the pharaoh, or the queen of Sheba, or something vaguely operatic, where you just knew that everyone in the production was doomed.

"Ah!" Isolde dived into the voluminous folds of her costume. "My mobile." She

56

fished out a preposterously minute plastic toy and activated it.

"Yes?" She listened. We all did, but she was the only one who could hear anything. She nodded in satisfaction. "You're outside the building now. Good. Yes, she's here. Come straight up. It's the penthouse."

"Pay no attention to us —" Evangeline was quivering like a volcano about to erupt. "We only live here!"

"Quite." It had obviously never occurred to Isolde to consider us at all.

"What Miss Sinclair is saying" — Martha hissed like a snake — a spitting cobra — "is: you are not welcome. Your friends are not welcome. In fact, we'd like you to leave. Now! Before we call the police!"

"Isolde —" Valeria seemed to have a slightly firmer grasp on reality. "Perhaps we ought to go. We can continue our discussion in the car. Come along, Jocasta. They don't want us here."

Nope, she was as flaky as Isolde. Or perhaps she hadn't looked at poor Jocasta recently.

"No!" Jocasta was galvanised into rebellion. "I'm staying here! Go away!" Her voice rose in a modified shriek. "I'm not going anywhere with you!"

"Nonsense!" Isolde said. "Tom and Mick

57

are in the car waiting for us. We have to have a consultation and decide the best way for you to break the news to Banquo. Come along now!"

"I won't! You can't make me!" Jocasta looked around for support. She needn't have worried — we were all on her side.

"She's staying here!" Martha moved to stand in front of her, defying anyone to touch her. "We have work to do — and you're interfering with it. If you're not out of here in thirty seconds, I'm calling the police!"

"I have Ron on speed dial." Evangeline flourished her own cell phone. "He can be here in just a few minutes. With plenty of reinforcements. Especially when I tell him this is an attempted kidnapping."

"Good," I said. We had met Ron — sometimes unkindly referred to as our Tame Policeman — at the time of an unfortunate murder case we had been involved in, and we had proved helpful to each other. Evangeline had added him to our roster of useful contacts. I felt that he occasionally deplored us but he had never failed us.

"And the next calls," I chimed in, "will be to the media. You may not know who we are, but they do. They'll be here for an impromptu press conference before I've had time to ring off. That will take care of your breaking any news to Banquo — he'll get it from the headlines in the morning."

"You can't do that!" Isolde gasped. "The shock might kill the poor boy."

I shrugged. That was her opinion. From what I had seen of their precious Banquo, I felt he belonged in the ranks of those who, as the old expression went, "you couldn't kill with a meat axe."

"Come, Isolde." Valeria's hand closed on her upper arm and drew her inexorably towards the door. "We obviously are not welcome here. Let us retreat and consider the situation."

"But —" Isolde didn't want to surrender without a struggle.

"The boys are waiting downstairs," Valeria said, moving them forward. Dame Cecile proved her worth by sweeping in front of them and opening the door. Their exit wasn't a patch on the one she would have made. She closed the door behind them, not quite slamming it, then leaned against it, closing her eyes and breathing a great sigh of relief, which the rest of us echoed.

"Now —" Martha said grimly. "Can we get back to the matter in hand? We have recipes to test."

"Not right now, dear," I said. "I don't

59

think any of us are quite in the mood. Let's give our unwanted guests ten or fifteen minutes to get clear of the vicinity, then I'll ring Eddie and treat us all to lunch at the Harpo."

CHAPTER FIVE

Everything looked better the next morning. Even Jocasta was considerably perked up by an afternoon and evening surrounded by friends and allies, out of reach of Banquo and his cohorts.

We had encountered old friends of Evangeline and Dame Cecile at the Harpo. They had recently become involved in experimental productions and had no trouble in persuading us to come and see their latest at a suburban fringe theatre. Except for Martha who, still in a bad mood, made her excuses and retreated. The rest of us, with a handful of free tickets, had piled into Eddie's taxi for the six thirty matinee. There had been a ticket for Eddie, too, and he obligingly joined us, although he kept shaking his head all the way back to Docklands.

But today the sun was shining and Jocasta was humming as she produced delicious walnut waffles smothered with maple syrup and topped with whipped cream, which had us humming, too.

Nigel, who had been roused out of a deep sleep last night and recruited to go out and circle the block to make sure no unwelcome would-be intruders were lurking, seemed especially blissed out, reaping his reward as Jocasta gave him a generous second helping. No one seemed to notice that Cho-Cho, perched on his lap, was helping herself to the whipped cream. I decided not to point this out. We were all happy — why spoil it?

Classical music throbbed softly in the background. In perhaps an hour or so, the up-to-date news bulletin would be allowed to interrupt, but not for long, and it would be followed immediately by something soothing and timeless. Just what we needed to brace ourselves for the day ahead.

It was all so pleasant and civilised — what a pity Martha had to arrive and shatter the mood. She had her own key, so we'd had no warning of her presence until she stormed down the hallway and slammed her shopping bag onto the unoccupied end of the table.

"Good morning, darling." I tried to defuse the situation, even though I knew the effort would be useless. Sleeping on her grievance had not done any good. It had only made it worse.

"*Good* morning," Martha snarled, making it clear that it was anything but. She underlined this with an especially venomous glare at Cho-Cho.

Oh, dear. As I'd feared, the recent revelation was still rankling. I cast around for something I could say or do to —

"Good morning, everyone." The tone was placating, the manner diffident, but there he was, Teddy. He must have come in with Martha and accompanied her up in the elevator. No wonder she was so annoyed with Cho-Cho.

"Don't mind me —" He smiled at us uncertainly, perhaps noticing that he wasn't exactly getting a rapturous reception. "I've just come to visit Cho-Cho. We didn't — That is, our visit was cut short yesterday with all the — Anyway, I've brought her a present." He fumbled in his briefcase and pulled out a large and odiferous kipper which he waved in her direction.

Cho-Cho, replete with sweet maple-flavoured whipped cream and comfortably ensconced in the midst of her new family, gazed at him with as little enthusiasm as the rest of us.

"Oh." He was crestfallen. "I — I thought

63

she'd be pleased." He flourished the kipper at her again, sending waves of stomach-churning odour over everyone at the table. Kipper definitely did not go with sweet waffles and cream.

He waved it again hopefully. I began to feel quite ill.

"I don't understand it," he complained. "She usually loves kippers. Look, Cho-Cho —" He flapped it in her direction again. "Daddy's brought you a kipper."

Daddy, indeed! Cho-Cho and I both looked at him coldly. Cho-Cho even more coldly than I, if possible. I didn't blame her. That fish didn't smell exactly, well, *fresh*.

"I'll put it in the fridge." Jocasta advanced on him with a plastic bag and deftly tweaked the kipper from his hand. "She can have it later. She isn't hungry right now."

"That's it," Nigel agreed. "We've been tucking into breakfast. She can't have any room left." He rubbed her tummy gently and she rewarded him with a loud purr.

"Breakfast . . ." Teddy looked longingly at the bounty on our plates. He swallowed and looked away again.

I moved out of range of Evangeline's sharp elbows before asking: "Have you had breakfast yourself, Teddy?"

"Uh, no, not really." He swallowed again.

"Frella had . . . already left for the theatre and there was nothing in the fridge. That is, only the kipper — and I wanted that for Cho-Cho." He looked at me hopefully, obviously starving. "And they don't have a proper dining car on the Brighton train anymore."

Martha made that growling sound again and I could feel a faint breeze as Evangeline's elbow just missed my ribs. But what choice did I have? I was not only sorry for the poor man, but I wanted to keep him well-disposed. Apart from which, it must have been an unrealistically early hour for even the most dedicated of directors to be off to the theatre. I suspect that particular bit of information could be translated as: Frella didn't come home last night.

"There's plenty," Jocasta murmured to me before fixing Teddy with a stern gaze and asking: "Just how long has that kipper been in your fridge?"

"Oh, I don't know." Teddy shifted uncomfortably. "Perhaps a day or two . . . or three."

"I see." Jocasta nodded grimly, her worst suspicions confirmed. Our eyes met and I knew Cho-Cho was safe; that dubious offering was going to disappear just as soon as Teddy's back was turned.

"Sit down, Teddy." I gestured him to a

chair. "We have waffles on the menu this morning."

"Well, if you're sure it's no trouble." He had leapt into the chair before he spoke. "Of course, you were going to have me help test recipes yesterday, before . . . before . . . That is, I'm quite happy to work my passage, as it were."

Some work! Eating the delicious food Martha and Jocasta produced. I smiled at him blandly as Jocasta poured a fresh batch of the mixture into the waffle iron and helped myself to another cup of strong black coffee.

Even though the quiet wasn't great, I should have known it was too good to last. True, Martha was slamming the utensils around with unnecessary force, but that was only to be expected. She had a lot of resentment to work off before she settled down to being her own sweet self again. I just hoped I had the patience to wait it out.

Jocasta had reverted to her subdued mood and was keeping a low profile, rushing to anticipate Martha's every wish, thrusting the desired ingredient or implement at her, then retreating into the background, avoiding eye contact at all costs. She had learned quickly, I thought. It was the only way to deal with Martha in one of her monumental snits.

Nigel, also sensitive to atmosphere, had removed Cho-Cho from his lap to Teddy's where she slept peacefully, too replete to do any socialising. Teddy dabbed tentative caresses at her, obviously disappointed with his reception.

"Off to dancing attendance." Nigel gave me a meaningful nod as he left. "All going well, should be good news soon."

Since Evangeline had retreated to her room, I wondered who he intended dancing attendance on. I supposed it was too much to hope that he had found someone who might be willing to take on sixteen ostriches.

In the distance, we heard the door close behind Nigel. The silence lengthened.

"Um, er . . ." Teddy stirred restlessly. "It looks as though Cho-Cho is going to sleep for a while."

"Cats do," Martha said crisply. "She could be out of it for hours now. Jocasta — the big kettle. We'll do the overnight marinade and then the preparations for the forty-eight-hour renewable stew."

Teddy flinched. She couldn't have made it plainer. The short-order kitchen was closed. "Er, perhaps I ought to be getting along. I can come back another time. When Cho-

Cho is awake."

"That sounds like a very good idea," I said. The way Martha slammed a large mixing bowl on the table made me aware that, anxious to be rid of Teddy at any cost, I had recklessly committed us to welcome him at another time. Of his own choosing.

"It might be a good idea if you telephoned first," I amended hastily. "Then we could tell you if Cho-Cho —" I broke off. "Was receiving visitors" seemed rather pompous, as well as being pointed.

"Anyway," Jocasta said soothingly. "Shouldn't you be getting along to rehearsals?"

Uh-oh! Major gaffe. We were going to have to teach that girl to read *The Stage* as soon as it was published every week.

"Not really." He scooped up Cho-Cho awkwardly, stood and replaced her on the empty chair, and straightened, attempting dignity. "I've been replaced in the role. Frella felt they needed a stronger actor for the West End opening."

"Oh, I'm sorry." Jocasta's cheeks flamed with embarrassment.

"No, no." He smiled weakly. "She's probably right. She usually is." He turned and left the room, managing to keep his shoulders back until he thought he was out of sight and then they slumped. A man on his way out — in more ways than one — and who was beginning to know it.

"Oh, no!" Jocasta looked at me in dismay. "I had no idea. I wouldn't for the world have —" We heard the door close firmly.

Cho-Cho opened one wary eye, looked around, then sat up and yawned before stretching, leaping to the floor, and heading for the living room where there were soft cushions on which to finish her beauty sleep.

Evangeline had refilled her coffee cup and retreated to her room. I was contemplating a strategic withdrawal myself, back to the peace and quiet of my own room and the mystery novel I was reading. Let Martha and Jocasta get on with their work.

I had nearly reached the safety of my room when the doorbell rang. I heard Martha's exasperated, "*Now* what?" from the kitchen behind me and a crash as something hit the floor, obviously falling from Jocasta's nerveless hand.

The bell rang again and I was nearest, so I opened the door. I was annoyed, but not surprised, to find Teddy standing there. An echo of Martha's *Now what?* surged into my mind, but I simply asked:

"Did you forget something?" hoping the answer wasn't going to be Cho-Cho.

"I'm sorry." Teddy lurched forward suddenly and stumbled into me. "Sorry, sorry, sorry," he babbled. "I couldn't help it. They . . . they were waiting downstairs. When I opened the front door, they — they pushed me back and forced me —"

"Right. That wasn't so hard, was it?" Someone plucked Teddy off me and gave him a push through the still-open door. "You can run along now. We'll take care of the rest of it ourselves."

There were two of them. They loomed over me. At first blink, I thought they must be brothers or, at least, cousins. After a second blink, I realised they weren't all that large, nor did they look that much alike. The reason they appeared to was because of the curiously mismatched skin on their faces. The lower halves were several shades paler than their foreheads and cheeks. It was a familiar phenomenon in the profession, given that so many "resting" actors tended to give their overburdened complexions a rest from theatrical makeup by growing beards in the intervals between jobs. When work beckoned again, they shaved, and the resulting mismatch — depending on how much outdoor activity they'd indulged in — necessitated some pretty close attention from the makeup person.

But you learn to recognise your own breed of cat — and these weren't actors. Given the circumstances, I had the uneasy feeling that I could make a good guess at their identities. I don't imagine you go in for the daily close shave in Arctic temperatures.

"Who are you?" one of them demanded.

"Just what I was about to ask you," I countered, giving no indication of how much I had surmised. "*I* happen to live here."

"Excuse my friend." The other one had a charming smile and knew how to use it. "We've been out of touch with civilisation for too long. It takes some of us more time to adjust than others."

I gave him a show of a smile back and waited.

"We're sorry to intrude," he apologised, "but it is most urgent that we see Miss Lambert. We understand she's here."

"Miss Lambert?" I said blankly.

"Jocasta Lambert," the other one snarled. "Stop trying to play games with us. We know she's here!"

There was an ominous silence from behind me and then I caught the faint snick of a bolt as Jocasta took refuge in her favourite retreat. What a good thing Evangeline hadn't decided she wanted to take a long leisurely bath.

"You still —" I drew myself up to my full height, which left the top of my head somewhere below the level of their noses. "You still have not had the courtesy to introduce yourselves."

"You're right." Another charming smile accompanied by a slight grovel. "I do apologise. I'm Tom —"

"Mother!" Martha charged down the hallway. She had a carving knife in one hand and a meat cleaver in the other. "Who are these people? What do they want?"

"I'm still trying to find out, dear." I was happy to see that her mood had not improved one bit. If anything, it had worsened. "They don't seem too anxious to identify themselves."

"Oh, don't they?" Martha swung on them, the light glinting off the sharp blades of her impromptu weapons. "Who are you?" she demanded. "What are you doing here? How dare you force your way into our home! Don't just stand there, Mother — call the police!"

"No, no." They both took a step backwards. "Please, it's all right, I promise you. We just —"

"Who *are* you?" Martha flourished the carving knife just a little too close for the

72

comfort of the charmer. His smile was cutting no ice with her.

"What's going on here?" Evangeline joined the fray, suddenly in our midst — and carrying the heavy brass dolphin candlestick which, as we joked when she bought it at an antiques fair, would make a perfect blunt instrument. She swung it menacingly as she strode up to stand beside us.

The two men looked from one to the other of us and retreated a few more steps. The unsociable one muttered something under his breath. I was sure I caught the words "monstrous regiment."

"We — we just wanted to have a few words with Jocasta. But obviously," the charming smile turned craven, "we've come at an inopportune time. We'll come back later —"

"Oh, no, you don't!" Evangeline moved swiftly to block their exit. "Name, rank, and serial number!" she snapped. "Now!"

They looked at each other as though they really were prisoners of war. "Look, you're taking this the wrong way —"

"Now!" Martha echoed. The meat cleaver swished through the air, but didn't quite connect with the door, I was glad to see. The situation with our landlord was delicate enough at the moment without upsetting

him further.

"I apologise most sincerely —" He spoke directly to me, probably because I seemed the least threatening, being the only resident facing him who wasn't armed. "We've obviously gone about this the wrong way. You see, we're friends of Banquo Fitzfothergill. In fact, we were on the expedition with him. I'm Tom Hampton, official photographer for the expedition —"

"And I'm Mick Quinlan, nursemaid, dogsbody, and general handyman," the other said morosely. "*Now* can we speak with Jocasta?"

"Cook, dog handler, troubleshooter, and general keeper-up of our morale," Tom corrected. "Old Mick always undersells himself. We'd have been lost without him."

He kept up anyone's morale? I looked at the gloom-laden face. Things must have been pretty bad if *he* could cheer anyone up.

"And he's right," Tom continued. "We really need to talk to Jocasta urgently. For Banquo's sake," he added, as though we cared as much about Banquo as they did.

"She isn't here," Evangeline said quickly. "If you'd had the courtesy to telephone first to make an appointment, we could have told you that and saved you an unnecessary trip." She still wasn't relaxing her grip on the brass dolphin, I noticed. I hoped neither of the men were going to call her bluff and try to get past her. I can't stand the sight of any blood that isn't Kensington Gore.

"When will she be back?" Abruptly, Mick shifted into troubleshooter mode. It suited him better than that of morale booster. This, I believed.

"How should we know?" Evangeline faced him implacably. "Some frightful women were here yesterday, bullying her. As soon as they left, she took off. No forwarding address and no indication when — or if — we'd ever see her again."

The performance was worth another Academy Award nomination and I saw acknowledgement of this flicker in the depths of the photographer's eyes. The troubleshooter seemed to take it seriously, however. He frowned.

"The Graces," he identified. "They told us —"

"A most unsuitable nickname for them," Evangeline said. "Any creatures less graceful, I've never seen."

"It's their surname," Mick said. "They're all cousins of Banquo's on his mother's side. They —"

"We don't need the genealogical details,

thank you," Evangeline said crisply. "We have no plans to see any of them again. Ever. And that goes for you, too."

"Why?" I asked.

"Because they're boring me, because they have no business being here, because I'm sick of the sight of them, because —"

"Not you, Evangeline." I cut her off. "Them. Why is everyone so anxious to talk to Jocasta?" I knew the answer, but I wanted to hear their version of it.

"She worked closely with Melisande. She was the last to see her, to be with her, before —" Tom broke off and took a deep breath. I wondered suddenly what Melisande had been to him.

"Jocasta was there when . . . it happened," Tom went on. "The only reliable eyewitness. She has to understand that it's up to her to tell Banquo what happened — every last detail. She might be able to give him some comfort —" He was trying hard, but didn't sound as thought he believed it himself. "It's going to hit Banquo hard when he finds out Melisande is dead."

"It is *my* understanding" — Evangeline wasn't buying it, either — "that all of this took place some months ago! Why had no one told the wretched man that he's a widower long before this? It sounds as though you knew. Why keep it from him?"

They flinched, looked at each other, and Tom lost the mental toss of the coin.

"All sorts of reasons," he admitted miserably. "Banquo was just starting out on the expedition. We didn't want to upset him. There was nothing he could do back in England. It was all over. And there were other things to consider: the book deal, the window of opportunity in the weather it might be fatal to miss . . . It wasn't just our decision, the Graces told us to keep it from him. No one wanted to upset him . . ."

"Also," Mick, the troubleshooter, said, "he was supposed to be solo — and incommunicado. So he'd have no way of knowing then. If he came back and knew all about it, it would be a dead giveaway. As it is, he's behaving naturally. Sure, it's going to be a terrible shock to him. But Jocasta is the one who should tell him. Maybe Tom could get a good shot of her breaking the news. It would add a lot of human interest to the book."

What would he know about humans? Another one to whom the Arctic would seem homelike. Ten degrees below zero Fahrenheit was probably blood temperature for him.

"That's enough!" I wasn't the only one

sickened. Martha waved the carving knife at them in a fury. "Out! Out! Damned blots!" She threw a defiant look at Evangeline, perhaps hoping she might get away with it because of the slight change in the quotation.

"Stand not upon the order of your going —" No, she knew just what she was doing, but she didn't care.

"But go!" She advanced on them, brandishing both carving knife and cleaver in a way that meant business. I wouldn't swear to it, but I had the feeling that even Lady Macbeth hadn't speeded the parting guests quite so vehemently.

"All right! All right!" Tom fought the door open and they both crowded through it.

Mick turned as the door closed behind them and snarled: "We'll be back."

I didn't doubt it.

The door slammed and we all looked at each other, one thought in mind.

"I think —" I voiced it. "It's high time we had an in-depth conversation with Jocasta."

CHAPTER SIX

"I won't tell him!" Jocasta cried. "They can't make me! Everyone can stop saying they don't shoot the messenger anymore. I know that. And Banquo would never do such a thing anyway. But . . . but . . . he'd hate me forever!" She burst into tears.

She was probably right. Banquo hadn't struck me as the reasonable forgiving sort.

"Every time he looked at me, he'd remember," she wailed. "He'd never want to see me again . . . to speak to me . . ."

"That's nothing to complain about." Evangeline spoke with her usual sweet sympathy. "I could live quite happily if he never spoke to me again — or if I never saw him again. Especially if I never saw him again."

"You're not me," Jocasta sobbed.

"Thank heaven for that!" Evangeline muttered.

"You don't understand . . . you don't

know anything about it."

"Suppose you tell us," I said. "Remember, we walked in in the middle of the movie."

"What movie?" Jocasta looked at me blankly and I realised that the familiar expression of my younger days conveyed nothing to her.

She was of the hard-ticket generation. Too young to have known the days of continuous performance cinemas when one could buy a ticket and walk in at any time. They showed a feature film, cartoons, supporting B film, newsreel, previews, then feature film again, over and over. Not for this generation the extra fun of arriving in the middle of a film and watching the last half hour or so while trying to figure out which might possibly have gone before to bring the characters to this pass. Then the fascination of watching the film start and seeing what had happened, how the characters had developed and what led up to the now-comprehensible ending. It was as good as a course in fiction writing: plot, characterisation, action, and resolution. The current generation would never know what they were missing. Yes, and they used to give away a dish with every ticket, too.

"Movie . . . ?" Jocasta was still wondering.

"Never mind," I said. "Just tell us what

happened. And —" I added carefully, I already knew the answer, but did she? "And why everyone wants you to be the one to carry the can for it."

"It's so unfair!" Jocasta might not have been familiar with that expression, either, but she had less trouble grasping it. "I wasn't even supposed to be there that night. I was doing Melisande a favour after Edytha had let her down. Edytha was supposed to be helping with the demonstration, not me."

"The Edytha who's in Ibiza?" It was a silly question, as though Jocasta might know any number of females with that name.

"Yes, but she wasn't in Ibiza then. She had to rush to Glastonbury. She said it was an emergency."

"Glastonbury . . ." Evangeline echoed thoughtfully.

"At the festival?" I asked.

"Wrong time of year." Jocasta shook her head. "It was something to do with the shop Edytha had there. A burglary, I think." Her head went on shaking. "I don't know. I can't remember. It seems as though everything went out of my head after —"

"Jocasta, sit down." She was still in shock, I suspected uneasily, either post-traumatic or the original shock lingering.

"Martha, get her some brandy!" Evangeline ordered.

"No, please —" Jocasta flinched, obviously remembering her first encounter with Evangeline's favourite remedy for everything. "I'm all right. Really, I am —" She spoiled it by bursting into tears again.

Evangeline divided an exceptionally nasty look between Martha and me as she saw that Martha had bypassed the ordinary brandy and taken a bottle of the best cognac from her private stock. Not only that, Martha had filled a snifter well past the halfway mark and held it to Jocasta's lips, while I put a steadying arm around Jocasta's shoulders as she sipped at first, then took a deeper draught.

"Slowly . . ." I warned and Martha withdrew the snifter. "Now tell us about it, Jocasta. Start at the beginning. You had been assigned to work with Melisande on the cookbook and there was no problem with that . . . ?"

"None at all," Jocasta agreed faintly. "It was a standard nine-to-five job — to start with. Of course, if we had an experiment in the oven, I had to stay a bit later — until it came out and I could see if it had worked properly. But that didn't happen too often. Melisande liked her free time. And she had other irons in the fire. She had that early-morning radio stint, but at least they patched her in on a telephone line so that she didn't actually have to be in the studio at some ungodly hour. Then there were the freelance appearances at women's clubs for talks and . . . and . . . demonstrations." She broke off and lunged for the cognac, taking both Martha and me by surprise.

"Take it easy," Martha said nervously, as the level in the snifter went down by an alarming degree.

"Just keep going," Evangeline said. "You're getting to it." She reached for the bottle and topped up the glass. "Tell us what happened."

"I was at home." Jocasta swallowed and seemed to become a bit unfocussed. "Well, I would be, wouldn't I? I'd finished for the day, I thought. Then the telephone rang — and it was Edytha. She and Melisande were booked to give a demonstration at a high school in Marylebone, a cooking class, as usual. Only this sudden emergency had come up in Glastonbury and Edytha had to see to it. So they thought it wouldn't be any problem for me to take her place, since I was already broken in . . . broken . . ."

"Easy. Take a deep breath . . . and another . . ." I caught Evangeline's wrist just as she was about to splash more brandy into

Jocasta's glass.

"Keep going —" I gave Evangeline a warning frown. We needed Jocasta coherent and talking. After that, it might be kinder to give her enough to knock her out for a while. "We need to know what happened. Tell us . . ."

"Yes . . ." Jocasta hiccoughed. "Yes, I know. Well . . . I'd helped out a couple of times before, so I knew what I had to do. And . . . and nothing was any different this time until —"

"Deep breaths," I reminded her. "Keep going."

"I met Melisande at the school." Jocasta gulped and tried to carry on. "I helped her unload the car. She'd brought all her own equipment and ingredients from home. She always did because you couldn't depend on what might be available at these classes. Some schools had everything necessary on hand, other places had nothing at all because they were regular schools during the day and most of them don't have cookery courses anymore. It's only starting to be popular again now that there are so many television chefs. That's really why Melisande was taking on the extra work. Goodness knows she didn't need the money — she was hoping to get noticed and perhaps get

84

her own programme —"

"Sip!" Evangeline advised sternly.

"Deep breaths," I said at the same time.

"Yes —" Jocasta tried to do both at once and had a coughing fit. It took her a moment to recover.

"You unloaded the car —" Martha prompted.

"Yes. It was going to be mushroom quiche. It usually was. Quick and easy, minimum cooking time, and everyone could have a little slice to end the class."

"And . . . ?" Martha wanted to know.

"And . . . and . . . I just don't understand it. Everything was going on as usual. I sautéed the mushrooms and shallots, while Melisande talked and beat the eggs and cream together, and all that. Then she put it in the oven and gave the rest of her talk while I washed up all the utensils we'd used. The quiche looked great when Melisande took it out of the oven and cut it into little slices. A taste for everyone. There wasn't enough for me, but I didn't mind. Truthfully, I was a bit bored with mushroom quiche. It was Melisande's party piece and she finished up the last slice, while I packed up the pots and pans so that we could leave fast. She was beaming and everyone was crowding round and telling her how delicious it was and what a good talk and asking their last-minute questions. Some just slipped away quietly. It was the same as usual, except . . ."

"Except?" This time I didn't try to stop Evangeline from pouring. Jocasta looked as though she could use it.

"Well . . . Melisande began to get sort of huffy and irritable. She started giving short and sharp answers. Then she snapped at me to hurry up — although I was working as fast as I could. I didn't want to hang around any more than she did. And it was starting to rain. We both wanted to get out of there —"

"Sip . . ."

"Breathe . . ."

"Go on." Martha was implacable.

"She was breathing hard. And then she said she wanted to go to the loo and she'd meet me back at the car. I . . . I was relieved because I could get everything packed away much faster without her. And, as long as she stayed, some of the pupils would hang around trying to talk to her . . . So . . . so . . . I got all the equipment into the boxes and began carrying them out to the car. I was on the second trip when one of the students began screaming —"

"Sip . . ."

"Breathe . . ."

"Go on."

"I . . . I followed the screams. So did the other students. Luckily there were only two or three still around. The screams . . . the loo . . . Melisande was lying on the floor. Her . . . her face . . . was blue . . . One of the students dialled nine-nine-nine on her mobile phone . . . I . . . I tried to lift Melisande up . . . to talk to her . . . I tried. But I really didn't know what to do. I — I've *got* to take a first aid course. I . . . I felt so . . . useless —"

The tears came again.

We looked at each other. She wasn't the only one to feel useless. There was nothing we could do to help or comfort her.

"Presumably, the emergency services arrived quite quickly," Evangeline said.

"Oh, yes." Jocasta gulped. "We were right in the centre of town. They took her to the nearest accident and emergency department, but . . . but . . . it was too late. Even though they'd put an oxygen mask over — It . . . it all happened so fast. They'd done everything they could, but . . ."

"Breathe . . ." Oops! Perhaps that wasn't the best thing to say under the circumstances.

87

"Sip — gulp!" Evangeline was on surer ground.

Martha said nothing.

"It was awful . . . so awful." Jocasta slumped forward, her arms on the table, her head lowering to rest on them. She was just about finished. I felt guilty because there were still questions I wanted to ask.

"What did the autopsy reveal?" Evangeline had no such qualms. "There had to be one — in the event of the sudden death of a perfectly healthy young woman."

"Oh, there was." Jocasta raised her head and spoke wearily.

"The police thought mushrooms at first, but everyone there had had a taste of the quiche. Except me — and that made them pay extra attention to me —" She shuddered. "But no one else had had any ill effects, so they had to think again . . ." She was beginning to fade.

"Although —" With an effort, she forced herself to go on. The memory was obviously very painful. "Although there was still the possibility that there had been just one bad mushroom in the lot — and she'd had the rotten luck to be the one to get it."

"Mushrooms are always suspect." Martha gave a professional nod. "Where did she source them?"

"I don't know. It doesn't matter. They probably weren't what did it. The . . . the autopsy . . . showed anaphylactic shock. It seems she was desperately allergic to nuts. I didn't know! How was I to know? Edytha said I should have known — but no one ever told me!"

"You gave her some nuts?" Evangeline asked.

"In a mushroom quiche?" Martha frowned.

"Of course not! No one knows how she could have got any. She wouldn't have gone near them — she knew they were deadly to her. There was a theory that one of the students might have been eating peanuts just before they met her and then shook hands with her. But all the students had scattered and probably wouldn't even have remembered such a little thing. And they couldn't test the mushroom quiche to see if it had been tainted in some way — because there wasn't any left. Everyone had eaten it all."

"Disposing of the evidence!" Evangeline came dangerously close to licking her chops at the thought.

"But no one had any ill effects," I said. "So the quiche was probably innocent. I'd go with the idea of the sloppy student."

"But the police would have liked to make sure — and they were annoyed with me because I'd already washed all the pots and pans."

"So there was nothing left to test," Evangeline said slowly.

"Edytha would have washed up, too!" Jocasta defended. "We always did. Those pots and pans were Melisande's demonstration set, her best. They'd been donated by the manufacturer for the publicity. She always used them and took them home all clean and ready to use at her next appearance."

"Neat." Martha nodded and I had the uneasy feeling that she was making mental notes for future use herself.

"She was." The tears were close again. "Neat and tidy and organised . . . everything I'm not. Banquo adored her!" Jocasta wailed.

"I'm not going to be the one to tell him she's dead. Edytha says — they all say — it's *my* duty to tell him because it happened on my watch. But it's not! And I won't! I can't!"

She gulped down the last of her brandy, slumped back in the chair, and sobbed herself comatose.

"You might as well put her to bed." Evangeline divided her imperative look between Martha and me, distancing herself completely from the proceedings. "We'll get no more out of her today."

CHAPTER SEVEN

I woke in the morning with the feeling that today had to be better. How could it not be? Yesterday had gone from bad to worse after we got Jocasta to bed. Martha's mood had not improved, even though I'd taken Jocasta's place as her assistant. Evangeline, naturally, had disappeared after she announced that she had a few errands to do and couldn't say when she'd be back and not to bother about supper for her. I had looked again at Martha and envied Evangeline's escape.

Yes, today had to be an improvement. I sighed deeply and shifted Cho-Cho so that I could get up. She made an indistinct sound, somewhere between a purr and a grumble, then jumped down and followed me into the kitchen.

There was no sign of Jocasta, not that I'd really expected there would be. Martha hadn't arrived yet, but from the mood she'd been in when she left yesterday, I wasn't expecting her before noon. If then.

Savouring the momentary peace, I fed Cho-Cho and brewed a pot of coffee. As well as the bread, there were a couple of muffins in the bread box, but they didn't tempt me. I looked around for something more interesting and noticed the packet of sesame seeds on the counter.

Yes! It had been a long time since I'd had it, but I'd treat myself to sesame semi-toast. I took a slice of bread from the loaf, buttered it more enthusiastically than usual, and sprinkled a lavish handful of sesame seeds over it, pressing them down into the butter, then popped it seed side up under the grill. A delicious aroma seeped into the kitchen as the savoury seeds turned brown. When they were somewhere between mid and deep brown, I turned the grill off and took out my prize.

Cho-Cho leaped up on the table to investigate, sniffing the air delicately.

"It's delicious," I told her, "but I don't think you'd truly be interested." Just in case, I broke off a corner and offered it to her. Let's face it; I was already planning a second piece as soon as I'd finished this one.

"Mmm . . ." Cho-Cho might not be that interested, but Evangeline stood in the doorway, also sniffing. "Whatever that is, I'll have some." She poured herself a cup of coffee and sat down opposite me, waiting for the food to appear magically. The woman has spent too much time in fancy restaurants.

"Did you have a productive afternoon yesterday?" I finished my own semi-toast before getting up to make more.

"Oh, good enough." Evangeline yawned hugely. "How about you?"

"Oh, just ginger-peachy," I said bitterly. "Jocasta never surfaced again —"

"Did you expect her to?"

"And Martha . . . Martha . . ." I shook my head and pushed back my chair. The grill was easier to cope with.

"Would you pour me more coffee while you're up?" No "please," of course, but she actually smiled.

There was something wrong here. She was too casual, too polite, too . . . complacent. I looked at her suspiciously.

"You needn't narrow your eyes at me, just because you had a boring afternoon and I didn't."

"Oh, it wasn't boring," I assured her. "Fraught, walking-on-eggs fraught, tiring — in fact, exhausting — but definitely not boring." I took a beat, then asked, "And what did you do?"

"Oh, nothing much." She was elaborately casual. "Browsed in a library for a while, them met Cecile for a matinee at some ramshackle experimental theatre, then we had a leisurely dinner at the Harpo. I didn't get back all that late, but you were all asleep."

There was something wrong with that story but, before I could put my finger on it, the door rang.

"Martha forgot her key?" There was an odd note in Evangeline's voice.

"Possibly." But why should that make Evangeline look so uneasy? "Unlikely, though. I'm not expecting her this early."

The doorbell rang again. Cho-Cho looked in the direction of the sound and her ears twitched irritably. She turned and stalked back into my bedroom.

Now I was feeling uneasy, too, as I went down the hall to answer the bell. So much so that I actually bothered to stand on tiptoe to look through the peephole. I was swept by an irritation to match Cho-Cho's as I saw who was waiting outside. And pressing the damned doorbell again.

"Good morning, Teddy." I tried not to snarl as I opened the door.

"Good morning, Trixie." Encountering my

95

frown, he flinched nervously. "I hope I'm not too early."

"Too early for what?" I briefly considered slamming the door in his face, then remembered that I shouldn't antagonise him. It would be terrible if he changed his mind about letting me keep Cho-Cho-San. "We're just having breakfast."

"Ah, splendid, splendid!" Stepping forward, he seemed to barely refrain from salivating. "I was rather afraid you might be going out."

Why hadn't I thought of that excuse? I gave him a weak smile and turned. He followed me back to the kitchen. Evangeline looked up as we entered.

"Oh," she said flatly. "It's you. Again."

"I'm afraid Cho-Cho is asleep." I don't know why I bothered trying. Did I really think that item of information would make him turn around and leave?

"That's all right. I'll just wait. She never sleeps too long during the day. Just little catnaps, you know. Ha-ha."

"Ha!" Evangeline's answering smile could have curdled milk. I began to revise my earlier too-hopeful opinion. Today was not going to be better, after all.

"Something smells good." Teddy sniffed the air wistfully.

96

"I'm afraid we've just finished the loaf," Evangeline said.

No, the day wasn't going to get any better.

"Oh, well . . ." He looked so crestfallen I felt sorry for him.

"Actually —" I pretended to rummage in the bread box. "There's an end crust left." It was the best I could offer without showing up Evangeline as an outright liar. "If you wouldn't mind that?"

"Oh, no, no." He brightened. "That would be fine." I lathered on extra butter and plenty of sesame seeds and shoved it under the grill. Evangeline looked daggers at me. Teddy was oblivious.

"You rang our inside bell," Evangeline said abruptly. "But how did you get in downstairs? You don't —" She shot me an accusing look. "You don't have a key, do you?"

"No, no such luck. Actually," he continued, somewhat abashed, "jolly old Nigel was just leaving as I arrived. He held the door for me."

"Hmm . . ." Evangeline's lips tightened. Old Nigel wasn't going to be quite so jolly after she got through with him.

"Ah!" Teddy brightened. "Here she is now."

Cho-Cho strolled into the room with the

97

jaundiced look of someone doing her duty despite her better judgement.

"Come to Daddy, Cho-Cho." He patted his lap and Cho-Cho circled him a couple of times, not in any hurry to get into it.

"She's looking awfully well." Teddy sounded regretful, as though he might have welcomed signs of neglect as an excuse to take her back into his custody.

"She loves it here," I said. "And we all love her."

"It makes all the difference," Evangeline said pointedly, "when they know there's not someone in the background ill-wishing them. They can tell, you know."

"Yes." He nodded resignedly. "Frella just isn't a pet lover, I'm afraid. If she were . . ." He let the thought trail off, but I had no trouble following it.

If she were . . . then Cho-Cho would be living happily with them. Not an option, however, when his wife had tried to kill the cat — and would try again if Cho-Cho got too close. I hope he remembered that.

Abruptly, Cho-Cho alerted me. She raised her head and turned it to the far doorway. I followed her gaze to find Jocasta standing there, looking a bit blurry-eyed and still exhausted.

"Good morning, dear," I said. "Come in."

"Morning . . ." She nodded vaguely, then seemed to wish she hadn't. She groped her way to the nearest chair and sank into it.

"Apologies, apologies," Teddy babbled. "Can't stand up for a lady because I'd dislodge the lady in my lap. And I fear I've just eaten — literally — the last crumb crust. But I'm sure there'll be plenty of other choice bits still around." He was obviously looking forward to sharing in some of them.

"I'm not hungry." Jocasta dashed his hopes. "Just coffee, I think." Her eyelids lowered and she swayed. "Maybe not . . . if it's too much trouble."

"None at all." The only trouble, I suspected, would be in getting her to actually choke down the coffee I had loaded with extra cream and sugar.

"Thank you." Her eyes were still closed. I took her wavering hand and guided it to close around the cup. "Yes . . . thank you." She didn't even try to lift it to her lips. Oh, well, it was so hot it could do with a bit of cooling down.

Cho-Cho stirred restively under Teddy's restraining hand. Jocasta needed some active comforting. Teddy was just being self-indulgent.

Evangeline, as usual, had withdrawn from

99

the whole situation. She had this way of simply packing up her mental bags and retreating into some distant and unreachable corner of her mind. The effect is as though she has stood up and walked out of the room, even though her body remains sitting there. And yet . . . and yet . . . some quiver of wariness was still emanating from her. She was expecting something else . . . waiting for it. An uneasy instinct warned me that it was not going to be something pleasant. With Evangeline, it hardly ever was.

The silenced lengthened.

Evangeline wasn't going to break it. Jocasta didn't even notice it. And I'd used up just about all the small talk I had where Teddy was concerned.

Unable to get away, Cho-Cho had taken her other route of escape, closing her eyes and going to sleep. She didn't bother to purr. I couldn't blame her.

"Well . . ." Teddy pulled tentatively at Cho-Cho's ears, but couldn't tease her eyes open. "Someone's very tired."

Or bored. Like the rest of us. Why should she be any different?

"She had a busy day yesterday, supervising the cooking." I held back a yawn with some difficulty.

"Ah, yes . . . the cooking." He looked hopefully from Jocasta to me.

Silence fell again.

The sudden rasp of a key in the lock rang through the room like a shot, making us all jump.

"Startled me." Teddy gave a nervous apologetic titter.

"Martha," Evangeline said.

I checked my watch. As I had thought, it was still awfully early for Martha to make an appearance. Especially after the mood she had been in yesterday. But no one else had a key —

"Oh!" I didn't want to believe who was standing in the doorway, looking faintly embarrassed but determined.

"Jasper." Evangeline greeted our landlord with some reserve. I knew that she was recalling, as was I, his ultimatum. We hadn't done anything about it yet. "What a surprise."

"Surprise?" He frowned. "I rang yesterday and left a message. I said I'd be by this morning with a prospective buyer who wanted to view the property."

"I wasn't here yesterday and I've heard nothing about this." Evangeline looked to me. "Have you?"

Numbly, I shook my head.

"Martha — acting up again!" Evangeline's face was grim. "I'll sort her out!"

"Oh! Oh, dear! Oh, I'm sorry —" Jocasta came to reluctant life. "I talked to him. But I forgot. I'm so sorry."

I remembered then that I'd heard the telephone ring late yesterday afternoon, just when Martha had nearly dropped a tray of cookies she was pulling from the oven and I had rushed to help her. It had stopped after three rings and I had assumed that it was one of those automatic calls insistent on selling us something — but not if we didn't leap to answer the phone within the obligatory three rings. It had never occurred to me that Jocasta might have picked up her extension and taken the call.

And then forgotten to pass on the message.

"In any case, I did my part," Jasper said stiffly. "Have you, um, made any alternative arrangements yet?"

"We've hardly had time," Evangeline said coldly. "You sprang this on us rather suddenly, you know. We have the right to expect a reasonable amount of time to make our arrangement."

"How are Juanita and Beau?" I tried to inject a more social note into the proceedings by asking about his grandparents, our

102

old colleagues. "We haven't seen them for ages."

"Oh — fine. Fine." He blanched and looked at me as though I had just threatened him in some way.

"Good." I tried a disarming smile. It isn't often anyone makes me feel I'm more dangerous than Evangeline. "We must get together sometime. Soon."

"Yes. Right. I'll tell them." His gaze implored me not to tell them anything.

Poor Jasper, caught in the middle, not wanting to upset his grandparents by evicting their old friends, yet not wanting us in residence here, either. Docklands had been in a slump when he moved us into the penthouse in a partially completed building because he'd sold the St. John's Wood house we had been renting out from under us. It had been intended as a stopgap measure, but we got involved in other things and stayed on. Then Docklands started booming and prices said good-bye to the roof and headed for the stratosphere. Naturally, he wanted to cash in on it, but we were still in situ. Now, in a few short weeks, the market had veered and was beginning a descent — and he wanted even more to unload it. Poor Jasper. The life of a landlord wasn't an easy one.

"May I come in now?" The voice from the doorway behind him seemed to send an icy chill through the room.

"Oh, God! Edytha!" Jocasta looked up and screamed.

"But you're in Ibiza!"

"Not anymore. I got word that I was needed here, so I came immediately."

CHAPTER EIGHT

The woman eddied into the room, head high, multiple scarves and draperies fluttering around her as she moved. She didn't quite elbow Jasper out of her way, but he stumbled awkwardly as she passed him. She was good, I'll give her that. She crossed the room in a way that almost made you believe she was floating, and stopped in front of Jocasta.

"So! What have you to say for yourself?" she demanded. "Why have you upset Banquo?"

"I haven't upset him." Even just sitting in a chair at the table, Jocasta gave the impression of cowering in a corner. "I haven't even seen him."

"Precisely!" Edytha's head snapped up and down in an emphatic nod that did rather more to disperse the ethereal image she tried to create than she would have liked. "We agreed that you would meet with

Banquo when he got back and break the news about Melisande to him gently and explain what had happened."

"*I* didn't agree." Jocasta set her chin stubbornly. "And I can't explain anything. I don't understand what happened myself." I noticed she didn't mention anything about bringing Banquo's everlasting loathing down on her head if she gave him the bad news.

"That's beside the point," Edytha said sternly. "It was your duty . . ."

She began covering the same arguments the others had covered before her and I stopped listening. We'd heard it before, from all the other members of Banquo's crew. And now we knew what they hadn't mentioned — the secretly planned photo session.

A different wave of déjà vu swept over me as I studied Edytha. Bemusedly, I tried to count the number of scarves and bits and pieces she was wearing. I hadn't seen a costume like that since I played an innocent country girl who had just arrived in the big city and been taken under the protective wing of an older woman who turned out to be a female Fagin intent on training me to be a shoplifter in *She Lifted His Heart*.

"You two know each other?" Jasper stared

at them, completely bewildered. "I, er, I'm not sure — Don't you want to view the premises? I, er —" Pulling himself together, he frowned at his watch portentously. "There *are* other interested buyers —"

"Forget it, Jasper," Evangeline advised, coming out of her trance. "She's not interested, she never was. You've been had."

"You . . . you mean . . ." Jasper spluttered. "I've been wasting my time?"

"Sorry!" Edytha wasn't, not for a minute. "But it was necessary. The others told me of your appalling treatment of them —" She divided an accusing glare among us. "I knew I had to gain entrance by other means."

"You tricked me!" Jasper looked thoroughly disillusioned. I could almost sympathise. He'd thought he had a wealthy, if slightly eccentric, prospect for the quick sale of the penthouse. One who'd just returned from foreign climes and hadn't yet realised the property market was tottering. Furthermore, it would have been a direct sale without any estate agents stepping in to take a share of the proceeds. He should have known it was too good to be true.

"It was necessary," Edytha said again. Her eyes were colder than the ice-blue crystals around her neck.

"Now —" She turned back to Jocasta but,

while she had been distracted, Jocasta had slipped away. We heard a bolt shoot home in the distance.

"Come back here!" Edytha surged towards the sound.

"*What* on earth is going on here?"

I hadn't heard Martha come in. She looked around, her frown deepening as she saw Teddy.

"Where's Jocasta?"

"She ran away!" Edytha snarled, a tigress robbed of her prey.

"Ran away — where?" Martha was startled. "We have work to do."

"Who are you?" Scenting fresh prey, Edytha whirled on her.

"Who are *you?*" Martha countered, her mood visibly worsening. "Mother, who is this — this — *person?* What is she doing here?"

"Jasper brought her in." I disclaimed any responsibility.

"She told me she wanted to inspect the premises with a view to making an offer." Jasper had a grievance of his own. "But it was a lie. She tricked me!"

"Offer? View? Premises?" Martha advanced on Jasper dangerously. "What does this mean?"

"Um, er . . ." He groped desperately for

108

an answer, but knew he was on the wrong foot. All four of them, in fact.

"You're trying to sell this place out from underneath Mother!" She'd already arrived at the correct answer herself. That's my girl!

"It's not that bad," Jasper defended. "A couple of the people who are interested want it for a buy-to-let. Trixie and Evangeline could stay on here. They'd just be paying the rent to someone else instead of me."

Oh, yes — and how much would that rent go up?

"You're despicable!" Martha snapped.

"I'm only trying to make an honest profit," Jasper said, in an uncanny echo of the shoplifting Fagin defending herself when caught. Her rationale had been that the profit was honest, only her way of achieving it was slightly suspect.

"Faugh!" Martha turned from him in disgust. "We'll see about that!" The atmosphere was getting to Cho-Cho. She opened her eyes and looked around, as close to irritation as her normally placid nature allowed. Then she leapt to the floor, shook herself, and stalked off in search of a more peaceful spot.

Teddy looked down at his empty lap, then around at the rest of us, as though suddenly aware that he no longer had a viable role to play.

"Perhaps I should be getting along myself," he said. "This seems to be another bad time . . ." He let the thought trail off, plainly beginning to suspect that there were nothing *but* bad times around this establishment.

"Perhaps you should." Evangeline showed sudden animation.

"Um . . . er . . ." Teddy pushed back his chair. "Yes . . . well . . ." On his feet, he looked towards me, but I managed to avoid his eye. I wasn't about to urge him to stay longer, nor to invite him to return soon.

"Well, good-bye then . . ." At last, he was heading for the door. "Er . . . see you soon . . ."

"Not if I see you first!" Evangeline muttered. Thank heavens he was out of earshot. We heard the door close behind him.

"And now —" Evangeline turned her attention to the other intruder.

"Yes!" Martha swung around, for once of the same mind as Evangeline. It was a frightening sight. At least, it frightened me.

"Yes!" Edytha was made of sterner stuff — steel beneath the fluttering draperies, I would suspect.

In the pregnant silence — and I didn't

want to see what it would whelp — a tiny head poked around the corner and looked to see if the coast was clear yet. She inspected the martial stance of the women squared off against each other and then met my eye questioningly. I shrugged. Her guess was as good as mine.

The doorbell shrilled abruptly and we all jumped.

"Teddy must have forgotten something," I said.

"That would be his story!" Evangeline snapped.

"He might have." I just hoped it wasn't Cho-Cho.

"Any excuse!" She was not to be mollified and I wasn't feeling too good about it myself.

The bell shrilled peremptorily again, demanding instant attention. A bit too forceful for Teddy — unless his hand had slipped.

"I'll see to him!" Spoiling for a fight, Martha charged down the hall. Any fight would do.

Cho-Cho prudently withdrew. I watched wistfully as she melted away like the Cheshire Cat. I wouldn't mind disappearing myself.

There was a brief explosion of voices at

the door, then determined footsteps striding towards us, followed by a protesting Martha.

I wouldn't say he was the last person I wanted to see. By now, there were so many candidates for that honour that it would be difficult to choose any particular one.

"How did you get in downstairs?" Evangeline demanded.

"Chap going out held the door for me," he said. "Bit of a wimp, if you ask me. Wouldn't have lasted ten minutes on the frozen tundra."

"Not everyone has your courage and stamina, Banquo," Edytha said fondly.

"I wish to make a complaint to the management about the security around here." Evangeline skewered Jasper with a steely look. "There isn't any. This place leaks like a sieve!"

"That isn't fair." Jasper tried to defend himself. "Your guest let him in."

"Not mine." Evangeline switched her attack. "Hers!"

There I was, back in the direct line of fire. I wondered if there were a quiet amiable convent somewhere which would accept a peace-seeking applicant and her cat.

"Right!" Jasper frowned at me with something like an underlying relief. I was obviously much less intimidating than Evangeline. "You've got to be more careful. This just isn't on."

"You leave Mother alone!" Martha stormed to my defence. "She can't be responsible for what other people do when she isn't even there to see them do it."

"Poor boy . . . there, there . . . poor boy . . ." In the background, a low monotonous murmur had begun. I was vaguely aware that Edytha was stroking Banquo's brow. "Poor, dear boy . . ."

"The shock!" Banquo moaned. "The shock! I can't believe it!" He waved a piece of paper he was clutching in one hand. "Tell me it isn't true!"

"Poor boy . . . dear boy . . . I'm sorry . . . so sorry . . ."

I gathered that Jocasta was no longer required to break the bad news. That would be a relief for her. Perhaps we could all get back to something resembling normality now.

"And to do it so unfeelingly —" Edytha's voice rose as she realised she had our attention. "So cruelly. Just a photocopy of the obituary . . . sent to you anonymously . . ."

Evangeline had gone very quiet. I suddenly put my finger on what had been wrong about her recounting of her afternoon yesterday before she met Dame Cecile. The library! When was the last time she had gone voluntarily into a library? She didn't even know where one was. Easy enough to find out, however, and libraries kept back numbers of newspapers — and photocopying machines.

"Evangeline . . . ?" I whispered.

"One could hardly sign it 'from a well-wisher'. Could one?" She chose to defend the anonymity rather than the enormity of her action. Fortunately, she kept her voice low and Edytha had everyone's full attention now.

"It should have been broken to you gently —"

"You should have told me." He pulled away from her hand and glared at her accusingly. "Someone should have told me."

"We were working towards it." Edytha looked around in growing frustration. All this emotion — and not a camera to record it. This wasn't going according to plan at all. "When the time was right . . ."

When they had talked Jocasta into doing their dirty work, she meant. When Tom was standing by with his camera to record every tragic reaction.

"You needed time to recover from the exertions of your expedition, to get back

114

into the rhythm of everyday life before you had to face . . . something like that.

"And now," Edytha announced, turning to us quite as though we were waiting breathlessly for her diagnosis, "he is in shock!"

Banquo, his head recaptured and buried in her shoulder, nodded so vigorously that she staggered and had to brace herself.

"He should be lying down in a darkened room," she prescribed. "With a cool compress on his brow and a glass of warm milk with brandy and freshly grated nutmeg. Lots of nutmeg!"

She glared at us challengingly, obviously waiting for someone to jump to it. Martha stared back stonily.

Evangeline had frozen at the word "brandy" — he wasn't getting any of hers.

"Now —" Edytha prodded. "He needs it *now!*"

"Then you'd better get him home and see to it," Evangeline said.

"He shouldn't be moved," Edytha insisted. "He's too deep in shock. It's a wonder he made it this far."

"I had to see *you*." Banquo's voice was muffled. He tried to raise his head, but Edytha caught it and shoved it back into her shoulder.

115

"Told me . . . you were here . . . had to come . . ." His voice faded and choked off, probably from lack of oxygen as Edytha kept his face rammed against her.

"You see? He's at the end of his endurance. After the ordeal he's been through — to come home to this! If you haven't a spare bed, he can take one of the sofas in the living room."

"Oh, no, he can't," Evangeline countered. "We're not having anyone else move in here!"

"And that's final!" Martha agreed. Again, they were implacably alike — and dangerous.

"*You* must see . . ." Edytha swung to face me.

"No!" I wasn't the weakest link people sometimes mistook me for. "No, no, a thousand times, no!" I just barely refrained from breaking into the song.

"You're brutes — all of you!" But against our united front, Edytha wavered. "Then, at least, the warm milk and brandy before I take him out into the cold."

"The cold shouldn't be a problem," Evangeline said. "He's used to it."

"Heartless." Edytha paused, but we weren't to be shamed into anything. "Just

116

the brandy then. Surely you can do that much."

"No." We spoke as one. We wanted these people out of here as fast as possible.

"It's all right," a defeated voice said from the doorway. "I'll see to it."

CHAPTER NINE

I might have known Jocasta would have been behind the door listening. The sound of Banquo's voice would have drawn her out of her refuge, however ill-advised the move. She might not have wanted to face him, but she wanted to see his face again. "Moth to the flame," as the old subtitle used to say. He had been gone a long time and, poor child, she was badly smitten.

"We're out of brandy," Evangeline lied firmly.

"And there's no more milk." Martha backed her up.

If this went on, Edytha and Banquo might begin to get the idea that they weren't welcome here. One could only hope.

"Really? That's strange. I was sure there was —" Jocasta started for the fridge. Martha stepped in front of her, blocking her way.

Jasper had been awfully quiet during this whole confrontation. Not surprisingly, perhaps. The children of highly dramatic theatrical people learned at an early age to lie low and melt into the scenery when temperaments began flaring. They brooded a lot, though. I considered it a tribute to both Juanita, who had brought up Jasper because his parents were endlessly touring, and myself that neither Jasper nor Martha had ever wound up at juvenile hall as so many of their peers had.

"What happened?" Banquo wrestled himself free from Edytha's encircling arm and came up for air. "Melisande was young, healthy, strong — how could she have died?"

"I don't know!" Jocasta shrank back, shaking her head in denial. "They called it misadventure. Anaphylactic shock. At first they thought it was something she ate. But everyone ate the same thing —"

"Except you!" Edytha said pointedly.

"There wasn't enough for me. Melisande ate the last piece."

"Piece of what?" Banquo demanded. "She was allergic to nuts. I thought everyone knew that."

"There were no nuts in the mushroom quiche," Jocasta said. "That's why they decided one of the students must have snacked on peanuts before class and then shaken hands with Melisande. Or perhaps just breathed on her too heavily. I never knew she was allergic to nuts. No one did — or, or it might not have happened."

"Nonsense!" Edytha said. "We all found out at that terrible scene she threw at their engagement party. Just because Isolde offered her the Brazil nut crisps she'd made especially for the occasion. A disgraceful scene! The hysterics could be heard for miles around! No one could avoid knowing she was profoundly allergic."

"I didn't know. I wasn't there. I never met Melisande — or any of you — until after the marriage." There was a world of regret in Jocasta's voice — and something else. Regret that she had not met Banquo first, but also a sad recognition that she could never have offered any competition to Melisande's beauty, ambition — and money.

"A terrible, disgraceful, *public* scene!" Edytha reiterated. "You'd have thought Isolde did it on purpose! Poor Isolde was quite, quite shattered! Those Brazil nut crisps were her special party piece."

"Brazil nut crisps?" Martha's professional interest was aroused. "I haven't seen a recipe for those in the files."

"You wouldn't. Isolde was magnanimous enough to offer it, but Melisande rejected it — quite rudely. She said she wouldn't use anything she couldn't test personally."

"I noticed there were never nuts in any recipe," Jocasta said. "But I thought perhaps it was because peanuts seemed to be the only available nuts you find when travelling."

"I'll try that recipe," Martha said quickly. "If Isolde —"

"No need, I can tell you right now," Edytha said. "Any of us could. We have reason enough to remember it."

"Yes?" Martha was already reaching for her pencil.

"Just as many Brazil nuts as you think you need. Shelled, of course. Put them in a pan of cold water, bring it to the boil, simmer for three or four minutes. Then drain and slice them lengthwise —" She paused thoughtfully. "That's the tricky bit — they slide around, so watch your fingers and the knife. Then just spread the slices out in a baking dish, dot with butter, sprinkle with salt, and bake in a moderate oven —"

"That would be about a hundred eighty degrees Celsius," Martha translated, writing briskly, with one eye on Banquo, who looked as though he was coming to the boil himself.

"For fifteen minutes or so, stirring once in a while," Edytha concluded.

121

"It sounds as though that would work under a grill, or even in a frying pan," Martha said thoughtfully. "And olive oil could be used. I'll check it out and —"

"What about her EpiPen?" Banquo boiled over. "She always carried one. Why didn't she use that?"

"What's an EpiPen?" said Evangeline, as well she might.

I'd wondered, too. She and I were of a generation where all these new problems had never existed. I wondered if it were true, the theory that claimed the present generation had sanitised themselves out of the protection a few healthy germs used to give.

"It's a preloaded syringe, ready for use, with an extra-long needle so that it can be used through clothing." Edytha knew. "She always carried one with her. So did I, when I was working with her." Jocasta got another accusing glare.

"No one ever told me," Jocasta said. "That must have been why she rushed to the ladies' room. She wanted to inject herself in privacy when she realised what was happening. Only . . ." Her voice faltered. "Only it was too late . . ."

"Oh, what does it matter?" Banquo threw out his arms dramatically. "Melisande is gone. My darling — dead! And I — I am left alone. Bereft! Robbed of my expectations, my plans, my future!"

It hadn't done Melisande any good either.

"Poor boy . . ." Edytha's hand snaked towards his brow again. "Poor, dear boy . . ."

"Gone!" He moved out of reach, a flicker of irritation in his eyes. This was *his* scene and he was not going to be upstaged. "The love of my life! My soul mate!"

He had a use for his brow himself. He smote it — actually smote it. I hadn't seen a gesture like that since the days of the old silents.

"Dear boy, don't upset yourself so. You'll make yourself ill."

"*Make* myself ill? I *am* ill! Heartsick. Heartbroken. The only woman I ever loved is dead. I am dead, too. My life is over. There is nothing left for me until I join my darling Melisande in the grave. No other woman will ever touch my heart again. I will never love again!"

Jocasta gave a strangled sob and stumbled towards her room. Edytha didn't look any happier herself.

"My next expedition shall be my last!" Banquo declared. "I will make sure I do not return!"

"Can we depend on that?" Evangeline

123

murmured.

That did it. Edytha glared at her and laid a possessive hand on Banquo's arm.

"Come away, dear boy," she urged. "You need rest, a calming tisane, and a place of refuge to restore yourself. The atmosphere here is unsympathetic. The vibes are —" She shot a venomous glance at the retreating Jocasta. "Evil. Unhealthy. Poisonous!"

She began to shepherd Banquo down the hallway, then stopped, seeming to notice that something — or someone — was missing. She turned to focus expectantly on Jasper.

"Well, come along," she ordered. "We're leaving now."

"Er, I'm . . . I wasn't planning to leave just yet," he said. "You go along."

"Along where?" She was incredulous. "We're in the middle of nowhere here. You can't mean to let me try to find my own way back!"

Oh, couldn't he?

"You got me to bring you here under false pretences." His lips set in a stubborn line. "You had no intention of buying the property."

"That has nothing to do with it!"

Wrong. For Jasper, it had everything to do with it. She had deliberately tricked him and, so far as he was concerned, she was on her own. She could walk home, he wasn't wasting any more petrol on her. He was a chip off the old block, all right.

"But — we're miles from anywhere here!" Jasper shrugged.

"How — ?" She turned to Banquo. "How did you get here?"

"Taxi," he said. "I never thought of asking him to wait. I was too upset."

"Of course you were, dear boy. That's another reason why —"

"Just go down to the embankment," Jasper said helpfully, "and follow the river. You'll come to civilisation — eventually."

"You unfeeling brute! You hulking oaf! You —" Edytha took a deep breath. She was just warming up.

"Jasper has reason to remain here." Ice dripped from Evangeline's voice. "We have some unfinished business to discuss. Privately."

Jasper quivered and paled.

"Actually —" In one convulsive movement, he was down the hall and reaching for the door. "You may be right. I can't abandon you. I don't know what I was thinking . . . momentary lapse . . . sorry . . ."

"I should think so!" Edytha was not quite mollified. "We want to get away from this

125

place to somewhere —" She sent a nasty look at us, one that stopped at the door through which Jocasta had exited. "Somewhere healthier."

The door slammed behind them to give emphasis to her parting shot.

Evangeline and I looked at each other.

"Do you think she hates poor Jocasta for herself alone?" I wondered.

"Or is she like that to any woman who shows an interest in Banquo?" Evangeline finished the thought.

"You can't say that," Martha objected. "She seemed very fond of Melisande — and Melisande was married to him."

"And the obituary noted that Melisande had been the sole heiress to a large fortune," Evangeline reflected.

"And Melisande is dead now," I chimed in. "Which leaves Banquo a —"

"Wealthy Widower!" we finished together, the title of, theme of, one of our early films.

"Now stop that! Both of you!" Martha snapped. "This isn't the scenario of one of your stupid movies!"

"I will ignore your slur on our cherished profession." Evangeline was at her most glacial. "And merely point out that it is an indisputable fact that Melisande is dead. And in circumstances no one seems too comfortable with."

"The verdict was misadventure. An accident." Martha was beginning to sound harassed. "A terrible, terrible mischance. Everyone agreed about that."

"Edytha doesn't seem too agreeable about it," I said mildly.

"Oh, Mother!" Not mild enough. "Really!"

"Really," I said. "And perhaps it escaped your notice that — even if she doesn't believe it — Edytha is doing a great job of making Banquo distrust Jocasta."

"Well . . ." Martha couldn't deny it. "I still think you're making too much of it. She's just a thoroughly unpleasant woman, that's all."

"If only it were," Evangeline said. "Can't you see where this is leading?"

"I don't know what you mean." Martha was puzzled. Nothing new. She hardly ever knew what either of us meant. The poor child was distressingly literal.

"She all but accused Jocasta of being responsible for Melisande's death." Evangeline spelled it out for Martha.

"Nonsense! She did no such thing!"

"She implied it — in several different variations." I weighed in behind Evangeline. "But she didn't say anything outright that she could be sued for. That was the beauty of it."

"As neat a hatchet job as anything I've seen since the days when every studio had its own tame mobster or two," Evangeline confirmed.

We met each other's eyes and nodded.

"You're both being melodramatic again! No one would ever believe a story like that!"

"Oh, I don't know —" Evangeline pursed her lips. "Give Banquo a bit more time to brood over it. Depending on how much he's prodded, he might come up with some interesting conclusions. Possibly even a murder charge."

"And with a ready-made scapegoat in Jocasta," I said. "It would certainly give his book that bestseller zing. Especially if they can fake some juicy pictures of Jocasta breaking the news. And then comforting him."

"Have you given any thought to auditioning another assistant to help test your recipes?" Evangeline wondered. "It wouldn't do any harm to have an understudy waiting in the wings."

"Now that's enough!" Martha slammed both hands down flat on the table, making an impressive noise. Out of the corner of my eye, I saw a furry blur as Cho-Cho decided it wasn't as safe to rejoin the party as she had thought.

"I won't listen to another word!" Martha glared impartially at both of us. "So you might as well save your breath!"

A sudden gust of wind blasted against the building and it seemed to sway. But they were built to do that in high winds, weren't they? Surely, it didn't presage anything sinister. Abruptly, I found myself agreeing with Martha. I, too, had had as much drama as I could stand in one day. And the day wasn't over yet — or was it?

The sky had darkened without our noticing it and now large raindrops splattered against the windows, gathering force and intensity as I watched. There went any idea of escaping into town. If this wasn't a monsoon, it would do until the real thing came along. It was nothing to venture out in.

"Actually —" Evangeline turned away from the storm outside, obviously having reached the same conclusion. "I feel one of my headaches coming on. I shall retire to my room and lie down. Please see that I am not disturbed."

"I'll guarantee it," Martha promised grimly, underlining that she had no intention of seeking any more of Evangeline's company. She, too, had had enough of this day. And she still had her deadline to meet and a helper who was going to be no help at all. I felt for her but —

"Actually —" I echoed Evangeline. "I'm not feeling too well myself. And I didn't sleep much last night." Well, it might be true — I couldn't remember. "And this weather —" Obligingly on cue, a howling gale hurled the rain — or possibly hail — against the windows. "This weather is getting me down." I headed for the door.

"Oh, Mother," Martha was prepared to worry slightly more about me than about Evangeline. "Can I get you anything? Aspirin? A bowl of soup? Tea and toast? A — ?"

"No, no, thank you, dear. All I really need right now is a nice little nap."

"Don't worry about us," Evangeline said. "We'll be all right."

Righter than Martha knew. Neither of us had wanted to tell her but, when we found our fridge full of strange ingredients and our kitchen taken over, we had provided ourselves with mini fridges and hot plates for our private quarters. I knew for a fact that Evangeline kept a supply of caviar, smoked salmon, and half bottles of champagne in hers. I wasn't that fond of caviar, but I had a few tins of pâté and three-bean salad and red wine in mine. We were well stocked up for emergencies or unforeseen events.

I closed my door behind me and leaned against it thankfully. Peace. And quiet. At last. Outside, the storm continued to rage. In here, it was warm and cosy and the soft bed inviting. I flipped on the radio and picked up the mystery I was reading.

A faint mew of protest told me that I had nearly squashed my little chum as I stretched out on the bed.

"Push over, then," I told her and she obliged. I began to feel drowsy as I settled down next to the warm little body with the comforting purr.

I had intended, I really had, to review the events of the day — with particular attention to everything that had been said or implied. But . . .

But . . . the room was warm, the bed was soft, the storm outside closed us into a sphere of comfort and contentment.

Then Classic FM began to play the "Rose Adagio" and the smooth melodic strains wafted me into another world. I stood on a stage I had never known, wearing a costume I had never worn, facing a partner I had never seen before . . .

Another moment . . . I promised myself.

Just another moment and I'll pull myself together, open my eyes, and do some serious thinking about the situation.

"Prrr . . ." a little voice throbbed in my ear. *"Prrr . . . prrr . . ."*

Just another minute. The music swirled and soared and I soared with it.

I'll open my eyes in just another minute . . .

"Prrr . . ."

Just another minute . . .

CHAPTER TEN

I awoke to discover that the rain had dwindled from a monsoon to a mere downpour. An improvement, but still nothing one would want to go out in. A quiet evening at home stretched out before me. At least, I hoped it did. Given my personal opinion that Banquo and his crew were all mad as hatters, they might even now be heading in this direction.

I yawned, stretched, and decided I wouldn't bother to change for dinner. There would just be Evangeline and me and, judging from the finality with which Jocasta had disappeared earlier, I would be the one doing the cooking. Perhaps an omelette and crusty rolls and —

Something wasn't right. I was awake enough now to notice this. But — what? I inhaled deeply: bacon, eggs, coffee, toast. Morning smells. And the murmur of voices. Jocasta, sounding slightly plaintive, but in a reasonable mood. And lower, soothing, a man's voice I couldn't immediately identify. But all the men had left earlier . . . or yesterday?

I couldn't have slept all afternoon and all night!

The clock, though, said eight and the sky had lightened as much as the rain would allow. Cho-Cho was nowhere in sight, so the visitor must be friendly — and not Teddy. Not yet.

As I entered the kitchen, a sudden burst of laughter halted me in surprise. In fact, amazement. To be fair, Jocasta looked equally surprised at herself. I realised it was the first time I had ever heard her laugh. I looked around to see who the miracle man could be.

"Good morning, Trixie." Nigel beamed at me — or, possibly, at his success in amusing Jocasta. "Ready for breakfast? We're having bacon, but there are sausages, if you'd rather."

Cho-Cho looked at me hopefully. She liked bacon, but she loved sausages.

"Split the difference," I said. "A couple of each."

"Coming up!" He seemed to have taken over at the grill.

"Oh, Trixie —" Jocasta greeted me.

134

"There's a message from Martha. She won't be here today. I'm to just go ahead with the next recipes to be tested. Nigel has very kindly volunteered to help me."

"Good! I mean —" Perhaps I had sounded too enthusiastic. "I mean, it's a filthy day for her to trail all the way over here. I'm sure you and Nigel will manage splendidly."

"Martha's sulking again, I'll be bound!" Evangeline appeared in the doorway, blinking as she took in the scene. It did not escape her notice that I was wearing yesterday's outfit. So was she.

"I can't believe I've slept the clock nearly round," I greeted her brightly.

"You, too?" Her eyes narrowed. "Martha must have slipped something into our private supply."

"Don't be silly!"

"I wouldn't put it past her!" Evangeline was spoiling for a fight, but not quite up to it. She yawned unwillingly.

"Here you are!" With a presence of mind that I wouldn't have expected of him, Nigel slid my plate in front of Evangeline and pulled out a chair for her, giving me a nod to say I'd have mine in just another minute.

I nodded back. Cho-Cho sidled over and leaned against my ankles. She was no fool; she'd rather wait for my serving than try to

135

cadge anything from Evangeline right now.

We hadn't long to wait. Nigel was shaping up nicely as a short-order cook. Perhaps it had been one of the temporary jobs he had tangled with somewhere along the way.

Jocasta settled down at the other end of the table with a cup of coffee and several sheets of paper, presumably the recipes for today's testing session. She seemed more relaxed than I had ever seen her. Was it because of Martha's absence — or Banquo's? Or Nigel's presence?

My plate was slid in front of me — with an extra sausage, I saw. I cut it into slices, transferred it to a saucer, and set the saucer down at my feet. Cho-Cho pounced on it, in a ladylike way.

I did some pouncing myself. Now that I thought about it, no wonder I was starving. I'd missed dinner last night and —

The buzzer of the downstairs entrance jarred like a Klaxon. We all jumped.

"Not Banquo —" Jocasta whimpered, shrinking back. "Oh please, not Banquo."

"Not Teddy!" I had my own preoccupation. "Not again!"

"I'll take care of this!" Evangeline pushed back her chair and advanced grimly on the intercom. "I've had enough!"

"Evangeline, please —" I began. She

mustn't antagonise Teddy. He was a mild man — but they're the worst when sufficiently aroused.

"Go away!" Too late. She was shouting into the intercom. "No one can come in! We're quarantined! The doctor says it's bubonic plague! Flee for your lives! It's too late for us — save yourselves!"

"And good morning to you, too, Evangeline." The deep amused male voice was too self-assured to be Teddy's, too professionally trained to be Banquo's. "In top form, as usual, I see. I was under the impression we had a date. Are you going to let me in? Or shall I take a rain check?"

"Good Lord — it's Jem!" Evangeline stabbed at the lock release button. "Is it Wednesday already?"

The Grey Pound was out in full panoply at the matinee. They filled the orchestra pit and dress circle, chattering brightly, waving to friends, stowing walking sticks under seats, and adjusting hearing aids. The more thoughtful unwrapped their boxes of sweets immediately rather than waiting until the show had started and the actors were in the middle of a key scene.

Dotted here and there amongst the sleek coiffures in every shade of white, from silver to palest blue, were a few more vivid younger heads, obviously theatre students and resting actors taking advantage of the professional courtesy that allowed them to occupy the unsold seats.

The house lights dimmed and the old familiar expectant hush came over the audience as we gradually slipped into total darkness and the curtain rose.

Okay — so it wasn't the greatest show I'd ever seen, but that didn't matter. It was theatre, it was lights, costumes, music — magic.

From time to time, I could feel Jem's eyes on me, so perhaps I overdid the enthusiasm a bit. He was our host, after all, and I wanted to show him we appreciated it.

I was subvocalising the chorus of the main song, which was sure to be a hit — or would have been once. Before the world went mad and accepted discordant notes and raucous shouting as the norm for what passed as music.

"Like to be up there yourself, would you, Trixie?" Jem smiled, aware that I had caught him watching me.

"Oh, boy! Would I!"

He nodded, as though I had confirmed a private suspicion, and turned to watch Evangeline as the non-singing heroine took

138

centre stage for one of her big dramatic scenes.

Evangeline was leaning forward in her seat, oblivious to everything but what was happening on the other side of the footlights.

Jem didn't speak to her, but nodded to himself again.

The cast took six curtain calls, perhaps two more than they really deserved, but the audience had enjoyed the performance, so why not?

"Thank you, Jem," Evangeline said as we emerged from the theatre. "I really needed that. I didn't know how much."

"Me, too," I said. This was our world — and we had been away from it too long.

"Over here." Jem steered us to the kerb where Eddie and his taxi waited, rebuffing the hopefuls trying to hire him.

The rain was more of a drizzle now, but I saw the street dotted with puddles and knew that there must have been another downpour while we were inside.

"Cecile can't join us for dinner." Jem nodded to Eddie and we slid out into the stream of traffic. "Her show is previewing this week and next and she had a working matinee today. She's invited us for drinks in her dressing room before she rests for the evening performance."

The champagne was chilled and the welcome was warm. What more could one ask? Dame Cecile and Matilda looked tired but happy. A successful matinee accomplished, a successful evening performance to come, they glowed with the growing realisation that they were starring in what was going to be one of the hits of the season.

In fact, the smell of success was in the air the instant we stepped through the stage door. A heady mixture of fresh flowers, expensive perfume, the sound of relaxed triumphant laughter, and the buzz of excitement, it was all there.

For a moment, I felt a pang of sympathy for poor Teddy, cut off from all this because of being replaced in the tryout stage. Then I remembered that Teddy had been dire in the role and that, if he had been allowed to continue in it, the show would have lost all chance of being a hit.

I gave a faint sigh for the unfairness of life in general and the theatre in particular.

Then a flute of champagne was pressed into my hand and I was waved towards a side table set out with a small bowl of caviar surrounded by the trimmings, a larger bowl of quails' eggs with celery salt, and dishes containing mixed olives and feta cheese, smoked salmon, pâte, a selection of toast triangles, buttered brown bread, and crackers.

"Good, solid . . . a bit old fashioned, though." Jem gave it a mock review while selecting a quail egg. "No Chinese rolls, no onion bhajis, no sushi —"

"Nothing that might put any strain on the digestion," Dame Cecile said firmly. "Tried and true — and safe. This is our usual matinee day meal between performances. We have to be careful. It looks as though we may be in for a long run. We have to pace ourselves."

"And we" — Evangeline took a couple of olives — "are going on to dinner at the Harpo. We mustn't spoil our appetites."

It was a good try, but paled in comparison to the prospect of a long run in a hit, and the hollow note in Evangeline's voice betrayed that she knew it.

"You and Trixie will be next," Jem said reassuringly. "You'll pull out the whole we-don't-applaud, we-just-rattle-our-jewellery brigade for your opening. How *is* the prospective vehicle coming along, by the way?"

There was an uneasy silence in the dressing room. Everyone except Jem knew that this was a sensitive subject. Evangeline and I met each other's eyes.

141

"Not too well, I'm afraid —" I began.

"A disaster!" Evangeline threw restraint aside. "That bastard playwright has decamped with our advance and his girlfriend and gone off to see the world. For inspiration, he said! We haven't heard a word from him since. Not one page of script — He hasn't even written a postcard —" She broke off and finished her champagne in a single gulp.

"Oh, my poor dears, how unfortunate," Jem said unconvincingly, hurrying to refill her glass. "How very awkward for you."

"Yes." I had the curious feeling that he was not displeased to learn this. That was the theatre for you — schadenfreude all the way, even with the best of them.

CHAPTER ELEVEN

"Oh, there she is!" Jocasta cried in a tone of unmistakable relief as I entered the kitchen next morning with Cho-Cho in my arms.

"What?" I also caught the edge of receding panic in her voice. "What's the matter? Where else should she be?"

"Nothing . . . nowhere . . . that is —" Jocasta broke off in confusion — or perhaps guilt — for a moment before continuing. "I . . . I thought . . . I was afraid . . . we might have lost her. She . . . she disappeared yesterday. I couldn't find her anywhere."

"Lost?" My arms tightened and Cho-Cho mewled a small protest. "Yesterday?" True, Cho-Cho hadn't come to greet us, as usual, when we returned last night, but I'd assumed she was asleep. Soon after I had settled in bed and turned off the light, there had been that familiar bounce of the mattress as Cho-Cho had leapt up on it and curled up in the crook of my arm. I'd no idea at all that everything hadn't been normal and serene. "How could she have been lost?"

"I was afraid she ran out when the door was open. I couldn't find her anywhere after they left."

"They?"

"Oh, not Nigel. He's always very careful to make sure she's out of the way before he opens the door, but that Teddy —"

"Teddy?" a voice behind me thundered. "Has he been here again?"

"He came yesterday afternoon . . ." Jocasta quivered and shrank back. "After you'd left."

"And you let him in!" It was an accusation and a condemnation.

"Well, you always do. No one told me not to."

"*I* do nothing of the sort! This is your fault —" Evangeline rounded on me. "I know you told him he could have visiting privileges — but I don't recall your inviting him to move in!"

"But he didn't let her out, after all," Jocasta defended. "Here she is. He may have upset her a bit, but there's no real harm done."

"That's beside the point," Evangeline said, at the same moment I said:

"What do you mean he upset her?"

"And *what*" — Evangeline pushed past me and swooped on a sinister tangle of narrow turquoise leather straps I hadn't noticed lying on a chair — "is *this?*" She held it aloft, wrinkling her nose in distaste.

Cho-Cho stirred in my arms and twisted to face me, uttering soft plaintive noises of distress.

"Oh, that's what he brought for Cho-Cho this time. It's a harness and leash, so that he can take her out for walks when he visits."

"The man's a fool!" Evangeline snapped.

No one was going to argue with that.

"That's what upset her so much." Jocasta turned to me. "He tried to, well, stuff her into it. And . . . and he *is* rather clumsy, you know. He . . . couldn't get her legs through the right openings — and she was fighting him. I was afraid he was going to break some bones — I don't think he realises quite how fragile her little bones are."

"That's it!" Evangeline pitched the harness into a corner. I felt Cho-Cho's tensed muscles relax. "The welcome mat is rolled up. The candy store is closed. That man is persona non grata around here from now on! If you don't tell him, I will!"

Sooner her than me, but —

145

"He didn't actually take her outside?" I asked anxiously. If he did, he'd obviously brought her back. This time. But . . . next time?

"He couldn't get her into the harness, she was fighting too hard. He kept pleading with her to cooperate, but she wouldn't. He got rougher and she got more frightened. I didn't know what to do.

"Then there was a great clap of thunder and a bolt of lightning that seemed almost overhead and the heavens opened again. He was so startled, he dropped everything and Cho-Cho took off. I hadn't seen her since. Not until you appeared with her just now. I was afraid she'd got out somehow — and was still running. She was *very* upset."

Evangeline was right. Something had to be done about Teddy. Short of murder, I couldn't think what.

The rest of the day was so quiet it began to make me nervous.

Even Martha, intent on testing a couple of promising recipes she'd found in an old cookbook was in a not-so-bad mood when she appeared. Teddy didn't show up at all.

The calm before the storm was the uneasy thought that kept running through my mind.

146

By nightfall, I was close to a panic attack and decided to make an early night of it.

Next morning the situation remained the same. I knew it had to be too peaceful to be true. The alternative possibility was that some mysterious plague had swept through the world and we, up here in our penthouse, quiet and unsuspecting, were the only survivors.

"It's too quiet." Evangeline felt it, too. "It's like waiting for the other shoe to drop."

I nodded agreement, conscious that we had both involuntarily glanced upwards, although there was nothing overhead but the roof. Then I looked around our space-age state-of-the-art kitchen, noticing that it seemed a little less daunting these days. Perhaps that was because of all the cooking clutter on the table and work surfaces, or Jocasta's homely little retro radio perched on a shelf, providing musical wallpaper while they worked. Or perhaps I was just getting more accustomed to it. Mind you, there were still several strange dials and switches I wouldn't like to fool around with.

"Prr-yah?" Queried a little voice, reminding me that there was nothing like a cat for the real domestic touch.

"Prr-yah?" Cho-Cho questioned again, twisting her head anxiously towards the

windows. I saw that it was growing darker outside.

"Just a bit more rain on the way," I told her soothingly, thinking that rain wasn't such a bad thing. It might discourage Teddy from another of his interminable visits.

"Oh, bother!" Martha's reasonable mood of yesterday hadn't lasted very long. There was a metallic clatter as she slammed the lid down next to the canister. "You should have refilled this as soon as the flour started getting low, Jocasta!"

"Sorry." Jocasta bent her head and continued beating something in a bowl vigorously, making it clear that she wasn't going to stop what she was doing and refill the canister now.

"I should think so!" Martha hesitated for a moment before getting the message and going over to the walk-in supply cupboard to do it herself.

Jocasta gave her a swift look and seemed to shrink. She added something to her bowl and became more engrossed than ever in beating it wildly.

"Jocasta?" Martha emerged from the cupboard, looking both annoyed and puzzled. "There was a large bag of flour in here last week. Where — ?"

"It's gone," Jocasta said. "We've used it all."

"All? But —"

"You may not have been here all the time —" Jocasta was veering close to insubordination. "But I have. And I've been working!"

That was true. She'd hardly stopped. And she hadn't been outside the place in days. I'd decided it was her way of dealing with the cabin fever which would have set in if I'd been forced to spend so much time in the same place. She was virtually under house arrest — even if it was her own choice.

"We need a lot of other things, too." Jocasta was mutinous.

"Someone ought to take a trip to the supermarket and do some shopping," Martha said. It was clear that someone wasn't going to be her.

"That's not a bad idea." Evangeline jumped at the chance for action. She pulled her cell phone out of her jacket pocket and pushed the speed dial. "I'll call Eddie."

"I'll come, too." She wasn't going to leave me behind. "Just make a list of what you want us to get, darling, and —"

"Oh, no!" Evangeline was speaking into the phone. "No. I'm so sorry to hear it. Is

149

there anything — ? Oh, well, perhaps he could give us the number of one of his cabbie friends to — Hello? Hello?" She lowered the phone and looked at me incredulously. "Would you believe it? That wife of his hung up on me!"

I'd believe it, but that was beside the point. "What's the matter with Eddie?" I asked.

"He's in bed with the flu, probably for the rest of the week. And she isn't going to disturb him. For anything."

"Poor Eddie." If he were that ill, no wonder his wife wouldn't let Evangeline talk to him. He was very loyal to us — and besides, he hated to think he might be missing out on anything. She undoubtedly feared that he would try to get out of his sickbed and ride to our rescue.

"Mmm . . ." Evangeline tapped her front teeth with a fingernail for a moment before asking: "Do you suppose Hugh would loan us — ?"

"Hugh is using the car himself today." She had spoken to me, but it was Martha who answered crisply. "Benson is driving him up to Peterborough to check out a new fringe production he's had good reports about."

"Mmm, then perhaps —"

The room suddenly flared with a white

150

brilliance brighter than daylight. Almost immediately, there was a violent crash of thunder directly overhead. Instinctively, we all ducked.

"The Met Office has just issued a Severe Weather Warning —"

Into the startled silence, the voice of the announcer on Jocasta's transistor spoke firmly. "For London and the southeast."

Another blaze of brilliance nearly blinded us, while the resultant crash of thunder blotted out the radio report.

"On second thought," Evangeline said into another silence, "perhaps not."

"Definitely not!" I said.

Overhead the first heavy drops hit the roof like an ominous drumbeat.

". . . torrential rain." The radio cut back in. "There will be flooding in low-lying areas. The public is advised against travelling unless absolutely necessary. High winds will add to the danger of falling trees, billboards, and overhead lines. The emergency services are on full alert —"

"Hugh!" Martha cried distractedly. "He's out in this storm! He could be killed!"

"Benson is a very good driver." I tried to soothe her. "He wouldn't let anything —"

"They're heading north," Jocasta said, more practically. "The storm may not reach

151

them for hours yet."

The rain was hammering on the roof now and running down the windowpanes like liquid curtains.

"Hugh is perfectly capable of assessing the situation and making arrangements for himself and Benson to put up for the night somewhere. And" — Evangeline added reluctantly — "it looks as though you'd better plan on staying here tonight."

Another blast of lightning and thunder endorsed her invitation. It hadn't seemed possible, but the rain had become even heavier. You could barely distinguish individual drops, it was all one great continuous downpour.

"I suppose so." Martha was nearly as reluctant. She looked around restlessly, then moved closer to the cooking implements, as though they gave her comfort. Like Jocasta. I suspected we were in for a marathon cooking session.

"But —" Martha picked up the flour sifter, then flung it down again. "There's no flour!" She glared at Jocasta.

"Why don't you try your butterless, eggless, milkless cake, darling?" I suggested.

"Because, Mother —" She barely refrained from grinding her teeth. "We have butter, we have eggs, we have milk. What we don't have is flour — and you need flour for practically everything! Even if it's only a little bit of flour!" She sent Jocasta another poisonous look; forgiveness was not going to be earned easily.

Jocasta shifted uneasily, fully aware of this. The next flash of lightning did not seem quite so bright and the thunder took a few more seconds before it sounded. That part of the storm was moving upriver, but the rain looked as though it was settling in for the night.

So was the wind. A wild gust hit the windows with what I swear was hurricane force, driving the rain into them like daggers.

"I hope those windows hold," Evangeline said.

I nodded agreement, not voicing what I really thought: I hoped the building held. I'd distinctly felt it begin swaying. And even though modern high-rise buildings are designed to accommodate natural phenomena, that meant earthquakes, didn't it?

Too many pictures rose in my mind of areas devastated by typhoons, tornadoes . . . and hurricanes.

I didn't even want to think about what the river might be doing. Presumably, they had raised the Thames Barrier against tidal

153

surges — but we were all in the lap of the gods. It wasn't very comfortable there.

"That does it!" Martha glared at the windows as though the storm was a personal insult. "There's no chance of getting any supermarket to deliver now."

"They couldn't," Jocasta said. "No vans will be allowed out on the road in this. It would probably violate all sorts of clauses in their insurance policies."

It also wouldn't do much good for any drivers foolhardy enough to attempt it. Evangeline and I exchanged glances. How nice that Martha and Jocasta were so concerned about their cooking that it hadn't occurred to them to worry about their basic survival. Nice for them, that is.

"Actually . . ." Jocasta got a faraway look in her eyes. "I wonder . . . ?" She headed back into the supplies cupboard.

It was just as well there were no windows in the cupboard. The next flash of lightning was blindingly bright and Jocasta's disposition was nervous enough. The subsequent crash of thunder wouldn't have helped either. The storm hadn't moved away; it was stuck overhead, circling us relentlessly.

"Found it!" Jocasta staggered under the weight of the cardboard carton she was carrying. "The movers brought it up here with the rest of the kitchen gear I brought from home. I thought they might have." She dropped it on the table and stood back, beaming triumphantly.

"What is it?" Martha frowned at it. I didn't like the look of it myself.

"It's Melisande's demonstration equipment. She kept all the basic ingredients in it, ready to use. So all she had to do was unpack them and measure them out — all *I* had to do —" she corrected. "Then I had to measure everything out for her. As I recall it, the flour canister should still be about two-thirds full." She lifted a round medium-sized tin from the carton.

"Wonderful!" Martha pounced on it and twisted the lid off. "It is! We have enough to carry us through today."

"What else is there?" Always curious — not to say nosy — Evangeline was peering into the carton.

"Sugar —" Jocasta lifted out a smaller canister. "Olive oil for sautéing the mushrooms and shallots —" A smallish bottle was deposited on the table.

"What's in there that's so heavy?"

"Oh, that." Jocasta reached in and, brushing a few other items aside, wrestled it out with some difficulty and set it on the table. "A camping gas stove with a spare gas

155

cylinder. Melisande never knew what conditions she might encounter, so she always brought this along to have in reserve. She even had to use it in a couple of places that didn't have their own cooker."

"You can make a mushroom quiche on this?" Evangeline looked at the two gas rings incredulously.

"Of course not. If there wasn't an oven available" — Jocasta took out a packet of basmati rice and a tin of chopped tomatoes in basil and herbs — "she went to plan B — which was a mushroom risotto. You can cook that on the stove top."

Risotto! The word made my mouth water. In weather like this, that was just what was needed. Only, perhaps, beefed up a bit. I drifted over to the freezer and removed a pound of mince and a packet of peas and put them on the draining board until we got round to thawing them in the microwave, then went back to the table.

Martha had been too impatient to wait any longer. She had used the little scoop in the canister to transfer an appropriate amount into the flour sifter which she was wielding over a bowl.

Not too successfully apparently. She was frowning at the result.

"What's the matter, dear?" I asked.

156

"It doesn't look right." Martha transferred her frown to Jocasta. "Have you mixed semolina in with this?"

"Certainly not!" Jocasta was indignant. "Why would I do a thing like that? Let me see!" She moved closer to Martha and peered into the flour sifter.

"How odd!" I closed in on Martha's side and looked, too.

"You see, Mother, there is something wrong, isn't there? It looks lumpy. No, not lumpy — grainy."

Our fingers met, then danced around each other, as we all simultaneously dipped into the sifter to take out a pinch of the flour and study it more closely.

"There's definitely more here than flour." I rubbed it between my fingers and sniffed. Odourless, so far as I could tell.

"Melisande didn't have a secret ingredient in this, did she?" Martha had done the same, obviously with the same results.

"Not that I know of." Jocasta was just as puzzled. "And" — she forestalled Martha's next question — "she didn't rub in the shortening in advance. There might be a long time between engagements where she needed her own supplies and it would go stale."

"Hmm . . ." Martha cautiously put the

stuff on the tip of her tongue and tested the taste. She frowned and took a bit more from the sifter and rolled it around her taste buds.

"Mother —" She paled visibly. "Mother, I think it's —" She tried one more pinch and looked ill.

"Darling, be careful —"

"Mother, it's ground almonds!"

"Are you sure?" I tried a pinch myself and, now that she had identified it, I could taste it. "Ground almonds — and Melisande ate the last piece of quiche with a crust made with ground almonds mixed into the flour!"

"Long-distance murder!" Evangeline said with relish. "Anyone who knew Melisande's habits could have tampered with her kit and then sat back and waited. Or gone off to Timbuktu, Glastonbury . . . or the North Pole!"

CHAPTER TWELVE

"No-o-o-o . . ." Jocasta wailed. "You can't think that! You don't understand. You don't know him. He's idealistic, brave, noble —"

Evangeline and I just looked at each other. She was off again.

"He's kind and courageous —" Jocasta went on listing his virtues. It didn't sound as though she was going to run out of them anytime soon.

"He always thinks of others. He —"

"Let me see that bottle of olive oil!" Martha cut across her. "I don't like the look of it!"

"Oh!" Jocasta stopped abruptly and looked at the small bottle critically before passing it over to Martha. "It does seem a little — different."

"I know this brand." Martha frowned at the bottle. "It's usually a darker colour than this."

"It seems to be a little lighter at the bottom." Or was I imagining it? "Doesn't it?"

"There's definitely something wrong about it." Martha unscrewed the cap and sniffed at the bottle. Nothing. She put her forefinger over the opening and upended the bottle swiftly and put it down on the table. She sniffed her finger, and then tasted gingerly with the tip of her tongue.

"Well?" Evangeline demanded. "What is it?"

"I'm not sure . . ." Martha licked her finger, a thoughtful look in her eyes.

"Something . . . some other oil mixed in with it, I think. Odourless . . . almost taste-less."

"Almost . . . ?" Evangeline prodded.

Martha upended the bottle again and took another taste, then poured a small amount into a saucer and studied it before tasting again.

"I can't be absolutely sure," she said. "This should really go somewhere for a professional analysis. But, if I had to guess — I'd say walnut oil . . ."

"Walnut!" Evangeline looked at the innocuous-seeming bottle. "More nuts! Someone wanted to be very sure. If the ground almond in the pie crust didn't get her, the walnut oil would."

"That's terrible!" I shuddered. "That's evil!"

"You see?" Jocasta said. "Banquo would never do a thing like that. He's too fine, too decent —"

"Stop worrying about Banquo and start worrying about yourself!" Evangeline snapped. "You sautéed the mushrooms and shallots in that oil. You handed her the pie crust mixture."

"And," I added helpfully, "Edytha has already begun hinting to Banquo that you were in some way responsible for Melisande's death. By negligence, if nothing worse."

You couldn't fault the stage effects around this place. As though on cue, the lightning flashed, the thunder crashed, the electricity flickered and . . . the doorbell rang.

We all jumped, stared at each other, and looked down the hallway as fearfully as though Beelzebub himself might be standing outside our door.

"Not Teddy," I moaned. It was the worst fate I could think of. "Oh, please, not Teddy." Did the building sway again — or was it me?

"In this weather?" Evangeline was incredulous. "Only a suicidal moron would go out in weather like this."

161

"That's Teddy," I said glumly.

The doorbell rang again, not with the imperative urgency Banquo used, but faintly, with an almost pleading note.

"Teddy." Now I was certain.

"Oh, for heaven's sake!" Martha started down the hallway. "I'll answer it." I stared after her, wishing I could tell her not to — and she'd obey.

"Nigel!" Martha's startled cry rang out as a figure stumbled past her, reeled down the hall into the kitchen, and collapsed into the nearest chair. He slumped there, grey-faced, shaking and wheezing.

"Nigel, are you ill?" I asked anxiously.

"Nigel, is anything wrong?" Jocasta asked at the same time.

He shook his head. Which question was he answering?

"Nigel —" Evangeline spoke in her take-no-prisoners tone. "Have you just walked up eight flights of stairs?"

"Six . . . teen . . ." Nigel gasped. "Two . . . flights . . . per . . . floor . . ." His head drooped again and he leaned forward to rest his arms on the table and wheeze some more.

"A glass of water!" Jocasta rushed to get it.

"Brandy!" Evangeline moved in the other

direction at a statelier pace.

"Both!" Martha said. "Water first —" She took the glass from Jocasta and set it down in front of Nigel. He fumbled for it weakly.

"But why?" Jocasta asked.

"Storm . . . *gasp* . . . overhead . . ." He managed a gulp of the water. "Wanted . . . make sure . . . *gasp* . . . all safe . . . up here."

"I mean, why didn't you take the lift?"

"Ah . . ." Nigel took another gulp of water and began to sound more like his old self. "Same thing . . . storm overhead . . . electricity supply . . . never too . . . reasonable. Couldn't . . . risk . . . getting trapped in it . . . if . . ."

The lights flickered and went out.

"You see?"

"But you're here. You could have made it."

"Didn't know that, did I?"

"Never mind that!" Martha was exasperated. "Do we have any candles around this place?"

"I'm not sure." I tried to think. "There may be a couple of scented ones in the bathroom cabinet. Nothing too practical."

Now, when we could have used it, the lightning was moving off into the distance again. The rain remained, beating against

163

the windows more heavily and noisily than ever.

"*Braak-erk-erkk* . . . large areas of London are without power as . . ." Jocasta's little radio burst into sudden life, startling us all.

"Perhaps all the electricity hasn't gone out completely," Martha said hopefully. "The radio is still working."

"It's battery-operated." Jocasta was backing into the room, holding a flickering glass-enclosed candle which gave off the faint sickly scent of some unidentifiable bloom.

". . . lightning strikes at power plants . . . *erkk-erkk* . . . overhead cables brought down by high winds . . . *brakkerkk* . . . flood warnings are being issued for . . . *erkk-erkk* . . ." The static was getting worse, cutting in every time the lightning flared.

". . . Emergency crews are working to restore power but . . . *brrkk-brrkk* —" The radio erupted into staccato bursts of static, then went dead.

"Oh, dear," Jocasta said. "I'm afraid the batteries have gone. I can't remember when I put them in, but it was some time ago."

"Don't you have any spare?" Evangeline was impatient.

"Oh, dear, I'm sorry. I meant to get some but . . . I haven't been out much lately." She hadn't been out at all; she had been lying low in here.

"Never mind," I said. "The radio can't tell us anything we don't know — or can't guess."

"And it's not quite accurate information, either." Nigel was reviving by the minute. "Emergency crews can't do much until the storm is over. Work inside the power stations, of course, but all this lightning could knock the power out again as soon as they restore it."

"I could only find three candles and we're already using one," Jocasta said anxiously. "I do hope the storm is over soon."

"Not bloody likely," Evangeline quoted as the thunder and lightning moved closer again. "We'll use them one at a time and make this an early night, I think."

"Put the candle on the high shelf," I said, hoping that would place it far enough away to throw a faint radiance, but keep that dreadful scent from mixing in with any cooking smells. "Thank heaven you pulled out that camping stove. The gas rings will give us some light as well as cook our risotto."

"I'm not sure we ought to open the freezer door if the power is going to be off for any length of time." Martha was fretting over trifles again.

"Relax, dear," I told her. "I took out a packet of peas and a pound of mince before the lights went out. It won't be thawed yet, but we can use the old trick of tossing the block of mince into a hot frying pan and scraping off bits as they cook. If we cook the rice separately the usual way and add the peas, then combine it with the cooked mince and throw in that tin of tomatoes and perhaps any herbs you have lying around — presto! We've got ourselves a nice big kettle of risotto."

"But is that really risotto?" Jocasta frowned. "Or would it be Spanish rice?"

"Who cares? It will be a good hearty hot meal. Serve it with a bottle of red wine —"

"Two bottles," Evangeline corrected. "Possibly three."

"On a night like this, why not?" I agreed.

"Ah —" Nigel remembered his manners and made a feint towards departure. "Since everyone is all right, perhaps I should —"

"Sit down!" Evangeline ordered. "You're not walking down all those stairs. We don't want you killing yourself! Martha is taking the spare room and you can doss down on one of the sofas in the living room."

"Ah!" Nigel sank back in his chair with relief. "If you're quite sure —"

"There's plenty of food," I assured him.

More than he had down in his flat, I was willing to bet — and he had no way of cooking that.

"Furthermore —" I added. A sop to male vanity never goes amiss. "It's going to be a long night and we'd all feel much safer if you were here with us."

"Ah! Right! Of course!" Nigel nodded sagely. "Might still be an emergency before the night is over. Of course, you want a man around."

Evangeline snorted, but didn't say anything.

I wondered if she had the same mental image that had occurred to me: Nigel, with Evangeline under one arm and me under the other, staggering down fourteen — no, twenty-eight — flights of stairs. And then staggering up again to rescue Martha and Jocasta.

I coughed to disguise the bubble of laughter that threatened to break loose and bent to scraping the cooked mince off the frozen slab, then turning it over to cook another layer. Something brushed my ankles, then twined around them. Cho-Cho had caught the scent of cooking and rejoined the party.

And it was a party — or turned into one. Evangeline opened the first bottle of Sangiovese and poured it into our glasses for sipping while the meal was cooking. Jocasta tended the rice. I indicated the thawing packet of peas and she nodded and put them close to add when the rice was nearly done. Martha opened the tin of tomatoes and found another one, plus some herbs, then began setting the table.

The light from the gas hobs was brighter than the candle glow — and a lot warmer. Cho-Cho purred loudly with an occasional chirrup to remind us she was there. Nigel beamed impartially on us all.

It might have been a potluck, picnic-style meal, but it was delicious. The second bottle of Sangiovese had us nicely mellow and Evangeline trotted out some of her best anecdotes, while Nigel filled us in on the local gossip. Warm enough, well fed, and with the curious intimacy bestowed by the storm closing us in, we knew we were a lot better off than many people this night — loss of electricity notwithstanding. There were worse fates out there in the storm.

I was stifling a yawn and thinking of snuggling into the cocoon of blankets waiting in my bedroom when I saw Evangeline's jaw stiffen against a yawn and knew that she was ready to call it a night, too.

"I'll get you a pillow and a blanket," Jocasta said to Nigel. "Martha, your room is already made up."

"I'll say good night then." I stooped and gathered up Cho-Cho. "I hope everyone sleeps well through all this noise. This rain is —"

A different noise cut me off. A sharp shrill alarm bell drowning out all other sound, even the drumming downpour.

"The fire alarm!" Jocasta shrieked. "Some of that lightning hit us! The building is on fire!"

Nigel's face froze, a pale green tinge appeared in front of his ears and travelled up towards his eyebrows and down to his chin.

Green around the gills. I hadn't seen that reaction in years, not since a couple of the most bullying directors in the industry had terrified their last victims. I knew Nigel had suddenly shared my nightmare vision of him trying to shepherd us all down those endless stairs.

There was a pause, then another burst of unbearable sound. Cho-Cho squirmed in my arms and I tightened my hold on her. She wasn't going to run away and hide; we were going to leave together.

"Get your coats on!" Martha ordered. "We've got to get out of here!"

"No, no, it's all right." Nigel's face and complexion began to return to normal.

169

"There's no fire. That's the emergency alarm bell for the lift. Someone's trapped in the lift."

CHAPTER THIRTEEN

I went limp with relief. Cho-Cho dropped to the floor and fled to the sanctuary of our bedroom. I only wished I could follow her, but . . .

The bell shrilled again, more faintly this time.

"Ah! Emergency standby power's running down," Nigel diagnosed. "Only enough for a few blasts when the main supply isn't working."

That settled to his satisfaction, he turned to Jocasta. "Let me help you with that." He reached for the blanket.

"Those poor people!" Martha said. "We just can't stand here —"

"We've got to *do* something!" Martha started forward.

"Nothing we can do," Nigel said. "Not tonight. Not until the electricity comes back on. Whenever that is."

"Morning?" Jocasta sounded frightened.

"Surely in the morning we'll wake up and find everything working again."

The persistent drumming of rain on the roof overhead mocked that hope. And morning was a long time away — especially if you were suspended in space in a small dark box. I hoped whoever was in there wasn't claustrophobic.

"Wouldn't count on that," Nigel said. "Too much of London is out and who knows what's happening in the rest of the country. If the national grid has blown —" He shrugged. "It's anyone's guess how long it will take to get back to normal."

"And, meanwhile, those poor people are going to stay trapped in the lift?" Martha was horrified.

"Ah! Well, when they get the time, the fire department will come and wind the lift down to the ground floor manually," Nigel said knowledgeably. Too knowledgeably.

"You seem well acquainted with the procedure." Evangeline had spotted this, too. "Has this happened before?"

"Ah! Well . . . once or twice. But half the city wasn't knocked out then. Just a little local difficulty. Just here, in fact. The workmen weren't very . . ." He let the thought trail off.

Jasper had hired the cheapest available, I

172

translated. And an incompetent group of cowboys had messed up the wiring.

"Anyway," he said, "the firemen were pretty prompt and sorted things out. But we'll be fairly low on the list for rescue here. I mean, it's not as though a family with children were marooned in a car with the water rising around them."

"Children!" I gasped, but dismissed the thought almost immediately. There was no danger at all that my grandchildren might have been out in this. Only . . . who *was* in the lift?

"Do you know who's in the lift?" Evangeline was having the same thought.

"Ah! No, not really. I could guess, though."

"Teddy." I could guess, too. No wonder Nigel wasn't too concerned.

"Well, I'm going to find out!" Martha swept past us and down the hallway. She was out the door before we pulled ourselves together enough to follow her.

She had her ear against the doors to the lift when we reached her. Faint cries for help could now be heard. In more than one voice. But I couldn't identify the voices.

"Hello, down there!" she called. "Where are you?"

"In the lift," came a plaintive reply.

173

"I know that!" she snapped. "I mean, what floor are you at?"

"Don't know . . ."

"Can't see . . . it's too dark . . ."

"Between floors, I think . . ."

The voices responded, a faintly hysterical note of relief in them. At last, someone knew they were there.

"They can't be very far away." Martha tugged at the sliding doors, trying to pry them open. "We wouldn't be able to hear them so clearly if they were."

"Don't *do* that!" I caught her hands and pulled her back roughly. Perhaps too roughly, but I had a terrifying vision of the doors giving way suddenly and her tumbling through them and plunging down the lift shaft to sprawl, broken and bleeding, on the roof of the lift. And not a thing we could do to help her.

"Really, Mother!" Martha rubbed her wrists as I released her. "That was unnecessary."

"Ah, no! No, she's right," Nigel said. "Those doors are unreliable. They might spring open suddenly. It's been known to happen."

The candlelight flickered and flared, then flickered again. The candle was burning down rapidly. We were in danger of losing what faint light we had.

"Hello . . . ? Hello . . . ? Are you still there?" The voice seemed to echo in the distance. "Is anyone going to get us out of here?"

"Good question," Evangeline said. "Anyone want to answer it?"

The candlelight flickered and flared some more. I glanced at it nervously and discovered that it was actually a fairly fresh candle, not guttering out at all. The effect was caused by Jocasta's twitching.

"Hello . . . hello . . . has everyone gone and abandoned us?"

"They *don't* sound too far away," Nigel admitted. "Let's just see. If we can." He advanced on the doors.

"So it's all right for you to fool around with those doors," Martha said bitterly. "But not for me."

"Ah! But I know what I'm doing." He dropped to his knees and fumbled with some sort of concealed latch near the floor.

The lower third of the door slid apart slowly, revealing that something I had thought was just fancy trim actually concealed the divide.

"I say, you chaps —" he called, leaning into the shaft cautiously. "Any idea at all where you might be?"

"Tom says he noticed that we'd passed the tenth floor" — the furious snarl couldn't belong to anyone but Mick — "just before the lights went out and we stopped." He almost choked in his fury. What a situation for a troubleshooter — hopelessly frustrated by a trouble he couldn't shoot.

"Ah!" Nigel withdrew from the shaft and turned to us.

"They're somewhere between the eleventh and twelfth floors, from the sound of it, I'd say."

"That's quite close." Martha pushed him aside and knelt to take his place.

"Hello —" she called. "Are you all right? How long have you been there?"

"Days . . . weeks . . . months . . ." a plaintive voice answered. "We're starving —"

"I knew Teddy was here!" I'd felt it all along and now I knew for sure. That was his voice.

"Is there enough air?" Always practical, my Martha. Foodie, she might be, but she realised that air came first. Then water. "Are you thirsty?"

"We'll survive," a dry voice answered. "Plenty of air. We opened a panel in the roof. Thought it was an escape hatch, but it's not big enough. It let a lot more air in, though."

"What time is it?" Tom's voice asked. "How long have we been in here?"

"Weeks . . . months . . ." Teddy bleated.

"Oh, belt up!" The other two voices spoke as one. Teddy was having his usual effect on people. Even more so, if you were shut up in a small space with him for hours. The thought made me wince.

"I'll make some sandwiches," Martha said. "If we wrap them well and lower them onto the roof, do you think you can get them in through that hatch?"

"We'll manage —"

"No! No!" Teddy was cracking up. "We can't stay here! Never mind sandwiches — get us out of here!"

"Sorry, old chap." Nigel took over, a new authoritative note in his voice. "No can do. Power's out all over town. Lightning strikes. Flooding. Emergency services at full stretch. You're in the warm and dry. You won't rate high on their priority list."

"No! No! There must be something —"

"Belt up or I'll scrag you!" Teddy wasn't the only one losing it.

"Steady on," the other one said. "Count your blessings. At least we're only stuck in a lift with him. Imagine if he'd been on the expedition."

"Hah!" There was an explosive snort. "He

177

wouldn't have lasted twenty-four hours!"

"That long, you think?"

"Stop talking about me as though I weren't here!" It was perilously close to a shriek.

"Wishful thinking —"

"I'd better go and start those sandwiches," Jocasta said. "They'll all feel better when they get something to eat."

She started away, but I caught her arm and took the candle from her. It wasn't much, but it was better than nothing.

"We need this more than you do," I said. "You've got more in the kitchen. And the light from the gas stove."

"You don't need to stay here, Mother." Martha urged me along. "You'll be more help in the kitchen right now."

"I suppose so." She was right, as she so often was. "But we'd better let them know." I stooped to the opening and called down:

"We're organising some food now. We'll be back soon."

"No! No!" Teddy's anguished wail drifted up to me. "Don't go! Don't leave us! Don't — *Owwww!*"

"Teddy, are you all right?"

"Come on —" Evangeline tugged at my arm. "You don't want to know. There's nothing you can do, anyway."

178

She led me to the kitchen saying, "Be with you in a minute" to the others as we passed through.

"Right," Martha answered absently, groping in the fridge to discover what she could find.

"I don't want to get their hopes up," Evangeline said as we went into her room. "But I've just remembered our reading book lights. I'm pretty sure there's still some life in my batteries. How about yours?"

"I think so." I should have thought of that myself. When you're travelling, your own reading light and a paperback with decent-sized print is essential for those unexpected airport delays and the time aboard when the lights go down for sleeping.

"Here it is!" A sudden radiance glowed and she held it over her travel survival kit as she continued to rummage in it. She pulled out a small flask of brandy — another essential — and considered it thoughtfully, then shook her head. "Not enough for three people," she decided and rummaged some more, emerging triumphant. "Two unused batteries. No good for Jocasta's transistor — they're triple A, but they'll keep this light going."

"Great! Let's see what I've got." A quick search in my room found my own book light

— I'd been using it recently. I dimly recalled having changed the batteries a day or so ago, so I had no spares. This would have to do. Every little bit would help. And morning would come . . . eventually.

We returned to the kitchen in triumph, waving our lights, a lot brighter than the candles.

"Wonderful, Mother! Over here, so I can get the right things out of the fridge. I thought I knew where everything was but . . ."

I moved forward obediently, flinching as a distant shouting erupted. They must be using full lung power. Why hadn't we heard them before?

"Oh, dear," Jocasta said. "They're so impatient and we're just getting started."

"Throw them a bone!" Evangeline said. "Or, better still, a bottle of wine." She disappeared into the pantry, emerging with a screw-top litre-and-a-half plastic bottle of plonk. "This will do — and it won't break if we drop it."

"Wait a minute —" I had a brainstorm and darted to the far corner of the room, returning with the ridiculous harness Teddy had brought for Cho-Cho. "We ought to be able to truss it up in this and lower it to the open hatch. It has one of those expanding leads, so it might just reach."

"Good thinking!" Evangeline snatched at the harness and began strapping the bottle into it. After a couple of tries, it seemed secure enough.

"Ready?" Nigel looked up from his assignment of slathering mayonnaise on bread slices for the sandwiches.

"We need you here!" Jocasta said rather sharply, as he started to abandon his post to come with us.

"Ah! Right!" He sent us an apologetic shrug.

"We'll be right back," I told Martha and followed Evangeline.

"Let me go! I know I can do it!" I heard Teddy being unusually assertive. "Make them let me go —" he appealed to someone — anyone. "I know I can do it!"

"Do what?" I called down.

"Unscrew this thing here," Teddy said. "Then I can take off another of these metal plates and there'll be room to get out."

"No!" I screamed. "Don't let him do it!" I had a flashback to an old Red Skelton comedy when he and the girl were trapped in a lift in a deserted building. He had tampered with a few screws too many and it allowed them to clamber out onto the roof

181

of the lift but then, with a few ominous creaks, the whole lift had dropped from under their feet. Leaving Red and — surely it was Ann Rutherford — hanging perilously from a crossbeam while the lift cage smashed to smithereens below them.

"Don't let him do anything!"

"Don't worry," Tom called. "We won't."

"He may be crazy," Mick said. "But we aren't!"

"Stand by below!" Evangeline was leaning out into the shaft to lower the bottle. Thank heaven it was plastic. "Bottle of wine coming down. Sandwiches to follow in a few minutes."

I held the light steady while she paid out the leash. Down below, I could barely discern groping hands reaching out to grab it and guide it through the hatch.

The bottle swung just out of reach. Evangeline leaned a little farther out.

"Be careful!" I caught my breath.

There was a shout of triumph.

"Send back the harness," Evangeline called. "We need it for the sandwiches."

"Thanks!" Tom shouted as she reeled in the empty harness. "You're a star."

"I always was!" she retorted.

CHAPTER FOURTEEN

In the morning, I was not entirely displeased to find that we were still without power. If I could keep Teddy cooped up in that lift cage for the rest of his natural life, I would cheerfully do so. And that went for the others, too!

It was still raining, but not so heavily, and the wind had dropped. Without the electrical storm raging around us, Jocasta had managed to eke out the batteries in her transistor long enough to get us a position report on storm damage before the voice faded to a whisper and gave up.

"We'll try again at the top of the hour," Jocasta said. "When the batteries are this low you can sometimes get the first few sentences of the news bulletin before they fade out." She spoke with such expertise that I gathered forgetting to renew the batteries was a common occurrence in her life.

"We got the gist of it." Nigel looked on

the bright side.

"Such as it was." Evangeline was having none of that.

"The emergency services may be working full out, but it doesn't look as though much will happen in our area for hours yet."

"Naturally, they're working to get the hospitals back on line first," Jocasta said.

"Hours and hours yet." Martha sighed. She and Jocasta looked at each other. I knew they were mentally reviewing the provisions on hand. They wouldn't want to dip into the freezer too often for fear of speeding up the defrosting process.

"And three more mouths to feed in the lift," Jocasta brooded.

"Don't bother!" I snapped. "Let them starve!"

"Mother!" Martha was aghast. I am not normally vindictive, but in Teddy's case, I was prepared to make an exception.

"She has her reasons," Evangeline assured Martha.

"Obviously." Martha cocked an eyebrow at me. "Something tells me I missed something last night. I shouldn't have gone to bed so early."

"You missed the grand finale," Evangeline agreed.

184

"Well . . . ?" Martha looked at me expectantly.

"Not well at all," I said. "I knew Teddy was thoughtless, incompetent, weak, and selfish, but I never realised the full extent of it. I couldn't believe it when he pulled that on me. The nerve of him! The unmitigated gall!"

"What?" Jocasta was wide-eyed. She'd gone to bed early, too. "How could he upset you so much when he's stuck in the lift?"

"Cho-Cho," I told her. "He wanted Cho-Cho. He — he practically demanded her. He actually expected me to strap her into that ridiculous harness and lower her down to him —" I choked, too furious to go on.

"That's monstrous!" Martha said.

"Never!" Jocasta was also horrified. "The poor little darling would be terrified. How could he even think of such a thing?"

"The chap has no sense." Nigel was too kind. "No sense at all."

There was a moment's silence as we all contemplated the mental picture of a frightened Cho-Cho being forced into that hated harness and swung out into the blackness; being dropped into what would seem to her an endless distance to hover over that small opening while unknown hands snatched at her, trying to pull her inside another black

185

confined space filled with strangers. Her little legs would be flailing wildly, claws outstretched and slashing for something to catch hold of. Serve Teddy right if she took all the skin off his hands!

"The other men in the lift weren't too keen about the idea, either," Evangeline said. "All they needed was a hysterical cat dropping in. They weren't keen at all."

"They sure weren't." My lips curved as I remembered the anguished howls of protest from Tom and Mick. And, rising above them, Teddy's voice — that of a plaintive, whining, insistent five-year-old pleading for his comfort blanket. With any luck, if they all had to stay cooped up in that lift for much longer, he'd aggravate the others into throttling him.

Cho-Cho was looking from one to the other of us, sensing that we were talking about her but, fortunately, with no idea of what we were actually saying.

"Don't worry, darling." I scooped her up and hugged her. She responded with a loud purr as she rubbed her cheek against mine. "I'll never let that idiot get his hands on you again! No matter what!"

It was midafternoon when something changed in the quality of silence around us.

At first, I couldn't identify it, I was just aware that there had been some sort of change.

"The rain has stopped," Martha said.

"You're right." For a moment, I savoured the quiet, the absence of that steady drumming on the roof. But something else had replaced it, a sort of low hum that seemed to be everywhere . . .

"The fridge!" Jocasta dashed to it and opened the door. Sure enough, the light came on. "We're back in business!"

"Wonderful!" Martha was regaining her enthusiasm for the project. "We can —"

"Don't get too happy," Evangeline warned. "If the electricity is back, you know what that means —"

The doorbell rang. Abruptly jolted out of our initial euphoria, we all realised what that meant.

"Where's Cho-Cho?" I looked around wildly. "I'll shut her in my bedroom." I didn't want Teddy to see her, to get hold of her. He might take her away out of sheer spite because I didn't let him have her last night.

"Where is she? She was here a minute ago." But there was no sign of her now. Perhaps she had sensed Teddy on his way to her and, being as fed up with him as we were, had gone to ground.

The doorbell rang again.

"Someone is going to have to answer it." Clearly, that someone wasn't going to be Evangeline. "They know we're in here."

"Oh, all right." Martha sighed. "I'll go."

"No, no!" Nigel sprang to his feet. "I'll go. Do those chaps no harm to know you've got a man here to look after your interests."

Evangeline and Martha both bristled, but I thought Nigel was probably right, no matter how tactlessly he put it. Men who went off together on long polar expeditions were undoubtedly more attuned to dealing with other males than with a houseful of women.

There was what sounded like a stampede down the hallway and the men burst into the kitchen. Tom and Mick were in the lead.

"Where is it?" They looked around frantically.

It was my turn to bristle. How had Teddy enlisted them in his rotten cause? I'd thought they were beginning to hate him.

"She isn't —" I began.

"There's one behind the far door over there —" Nigel cut in over me, pointing to the corner. "And another one opening off the living room."

Tom and Mick dived for them. Oh. Of course. After all that time in the lift . . .

Maybe Nigel wasn't so tactless, after all. Answering the door had given them the opportunity to have a private word with him.

Only Teddy remained, lurking furtively — even guiltily — in the doorway.

"Not in a hurry?" Evangeline eyed him suspiciously.

"I, er, I can wait," he said evasively. "A bit."

"Can you, indeed?"

"Yes." He wouldn't look at her. He wouldn't look at any of us. His gaze travelled across the floor. "Where's Cho-Cho?"

"She's sleeping." If I had to lie to protect her, I would.

"Never mind the cat." Mick was back, a nasty glint in his eye, in full troubleshooter mode. "You've got a little job to do before you start fooling around with the cat."

"That's right." Tom came up behind, backing him up. "Someone get a bucket of soapy water and a mop. Our friend here is going to muck out the lift."

"Me?" Teddy was indignant. "Why me?"

"You did it. You clean it up," Mick said sternly. "Other people are going to want to use that lift now that the power is back."

"It was pitch black in there," Teddy protested. "You can't be sure it was me."

"But he could wait . . ." Evangeline's darkest suspicions were confirmed.

"It might have been —"

"You can't blame it on the cat," Mick said. "They were too smart to let you have it."

Was that why he wanted Cho-Cho in the lift with him? To take the blame? By this time, there was nothing I'd put past the miserable wretch.

"Here —" Jocasta had taken in the situation and moved swiftly. She thrust the bucket and mop at Teddy.

"Right you are," Mick said. "Stop arguing and get moving!" He started forward threateningly.

"I'm going, I'm going. You don't have to come with me."

"Oh, yes, I do. I don't trust you not to do a runner."

"No." Teddy set the bucket down and faced him stubbornly. "I've had enough of you. Both of you. All night in that lift with you ignoring me. Talking over my head as though I was too stupid to understand what you were saying. I hate people who think they're talking in code about other people and think no one can decipher it —" He looked around for support and settled on Nigel who, at least, seemed neutral if not fully sympathetic. "Don't you?"

"Lot of it around, old chap," Nigel said.

"Especially in theatrical circles," Evangeline added.

"We thought you were asleep," Tom said. It was more of an explanation than an apology.

"And we've had enough of you." Mick moved forward again. "You're not to be trusted. You need someone standing over you to make sure you're not dodging out on the job."

"Not you." Teddy waved the mop in a vaguely threatening gesture. "Or you, either," he said to Tom.

"I'll do it," Nigel volunteered to my surprise, although, certainly, none of us was going to.

"All right," Teddy decided after a long moment. He picked up the bucket again.

"Make sure he does a good job," Mick called after them.

"Don't worry." I hadn't known Nigel could sound so grim. "I have to use that lift, too. All the time." That explained it.

"And when the lift is clean again," Evangeline looked at Tom and Mick severely, "I suggest you be the first to use it."

"Hey, not so fast," Tom said. "We're here on business."

"What business?" Martha's hand went out to hover protectively over the mixing bowl and spices she had just set out on the table. "Nothing here could possibly be any of your business."

"Not that female stuff," Mick said dismissively. "We mean real business." He looked at Jocasta. "You've fooled around with this long enough. We need to get down to work on the expedition notebooks."

"And I've got the first batch of contact sheets," Tom said. "We need to go through them and mark up the ones we want to get blown up and printed."

I hadn't noticed before but, now that Teddy wasn't around to be the focus of attention, I saw that Mick was carrying a briefcase and Tom had a portfolio with him. He opened it and began spreading the contact sheets over the table while Martha glared at him. Myriad images of a lone Banquo, looking impossibly brave and heroic against the northern wastes, stared up at us. In a few of them — very few — the sled dogs got a nose in, too.

"This is the start of the trip," Tom explained. "See, you can spot the plane that brought us in. Over there, in the corner of the picture."

Sure enough, you could just make out the tip of a wing. Just barely. Behind Banquo, who was centre stage in every photo and wasn't going to be upstaged by his transportation.

There was a moan. I looked up to find everyone watching Jocasta, who seemed, once again, to be trying to crawl into the fridge without opening the door. She had gone pale, her eyes were wide and distressed, her breath coming in gasps.

"Come on," Mick said roughly. "The ball is in your court. Sit down and let's get to work."

"We *are* working," Martha said coldly. "Clear those pictures off the table and let us get on with it."

Poor Jocasta, caught between the devil and the deep blue sea. Generously, I allotted the deep blue sea to Martha.

"This is more important," Tom said.

"Not to me!" Martha's eyes flashed. "You have thirty seconds to take that stuff off my table or I'll tear it up and bin it!"

"Don't try it," Mick warned.

"Evangeline — no!" She had picked up a large frying pan and was hefting it thoughtfully. We didn't need a fight here. At the same time, I slid my hand under the photographs to pick up the jam jar. If that bully dared to lay a finger on Martha —

"All right, all right, if you feel like that . . ." Tom began gathering up the contact sheets.

193

"It's too bad, though. Banquo is going to be bitterly disappointed . . . terribly upset . . ."

Jocasta wavered. We all saw it. Her gaze followed the shots of her hero as Tom stuffed them back in his portfolio. The last thing she wanted was to upset Banquo.

"Yes, right." Mick recognised that Tom had found Jocasta's weakest point and changed tactics. "Poor old Banquo. He's been planning to get stuck into the book right away to help take his mind off losing Melisande. Now he'll have to hang around waiting, grieving — and having too much time to brood over his tragedy."

"Oooh . . ." Jocasta was on the verge of tears.

"We have a contract," Martha reminded her.

"So have we," Tom said. "And the original contract for that book was with Melisande."

Martha's head snapped back as though he'd slapped her. Oh, dear — and she'd just been coming to terms with her discovery that she had been second choice.

"And it's a tie-in with the expedition," Mick said. "That means that Banquo's book should come out first."

"It is *not* a tie-in!" Martha flared. "It is sponsored by the Lady Lemmings and the

194

proceeds are to go to their charity."

"That's what they thought," Mick said. "Banquo and Melisande had other plans for it."

"Well, Banquo can forget them!" Martha snarled. "*I'm* in charge now and I'm going to see to it that the Lady Lemmings are treated fairly!"

"The Lady Lemmings are the ones who can forget it! They only got a look-in because they were paying to part subsidise the book. Melisande might have had plenty of her own money, but she was . . . careful . . . with it — and the expedition itself was costing her a bomb. She wasn't —"

Shut up! was the angry signal Tom flashed at Mick just before he said mildly:

"The fact remains: notebook or cookbook, you've still got just one editor between you. Jocasta might have something to say about who takes precedence." He looked at her expectantly.

Evangeline still hadn't relinquished that heavy frying pan. I watched her uneasily. For a few nasty moments, I was afraid she might use it on Jocasta, who was looking from the Banquo faction to Martha and back again . . . and again . . . and again. Evangeline never could stand a ditherer.

"Ah!" Nigel had reappeared in our midst.

I had never been so glad to see him. Especially since he was carrying the bucket and mop, which provided an instant change of subject.

"Where's Teddy?" I asked.

"Ah, gone. Took off as soon as he finished the mopping up. I let him go. I didn't think anyone would want me to urge him to stay."

"Quite right," I said. Nigel was growing on me, or maybe he was just growing up. His judgement was improving no end.

"Good riddance!" Mick said. "We can do without blokes like that."

"Ah! He did say he'd be back," Nigel added, somewhat nervously.

"We never doubted that for a minute," I assured him wearily. However, any respite was welcome.

Cho-Cho appeared from nowhere, obviously sensing the coast was now clear, and sat at my feet.

Jocasta relieved Nigel of the mop and bucket and put them away where the cleaning service would eventually deal with them.

Martha was reaching for the mixing bowl when her cell phone rang. "Hugh!" Her cry of delight rang out and my eyes misted over. It was so good to see my darling so happy.

"Overnight? Yes, yes, we thought you would . . . No, everything was fine here. We lost all power, of course, but it's back on now. Otherwise, it was quiet . . ."

Mick snorted and Tom raised an eyebrow.

"Are you still here?" Evangeline turned to them. "Shouldn't you be on your —" Her own cell phone rang.

"Yes? Oh, Cecile . . . that's right. Completely dark, a bit — but nothing we couldn't handle. And you?"

Another cell phone tootled and Mick pulled it from a pocket, turning away from us to speak softly into it.

I began to feel left out, which was ridiculous. The most important person in my life, Martha, was right here with me. Evangeline, too, had been here all along. I had no need of anyone calling me.

"No, not yet . . ." I tuned in to Mick's conversation. An edgy note had come into his voice. "The subject hasn't come up. No, I didn't talk to her last night. There were . . . complications . . ." He listened again, then held the phone out to Jocasta. "The rest of this is for you —"

Automatically, Jocasta accepted the phone. "Hello?" An expression of horror crossed her face as someone spoke to her.

An unspoken communication passed between Tom and Mick. Mick shrugged.

"No!" Jocasta screamed. "No!" She hurled

197

the phone from her. It hit the floor, bounced, then skittered across the room.

Cho-Cho, spooked, ran off in the opposite direction, after sending me an accusing look, as though this further disturbance of the peace was somehow my fault. I turned that look where it belonged — on Jocasta.

"Murderess!" Jocasta choked. "She called me murderess!"

Chapter Fifteen

"I'll ring you back, Cecile," Evangeline said. "We seem to have a bit of a problem here."

Jocasta had burst into tears. I started towards her, but Nigel beat me to it.

"Did you have to let her talk to her?" Tom asked Mick.

"It was bound to happen, sooner or later." Mick shrugged again. "You know how she is."

"Who?" Martha asked. "Who called you a murderess?"

Good question. From where I stood, it looked as though there were three candidates — all of them Banquo's harpy cousins.

"Don't let them upset you." Nigel had a protective arm around Jocasta's shoulders, but she didn't appear to notice it.

"Who dared to say that to you?" Martha also had ended her call abruptly. "Hugh has the best lawyers on tap. We'll sue —"

"Hearsay!" Mick, the complete troubleshooter now, threw cold water on that one. "Only Jocasta heard her say it. You didn't hear it yourself. Her word against yours and, believe me, she'd deny it. No lawyer would be happy with that one."

"He's right, I'm afraid." Evangeline's depth of experience with the law was mostly from the divorce courts, but she'd learned a fair amount.

"I don't know —" Jocasta wailed. "I can tell them apart when I see them, but they all sound alike to me."

"You know who you were talking to —" Martha whirled on Mick. "Which one was it?"

"Yes," Evangeline chimed in. "Which witch was it?"

"We're not going to get anything more here right now." Mick looked to Tom. "Time we were leaving. I need a shower, a change of clothes, and a few hours' sleep."

"Not necessarily in that order," Tom agreed.

"You're not leaving here until you've answered my question!" Martha snapped.

It was an order that couldn't be enforced — and they knew it. They were already halfway down the hall.

"Stop them!" Martha cried. "Don't let them get away!" She looked around for help.

Nigel was patting Jocasta's back as she sobbed. It was doubtful that he'd noticed a thing.

Evangeline shrugged.

"Let them go, darling," I advised as she turned to me. "We'll find out, sooner or later."

"Come back!" Martha shouted after them, seething with fury and frustration.

The door slammed shut behind them.

"Please stop crying." Nigel started to offer his handkerchief, realised belatedly that it was in no fit state, and stuffed it back in his pocket. "They've gone now. It's all right."

"They'll be back." Jocasta sobbed, tearing a kitchen towel off the roll and using it. "They'll *all* be back!" She tore off another towel.

"Don't worry," Martha said grimly. "If they do, we won't let them in."

"You don't understand," Jocasta wailed. "We've *got* to!"

"Why?" Martha spoke for all of us. By now, we were getting as adept as Cho-Cho at scenting a rat.

"The pictures —"

"The pictures can wait. Banquo hasn't even written the book yet. And we have a contract."

"So have they." Jocasta reached for an-

201

other paper towel. "And not just for the expedition story. Tom is going to do the photography for the cookbook. Melisande arranged it all — it's all part of the deal."

"Melisande again!" Martha was working up quite a head of steam. She took a deep breath, attempting to control herself. "Well, we'll make sure he comes alone. We don't need two people to do the photographs."

"Actually —" Jocasta avoided eye contact with Martha. "We do. The food stylist will have to supervise everything."

"Food stylist?" Martha was almost snarling. "What do you mean — food stylist?"

"It's quite customary . . ." Jocasta faltered, shrinking back against Nigel's supporting arm, which she still hadn't noticed was there. "Real food won't stand up to the hot lights and the length of time it can take to set up a shot. So there has to be a . . . a certain amount of . . . substitution . . . with some foods."

"You mean fakery." Trust Evangeline to make a bad situation worse.

"Fakery . . . ? Substitution . . . ?" Martha's eyes narrowed. "Explain yourself!"

"Um, well . . . take lemon meringue pie." Jocasta had been unhappy before, she was miserable now. "It wouldn't stand up to an hour or so under the hot lights. It would

202

dissolve into a gooey mess. So, instead of the . . . the real thing . . . we just take an empty pastry shell and, since you wouldn't see the lemon filling anyway, fill it with mashed potato whipped into peaks and brushed lightly with gravy browning. It looks just like really delicious . . . meringue . . ." She faltered to a stop under Martha's basilisk glare.

"Let. Me. Get. This. Straight." Martha spoke between clenched teeth. "You mean, I've been slogging my guts out, not only to test these recipes, but working to make them look tempting, as well as being fast and delicious — and you're not even going to use the real results in the photographs?"

"Everyone does it." Jocasta flinched. "It's standard procedure. The photography session is the only time the food stylist comes into it —"

"And fakes the whole thing!" Martha was losing her precarious control. "All my work — disregarded!"

"We ought to be able to use your casseroles," Jocasta offered.

"It happens all the time. Everywhere." Evangeline belatedly tried her hand at peacemaking. "Look at the substitute for window glass in films. Good old sugar and water panes. Looks just like glass, but no one risks getting cut when they're thrown through them in barroom brawl scenes. That dates all the way back to the days of the silents, but they're still using the formula today. Couldn't be bettered."

Actually, I thought everything was computer generated these days, but decided that this was not the moment to try to bring Evangeline up to date.

Martha ignored her, still concentrating on browbeating poor Jocasta. "And just who," she demanded, "*is* this so-called food stylist?"

"That's the trouble —" Jocasta gave way to a fresh bout of tears. "It's Isolde!"

"Isolde!" Martha reared back, nostrils flaring. "I will not have that woman under my roof!"

Actually, it was my roof. Mine and Evangeline's but, again, this was not the moment to debate the point. Suddenly, I felt very weary, ready to go back to bed and pull the covers over my head. I hadn't had much sleep last night — none of us had. And it was showing.

"It's not my fault —" Jocasta defended herself. "I don't want her here, either."

"I won't have any of them here!" Martha stormed. "And that goes for your precious Banquo, too!"

"Especially Banquo," Evangeline said.

"Now wait a minute —" Jocasta began.

Martha's mobile rang abruptly. I think all of us breathed a sigh of relief.

"Yes?" Martha snapped into it. "Oh, Hugh." Her face softened. "Yes, yes, I'm still here. You will? Good. How soon? . . . Marvellous! No, no, don't come up. I'll meet you downstairs. I'll start down now. Do hurry —

"No, nothing's wrong. Not really. It's just —" Her gaze swept us all with impartial loathing. "I've had enough! I'm more than ready to leave. Ten minutes? I'll be at the door, waiting . . ." She rang off.

"And maybe I'll be back —" She addressed Cho-Cho, who was cautiously edging back into the room now that it had gone quiet again. The cat was obviously the only one of us she was still speaking to.

"And maybe I won't!"

CHAPTER SIXTEEN

Morning arrived. Martha didn't. Nor was Jocasta anywhere to be seen. Evangeline was obviously sleeping. The smell of coffee will wake them up, I thought. Then thought again and made myself a cup of tea instead.

Enjoying the peace, I shared scrambled eggs with Cho-Cho, then suddenly had what I thought was a bright idea. Jocasta had been working so hard — and rather against the odds. Plagued by Banquo and his importunate crew, putting up with Martha in one of her worst moods, cooking our meals — and we had all been taking it for granted. If anyone deserved a little treat like breakfast in bed . . . or at least a cup of tea and a blueberry muffin . . .

I tapped on her door and swung it open, carefully balancing the tray. The curtains were drawn back, so she must be awake and stirring.

"This isn't to get you up and back to

work," I said defensively. "It's more of a little thank you for the good care —"

I was talking to an empty room. Her bed hadn't been slept in.

"Don't be melodramatic," I told myself in Martha's most critical voice. "She's probably . . ."

I tapped on the bathroom door and, getting no answer, opened it. Another empty room.

Perhaps she'd arisen early, made her bed, and gone out for a breath of fresh air before starting breakfast for us.

Except that she hadn't been outside for days. And, however much cabin fever might have set in, she was still too frightened — or too wary — to venture out now.

Wasn't she?

I was still trying to convince myself that there was a reasonable explanation for her absence when a modified hubbub at the door of the flat announced the arrival of the cleaning crew.

I retreated to my room with the tray I had prepared for Jocasta and left them to it, trying not to worry.

There was nothing I was interested in on television, but my book was absorbing and Cho-Cho, curled up at my side, was comforting. I allowed myself to be soothed.

207

Although Jocasta was becoming increasingly distraught, she wasn't silly. There was bound to be a reasonable explanation for her absence — and we would all have a good laugh about it when she returned.

Cho-Cho's purr was hypnotic and my eyelids were fighting a losing battle to keep open and let me read a few more pages when there was a knock on my door.

"Jocasta?" I called hopefully.

"It's Mrs. Mopp," a voice fluted. "Can I do yer now?"

In my half-dozing, half-waking state, unreality seemed not only possible, but actually real. This was London, it was a foggy day, I was hearing a voice from its wartime past. Or was I? It seemed quite possible that time had slipped a cog and flipped me back into that past. At least, I'd be more comfortable there than if it had tossed me into some unknown technological future.

The door opened and a head popped round it. "I'm Mrs. Mopp," it announced. "And I'm 'ere to do you. Can I do yer now?"

Except that he wasn't Mrs. Mopp, nor even the actress who had played her. He was a pleasant-looking young man mouthing the tagline of a character from a famous wartime radio show he was too young to have heard at the original time.

I smiled vaguely at him, wondering if I should applaud. I woke up a little more and inspected him closely. There was something familiar about him. But the cleaning crew was always changing — the company employed young actors and they came and went, depending on who had landed a part in something and who was resting. I frowned, trying to recall what show I might have seen him in.

"Oh, I'm sorry." Sensitive to atmosphere, he caught my frown. "Is this a bad time? I didn't mean to wake you up."

"No, no, it's all right. I was awake. It's just — I know I've seen you before, but not here. I was trying to remember what show — ?"

"Oh, bless you!" he cried. "I haven't been in a show for ages — and that was up north. Before I came down to London to try my luck. You don't recognise me because I'm out of context. I'm your waiter at the Harpo. This is my day job."

"Oh, of course." I knew him now. He was shorter than I had thought, but most of us are when you see us offstage or -screen. The Harpo was obviously his stage for the time being and, when you're sitting at a table with the waiter hovering over you, he appears taller.

"Even if you had seen that show," he sighed, "you wouldn't have noticed me. I was in the background . . . in the chorus."

"Nothing wrong with that." I tried to cheer him. "I started out in the chorus myself."

"I know. That's why I was so thrilled to find you at home today." He advanced into the room and, looking back over his shoulder, closed the door behind him.

"I was hoping — if you don't think I'm too presumptuous. I was hoping you might give me a few tips —"

"Tip? Tip?" Evangeline's outraged squawk came from the doorway connecting our rooms. "Don't give him a penny, Trixie! He gets quite enough. His lot charge like the Light Brigade, as it is!"

"Not that kind of tip, Evangeline," I said wearily.

"Great Heavens, no!" He was horrified and embarrassed. "I wouldn't dream — I'm not that sort of —" He broke off, doubly embarrassed, remembering that, as a waiter, it was the kind of tip he would accept gladly.

Evangeline identified the flaw in his righteous protest, too. Her eyes lit with triumph and she opened her mouth — but the look I shot her made her close it again.

210

"The chorus —" I tried to wrench the conversation back to a more comfortable subject. "Are you a hoofer or a singer?"

"A bit of both, actually." He gave me a conspiratorial look. "As we have to be. I used to see myself moving up to a juvenile lead but . . ." He sighed. "I'm afraid I'm getting a bit beyond that now."

"Oh, you mustn't give up!" I said quickly, hoping he hadn't noticed Evangeline's nod of agreement.

"I've been giving it some thought," he assured me. "There's too much competition for the romantic leads. Juveniles come and go. But a good character actor can go on forever. And villains do even better." He narrowed his eyes, his face chilled ominously, and he gave me a stare I wouldn't like to see coming towards me on a dark night. I shuddered involuntarily. Then he relaxed his features back into his usual amiability.

"I'd aim for that, if I were you," Evangeline said. "For a moment there, you looked positively evil."

"Oh, thank you." He beamed.

"Yes, I think that's definitely the line you ought to work on —" I groped for the name he announced every time he told us he was our waiter for the night. Ah, that was it —

"Robin."

"Er, no. I'm sorry — that's my waiter name. Actually, I'm Toby — Toby Trent. It will fit on a marquee better. And Robin sounds a bit soppy for a villain."

"True." Evangeline nodded judiciously. "But why do you keep on at the Harpo? You must get more money doing this." Rancour returned to her voice as she remembered what the cleaning company charged us. "And it must be exhausting waiting on tables all night."

"Oh, it is," Toby said. "But the networking is great. Do you know, I've had Frella Boynton at one of my tables about three times a week lately — and with a different producer or prospective backer every night!"

No wonder poor Teddy was wandering around like a rudderless ship trying to limp into a port, any port. More and more, it sounded as though he was on the way out — and he knew it.

"From all over the world!" Toby continued enthusiastically. "The play looks a dead cert to transfer to Broadway when the London run ends. Berlin is talking about getting Frella over there — if not with this show, then another. Paris, Budapest, Rome, Warsaw — they're all after her. I tell you, that woman is *hot!* Er, professionally, that is."

He became aware of the way we were looking at him. "Well, I couldn't help hearing what they were saying." He was defensive. "You learn an awful lot from people talking at your tables. But I'm very discreet —"

"I'm sure you are." Thankfully, Evangeline kept a straight face as she agreed. "I'm just surprised now that you keep on with your cleaning job when there's so much going on at the Harpo. Or are there just as many networking opportunities doing this?"

"No, but the money is better," he admitted. "And I find it very interesting having a window into so many different lifestyles. Amazing, in fact. You wouldn't believe the way some people live. They look so poised and fashionable when you see them at the theatre or in photographs — but their homes are a tip. An absolute tip!"

That word again. This time, Evangeline ignored it. She had scandal on her mind.

"Who?" she demanded. "Who?"

"You become more aware of these things." Toby shook his head. "Not just in houses, but outside. Everywhere. Even here —"

Evangeline bristled.

"No, no, I don't mean *here* here," he said quickly. "I mean outside the building. In that little dock behind it. Someone has dumped a big bundle of old clothes into the river there."

He shook his head disapprovingly. "Pollution at its worst. Some people have no respect at all for the environment."

I met Evangeline's eyes and we started for the door as though joined at the hip. We didn't need to speak. The last time we had gone past the little dock, the water had been as clear and clean as a public reservoir.

"What was it? What did I say?" Toby followed and caught up with us as we waited for the elevator. "I didn't mean to offend —"

"No, no," I assured him. "It's just —"

"JAKE!" a voice bellowed from behind us. "Jake! What do you think you're doing? Get back here!"

"Ja-a-ake?" Evangeline made it sound suspiciously close to "haa-aa-and-ba-a-ag."
"Who's Jake?" She looked around.

"Oh, that's me," our waiter/actor/cleaner said. "That's my cleaning name. I think it's so important to keep one's personas separate, don't you?"

"JAKE!" The bellow came again, just as the lift arrived.

"I'd better go," he sighed. "I really need to keep this job, you know." He turned and headed back into the penthouse.

"Robin . . . Toby . . . Jake," I said. "I

wonder which name he really wants to be called."

" 'Hey, you!' would seem the safest option at the moment." Evangeline stabbed savagely at the G for ground button. "That boy has a serious identity problem."

"We have a problem of our own," I told her. "Jocasta has disappeared. Her bed hasn't been slept in."

"And you think — ?" Evangeline glanced at me sharply.

"I'm trying not to think. But she's been under a terrible strain lately. Veering close to breakdown, perhaps."

"Enough to send her over the edge?" Evangeline raised an eyebrow. "I wouldn't be so sure."

"We've never had any rubbish dumped in our dock before. And we're a bit off the beaten track for casual litter louts." The lift stopped and the doors slid open.

"Come on," Evangeline said. "We'd better go and find out the worst."

The air was cold. The water must be colder still. Too cold for anyone to survive in it long. If Jocasta had slipped out last night . . .

"There it is!" Evangeline took my arm as she urged me to the far end of the dock. Now I saw it, too.

215

The semi-submerged bundle of clothes bobbed quietly in the water, so sodden it was impossible to tell what colour they had been originally. The piece of garment most in view appeared to be a coat. Would someone really put on a coat to throw themselves into the Thames?

On the other hand, why not? Instinct clung to the thought of comfort somehow. There were plenty of cases of suicides carefully placing a pillow for their head into the oven before turning on the gas.

"We've got to get her out!" I started forward.

"Not as easy as you might think." Evangeline held me back. "We might fall in ourselves. This is a job for experts. Let's go back upstairs and call Ron — he'll know what to do."

"But we can't leave her there."

A river barge chugged past on its way to the Thames Estuary with some sort of heavy cargo. The deep waves swelled out from its wake, rippling in our direction, into our dock, setting the bobbing bundle into motion.

As it rode the eddying ripples, rolling from side to side, it lifted out of the water just enough to allow us a partial glimpse of the face. Just enough to identify it.

It wasn't Jocasta.
It was Teddy.

CHAPTER SEVENTEEN

The welcome fragrance of freshly brewed coffee, frying bacon chops with sautéed potatoes and onions and fried eggs greeted us as we entered the flat.

"Martha?" I called tentatively. We had had to wait in the downstairs lobby until the river police arrived on the scene. I'll admit we were watching the river waiting for them, but I'm sure I would have noticed if Martha had driven up.

"Warmth!" Evangeline cried, elbowing me aside. "Food! I'm chilled to the bone!"

"We both are." I sent a bit more chill in her direction.

"Jocasta!" Evangeline stopped short in the kitchen doorway. I bumped into her. "We couldn't find you anywhere. Where have you been?"

"Ah —" There was the scrape of a chair being pushed back from the table. I moved around Evangeline to see Nigel rising to his

218

feet, wiping his mouth. "Actually —"

"I've been downstairs in Nigel's flat," Jocasta said. "Everything here has been so awful, I couldn't stand it another minute. And he offered —"

"Ah. I slept on the couch in the sitting room," Nigel said quickly, ever the gentleman.

"How sweet." Evangeline lost interest and abandoned the subject in favour of a far more important one: food. "Are those chops ready to eat?"

"Coming right up." Jocasta moved swiftly to serve them.

Nigel hovered uncertainly, still marshalling arguments of virtue, whether his or Jocasta's, I wasn't quite sure.

"Ah. Well," he said finally. "I'd better be getting along. Lots of work to do, but it's looking promising. Very promising." He gave us a look which was obviously meant to be significant.

"Good," I said automatically, since he seemed to expect it. He nodded a couple of times and went off, satisfied — and well fed.

Food . . . warmth . . . Evangeline and I slumped into our own chairs while Jocasta brought our breakfast.

"Prr-eow . . ." Cho-Cho leaped into my lap, a long strand of bacon dangling from one

side of her mouth like half of a Fu Manchu moustache. Her little pink tongue worked busily as she reeled it in.

"Cho-Cho! Darling!" I clutched her to me and the traitorous thoughts I had been trying to conceal from myself surfaced and engulfed me.

All right, I felt like a swine and a monster, but I couldn't help it. The joy and relief swamped all other feelings.

Poor Teddy was dead — and that was awful. I wouldn't for a moment have wanted anything like that to happen. But it had. And we would do everything we could to get to the bottom of what had happened. But the fact remained:

Teddy was dead — and Cho-Cho and I were safe. No one could take her away from me now.

It was perhaps the happiest breakfast of my life. Not only was the food delicious, but the atmosphere was ecstatic. Or was it just me? It didn't matter. Safe! We were safe!

And then the police arrived for a second round of questioning. With Martha hot on their heels.

"Mother! What does this mean? What are all these policemen doing here?"

"Please, Martha . . ." She was all I needed

right now.

"I saw the police cars downstairs and I knew — I just *knew* — they'd be up here with you again. There's even a police boat in the dock. Oh, Mother! What have you done now?"

That tore it! Good old tactful Martha. I saw a couple of officers exchange glances and then look at me with renewed interest. All the publicity for the revival of *Arsenic and Old Lace* had put people in mind of possible homicidal tendencies in the older generation. I could see them deciding that, if they were offered elderberry wine, they would accept it, but not drink it. In fact, they would bag it and take it away for forensic testing.

Evangeline ran a hand over her still windswept hair, trying to smooth it into some sort of order, and I knew she had caught the nuances of the situation, too. The vengeful look she slanted at Martha hinted of retribution when there were no uniformed witnesses around.

I must say I didn't blame her. I felt pretty much the same myself. I had brought that child up to the best of my ability. Obviously, my best had been none too good.

But Martha was not totally insensitive, just tactless and socially clumsy. She fell silent as the atmosphere finally got through to her and looked around uneasily, trying to decide how to retrieve the situation.

I willed her to just remain silent. She'd said enough.

"Um . . . would anyone like some coffee?" Jocasta offered tentatively.

The officers consulted each other in eye contact. They weren't keen on accepting anything in this flat at the moment. On the other hand, it wasn't alcoholic and they, too, were chilled almost to numbness from the icy wind blowing along the river.

"If everyone is having some . . ." one of them said cautiously. I knew they would wait until we had ingested ours safely before drinking theirs.

"I'm not really —" Evangeline began.

"We'd love to have a refill." I cut across her, taking pity on the officers. It wasn't so long ago that we were ourselves freezing after being out in that bitter cold.

I was just beginning to relax when I noticed that one of them was eyeing Martha strangely. He muttered something to his colleagues and they, too, surveyed Martha with renewed interest. Unhealthy interest.

"I've seen you before," he said. "In the St. John's Wood nick. Capital charge, wasn't it?"

222

"I was *not* under arrest," Martha said coldly. "I was merely helping the police with their inquiries."

Sure you were, sunshine, was written all over their faces. *That's what they all say.*

"More coffee, anyone?" I tried to distract them, but only succeeded in transferring their attention back to me.

Like mother, like daughter? We were now right up there with the Borgia family.

It was so unfair! Just because we had unwittingly been involved in a murder or two since we arrived in this country. Surely that didn't make us prime suspects in this case. Although I remembered reading that the person who discovered the body was always suspect. But Evangeline had been there, too. She was keeping a low profile, I noticed.

If we were likely suspects, what about Tom and Mick? They had left shortly after Teddy. And, if they had discovered him lurking downstairs, ready to continue with his grievances . . . ? Their tempers were already frayed by all that time in the lift with him. They'd had no sleep, they were sick of his whining — who could blame them if they snapped? Certainly not me.

Unfortunately, the police could. And would.

Martha slammed a spoon down on the table. I wished she hadn't. They were all looking at her again.

Martha, I realised, had also taken her departure shortly after Teddy. Martha, short-tempered, exhausted, in no mood to suffer fools gladly — or at all. If she had encountered Teddy . . . shoved him aside — into the water — and continued on her way, not looking back to see if he could swim . . . I tried to suppress the thought, in case it might escape into the atmosphere and be caught by one of the police.

They couldn't consider irritation a sufficient motive, could they? Of course not, they'd need something stronger than that. I took a deep breath and felt better — not one of us had a really strong motive for wanting to get rid of Teddy. It shouldn't take the police long to discover that.

A warm throbbing bundle of fur brushed across my ankles. Cho-Cho!

My motive. Now I never had to worry about Teddy taking her back.

Would the police believe that someone could care enough for her cat to murder to keep her?

Why not? Murders were committed for miniscule sums of money, for a few hours' supply of drugs, because some inane look or remark was considered disrespectful, for reasons most ordinary citizens would not consider credible. Why not for the possession of a faithful loving companion?

Another thought I tried to sweep out of my consciousness in case it was picked up by the men sitting at the table.

"Ron!" Evangeline's glad cry roused me from my forebodings. She started for the door, looking as though she would hurl herself into the newcomer's arms, were they not already laden with a stack of cake boxes.

"Sustenance, lads," Ron said, dumping the boxes on the table by the coffeepot. "It's cold, bleak work hauling bodies out of the Thames in this weather."

"It's bleak in any weather," one of them replied. The others were too busy opening the boxes to bother replying.

Doughnuts, lovely fragrant doughnuts. Dozens of them: jelly doughnuts, frosted, coconut encrusted, with cream and jam, chocolate speckled, cinnamon and sugar dusted, every variety except plain. Quite right, too. A good blast of sugar was what we all needed after what we had been through.

"And, in case any of you ladies are on a diet —" Ron pulled a large bag from an inside pocket. "The tasting menu. There's a

225

new shop in Upper Street. I thought you might like to sample their wares."

Shaking out the bag into a bowl, Martha cooed with delight to discover doughnut holes. Small delicious little balls with all the attractions of their larger companions.

But Ron had underestimated us. Evangeline had already thrust an arm into the melee and emerged with a coconut cruller. I had snagged a luscious lemon-filled doughnut. Martha and Jocasta, lagging behind, settled for the dainty holes. They had never had the practice we'd had on studio sets when the tea trolley was wheeled in.

"Ron, you're a darling!" Evangeline mumbled, her mouth full and her eyes already scanning the offerings for her next foray.

"You know these people?" the chief officer asked Ron.

"Old, old friends," Ron said. "Feels as though I've known them a thousand years . . . for my sins."

"And . . . ?" the unspoken question rested.

"And . . ." Ron had no trouble interpreting the silence. "I'll stand bail for them, I suppose." He sighed deeply. "Completely bonkers, but no harm in them. Theatre people, you know."

"Right." Apparently that explained everything.

Evangeline's eyes flashed but, before she could rise to the defence of our profession, there was a sudden opening in the crowd around the goodies. She dived in and surfaced triumphantly with a long doughnut, split and dripping with cream and jam. Bismarks, we used to call them, who knows why.

I eyed it enviously, then circled the crew waiting my chance for another lucky dip. Meanwhile . . .

"Martha —" I called over my shoulder. "More coffee and a cup for Ron. Especially for Ron!"

There! I elbowed in and fished out another jelly doughnut, raspberry jam this time.

"Apart from which," Ron continued blithely, taking his coffee black and latching on to a handful of holes, "there's no reason to worry about them. It's unfortunate that they discovered a corpse on their doorstep, as it were. But they're just innocent bystanders. There's no way they can be held accountable because some derelict decided to end it all in the Thames near them."

Uh-oh! Evangeline and I exchanged glances.

"Ron . . ." I said timidly, after he had

227

moved apart from the others and was getting comfortable with his coffee and doughnuts.

"Ron . . . I think we need to speak to you for a minute."

CHAPTER EIGHTEEN

I swear, I'll never get used to it. The way that man can change in the blink of an eye from Mr. Nice Guy to a bloodhound of the Torquemada strain. Faster than an actor getting into a role when the cameras start turning. And he didn't have to be so nasty about it. We were telling him, weren't we?

"Do you mean to tell me — ?" The fact that we had come forward voluntarily and helpfully cut no ice with him. "That the victim spent the night with you?"

"Certainly not!" Evangeline took violent umbrage. "We didn't even know he was here. He spent the night trapped in the lift with Tom and Mick."

"And who . . . ?" He was dangerously calm. "Are Tom and Mick?"

"They're Banquo Fitzfothergill's closest friends and members of his team."

"Fitzfothergill? You mean, the Heartbroken Hero? The Tragic Explorer?"

229

"Oh, so the tabloids are on to the story already." It wasn't a difficult deduction for Evangeline when Ron began speaking in headlines like that.

"What connection did the victim have with them?"

"None, really," I said. "He was here to visit Cho-Cho."

"Cho-Cho?" Ron looked thoroughly confused, although he had been feeding her the least sticky nibbles from his doughnuts since he'd sat down.

"Cho-Cho-San." I indicated her helpfully. "She used to belong to him, but Frella was, um, sort of allergic to her." That was putting it mildly, but the waters were getting muddy enough without any further explaining. "So he gave her to me."

"Who is Frella?" The doomed note in his voice suggested that he might suspect.

"Frella Boynton, the director. He's her husband. Rather," I clarified, "he is at the moment. I think he was about to be an ex-husband."

"Frella Boynton." Ron eyed us with distaste. "Don't you two know any ordinary people?"

"Of course, we do. Lots of them." Unfortunately, I couldn't think of one right now.

"What do you mean, victim?" Evangeline

230

zeroed in on a more salient point. "Wasn't it an accident?"

"You know I can't tell you that. It's for the autopsy to decide."

"Oh, please," Evangeline wheedled, going all kittenish. "You must have some sort of an idea. You can give us a teensy little hint."

"Well . . ." Ron looked around uncomfortably, but no one was paying any attention. "It looks as though he had a big lump on the back of his head."

"Struck from behind!" Evangeline pounded. "And then thrown in the water."

"It could still be an accident," he said unconvincingly.

"When?" She was relentless. "When he left here yesterday afternoon?" I knew she was lining up suspects from the mass exodus that had followed almost immediately. Practically everybody. Including Martha.

"Now that really is impossible to tell. I couldn't even guess. The autopsy will narrow it down."

"But you can —" Evangeline began.

"Right." He moved back. "Enough of the private consultation. You're going to have to tell the others. They'll have some questions of their own."

Questions, questions, questions. I don't

know how the police ever get any work done. They're too busy asking questions all day.

By the time they had departed, the sun had gone down, the lights of the city were gleaming below, and we were all limp and exhausted. Drained, utterly drained — and tomorrow we were going to have to report to some outpost of officialdom to read through our statements and sign them. Tomorrow didn't sound as though it was going to be worth getting up for.

Meanwhile, there was tonight to get through.

"We could ring up for seats and go to a show in town," Evangeline suggested listlessly.

"Or we could jump off the terrace," I countered with equal lack of enthusiasm.

"You're both too exhausted to do anything more today." Jocasta overruled us. "I'll thaw out some chicken soup from the freezer and make hot buttered toast."

"Sounds good," I said, more to encourage her than anything.

"And for dessert —" Jocasta looked inspired. "We'll have something luxuriously gooey. How about a slice of marble cake, drizzled with raspberry liqueur, with blended chocolate and vanilla ice cream on top and a thick chocolate sauce over all?"

"That *does* sound good." Evangeline showed the first spark of animation in hours. "Comfort food, just what we need. That river patrol can moan about pulling bodies out of the Thames, but it's no fun discovering them, either."

"No . . ." Jocasta gave a long shuddering sigh. "Especially when it's someone you know." She sighed again and I suspected that she had picked up on the point that Evangeline seemed to have dismissed as unimportant. Jocasta needed comfort as much as we did.

"Good old comfort food," I echoed. We were all going to need a lot of it.

Heartbroken Hero . . . Tragic Explorer . . . It didn't bode well. If that story had been leaked to the tabloids already, it meant that the pressure to rush Banquo's book into print had begun.

And the one facing the most pressure was going to be Jocasta. All other considerations aside, the basic unpalatable truth was that she was employed by the publishing company — and not by Martha.

If any project was going to be relegated to the back burner, it was the cookbook.

Martha was not going to be pleased.

My forebodings redoubled. Tomorrow was

233

definitely not going to be a day worth getting up for.

Oh, how right I was.

It began slowly, almost reasonably. Tom arrived by himself and began unloading what seemed to be a vanful of photographic equipment from the lift.

"We've settled on a compromise," he announced. "There's no reason we can't work on both projects at the same time. Most of my work was done on the expedition, so I can set up here and get some preliminary shots for the cookbook while the others —"

Others? There went the alarm bells.

"— work in the living room. We'll keep out from underfoot, stick to our own territory, and all will work out smoothly."

Evangeline sniffed, believing that no more than I did.

And what of poor Jocasta? She'd be ricocheting between the two factions, taking the heat from both sides. They weren't going to be satisfied until they'd given that poor girl a nervous breakdown.

Evangeline and I consulted each other silently. Any objections from us might make the situation worse for Jocasta. Besides, we would hate to miss any of the action.

"You'll have to tell Jocasta yourself." I

took the coward's way out.

"She'll already know," he said breezily. "We had a long talk with her principals yesterday. They'll have been on to her by now with the good old stick-and-carrot routine. Repercussions if she doesn't, a promotion if she does. She'll come round."

As though on cue — could she have been listening behind the door? — Jocasta appeared. Red-rimmed eyes downcast, head bowed, looking beaten but not quite broken.

My heart went out to her. She was obviously going to try to make the best of a bad situation. I wished her luck.

"There you are —" Tom greeted her. "Just clear this table and the counter so I can set up."

"You might let her have a cup of coffee first," I protested.

"Plenty of time for that when the others get here," he responded. "We want to be ready to roll. After all," he had noticed my frown, "the sooner we're finished, the sooner we'll be out of here."

"And how soon will that be?" Evangeline challenged.

". . . I'll do my best." But the pause had been revealing. "It isn't entirely up to me, you know."

"Isolde!" Both Evangeline and I realised it

at the same moment. "She's coming here. Today."

"Well, she *is* the food stylist." He shrugged.

I wasted a few precious seconds agonising as to whether it would be better for her to arrive before or after Martha, then common sense broke through and I rushed for the telephone. Perhaps I could reach Martha in time to put her off. Tell her we weren't feeling well, or something.

But I couldn't get through. No answer at home and she'd obviously turned off her cell phone. She'd be on her way.

"Too late," I told Evangeline, hanging up.

"Some days are like that."

"But why do *we* have to have so many of them?"

"What time are you expecting her?" Evangeline demanded of Tom.

"Um . . . they should be along any minute now." I gathered his constant use of the plural was his way of breaking the bad news delicately.

"They?" It wasn't going to work. "What *they? Who* they?"

This time Evangeline caught him up on it. "How many food stylists do you need for one little shoot?"

"Edytha and Valeria aren't stylists — nothing to do with food. They'll be helping Banquo with the book."

"I thought Jocasta was going to do that."

"She is, but it can take more than one. Banquo's handwriting leaves something to be desired — like legibility. Sometimes he can't even read it himself."

Jocasta had gone very quiet, spreading a pale blue cloth on the table, setting out a colourful selection of crockery and accessories, so self-effacing it was only too easy to forget she was there at all.

"Banquo is coming today, too?" Now she spoke with her first trace of animation.

"He'll be along with his Three Graces." Tom seemed barely to refrain from grimacing. "Mick will be driving them over."

So there was a dangerous chance they might collide with Martha in the ground floor entrance lobby. Ordinarily, I'd back Martha, but this time she'd be outnumbered four-to-one. Perhaps I should go downstairs and . . .

The downstairs buzzer sounded. I checked the video-scan. They'd arrived. Resignedly, I pushed the lock release to let them in and stood watching the screen anxiously to make sure Martha was nowhere in sight.

She wasn't. Not yet. Thank heaven for small mercies. Now, if we could get them

237

sorted into different parts of the flat before she did arrive — and realised how many of them were here . . .

Our own bell pealed.

"I'll do the honours." Tom went to answer the door. "They'll have equipment with them. At least, Isolde will. I'll help them unload it."

"Where's Cho-Cho? If they need to leave the door open, she might run out. Oh, there she is." I caught her up and retreated to my bedroom with her.

"I think I can feel one of my headaches coming on." Evangeline also was beating a strategic retreat. We had no intention of standing around where we might be mistaken for some kind of welcoming committee.

I settled in the armchair with my book, Cho-Cho curled in my lap, and tried to ignore the thumps and crashes sounding in the kitchen. What on earth were they doing, building a set? So it wasn't until a sudden lull in the noise that I noticed a lighter tapping, as of someone kicking delicately at the connecting door.

Shifting Cho-Cho to the arm of the chair, I got up and opened the door. Evangeline sailed through, a brimming champagne flute in each hand. Bubbles rose from the sugar cubes in the bottoms of the glasses.

Champagne cocktails — I recognised one of Evangeline's favourite crisis remedies. A sugar cube sprinkled with a few drops of Angostura bitters, liberally covered with brandy, the whole topped up with chilled champagne.

Champagne cocktails — at this hour! I spent about three seconds considering being scandalised, then reached gratefully for the flute Evangeline held out to me.

At this point, why not? The whole day was out of control anyway. We clinked glasses and took a big swallow.

"Plenty more," Evangeline said. "I opened a whole bottle."

Before I could reply, I heard a familiar battle cry from outside and the door burst open.

"Mother!" Martha stormed in. "Mother — what is that terrible woman doing here?"

Evangeline set down her glass and slipped back into her own room.

"Which terrible woman?" I asked.

"That — that —" Martha choked and fought for breath.

I took another calming sip and thought how wise it had been of Evangeline not to bother with half bottles.

"That awful frightful woman from Brighton!"

"Brighton?" I echoed blankly.

Evangeline returned in record time with another champagne cocktail which she thrust into Martha's unresisting hand.

"What did she say to you? What did she want?"

"Who, dear?" I took a deeper sip of my own. "I haven't seen any strange women today, from Brighton or not." It was true. I'd taken good care to avoid all those terrible women. But weren't they — or at least one of them — from Glastonbury, not Brighton?

"That ghastly woman from the theatre. Ella, Nella, something like that. She was prowling around the dock where you discovered the body. It's too much!"

"Frella," I said. "Frella Boynton." The not-so-grieving widow, I would bet.

"Yes, that's it." Martha looked down at her hand and realised what she was holding. "Champagne cocktails — at this hour!"

"Just drink it, dear," I advised. "It's going to be a long day."

"Is she coming up here?" Evangeline went straight to the pending problem.

"I thought she'd already been here. When she saw me watching her, she got into her car and drove away."

Evangeline relaxed and so did I. I took another sip of my own drink, aware that a blissful smile was creeping over my face — and not just because of the champagne.

For the first time, it had occurred to me that someone else had an even better motive for wanting to be rid of Teddy than I had.

CHAPTER NINETEEN

There was a resounding crash from the kitchen. The wall shook. Once again, I wondered how sturdily this place was built. In the last few days, I had lost any confidence I might ever have had in the competence of architects and builders.

"What on earth?" Martha swung around to face the trembling wall.

"Umm, didn't you see anything when you came through the kitchen, dear?" If she'd seen Isolde, she wouldn't be so calm. But what about Jocasta?

"No, the place was empty. I though Jocasta might be in here with you. Oh, yes — there was a strange pile of junk in one corner. I thought it might have something to do with Nigel; it must have toppled over." She started for the door.

"Umm, dear —" I followed her. I could hear voices now.

"Nigel left a while ago," Evangeline said.

"And there wasn't any junk there then."

Just short of the door, Martha stopped and peered closely at the wall. "Was that crack always there?"

"I've never noticed it before." Evangeline frowned.

Oh, fine! I forced myself to inspect it. It was a hairline crack, but it was there. More ammunition for Jasper to use to help speed our eviction.

"We'd better check the other side." Martha led the way, with Evangeline right behind her. I lagged back, fighting the awful feeling that I'd rather not know.

"What on earth is *that*? And what is it doing here?" Martha stared down at the large pile of junk against the wall. The chipped and flaking wall.

Cho-Cho advanced and sniffed cautiously at a jumble of straps on the floor. It looked like some sort of harness, much too big for her, but she was taking no chances. She backed away and, uttering a loud complaint, darted for the safety of my room.

"It looks like a runner." Evangeline bent to examine a wickedly glittering thin narrow strip of steel. It had certainly run down the hall, leaving a scar.

"Runner?" Martha stared at the thing blankly.

"As in sled —" Evangeline met my eyes grimly and I winced. This was worse than I had anticipated — and I hadn't been Little Mary Sunshine about the whole deal to begin with.

"Don't be ridiculous!" Martha snapped. "What would a sled be doing here? And what's all *this* clutter?" Martha turned to survey the table. "Where did all the ghastly peasant pottery come from?"

Well she might ask. Martha was a porcelain addict through and through. She wouldn't allow such tat in her house.

"Yes, look at that stuff." Evangeline, ever ready to fan the flames, picked up a leering cow that was masquerading as some sort of casserole. "Quite revolting, isn't it?"

"It certainly is!" Martha snapped. "What is it doing here?"

Evangeline turned her attention back to the cracked wall. She wasn't going to answer that one.

"Mother!" Martha's eyes widened in horror. "Do you suppose Jasper has succeeded in selling the flat out from under you? And the buyers are moving in already? Without even waiting for you to leave?"

"Oh, I don't think it's that bad, dear." I was immoderately cheered. Martha had come up with a scenario that was even

244

worse than the actual situation.

"He won't get away with it!" Martha raged. "I'll — What's that?"

"That" sounded like the invaders — as I was beginning to think of them — returning, with another load of equipment, to judge from the crash we had just heard.

Slowly, clumsily, inexorably, they were heading this way. I closed my eyes and waited for the explosion.

"Don't be such a baby, Trixie!" Evangeline's thump on my back opened my eyes as it sent me reeling forward. I managed to stop myself before I collided with Martha, who was barring the way out of the kitchen.

"Just what do you think you're doing?" Martha thundered.

I couldn't see beyond her, but there was a crash as they obviously dropped whatever they were carrying. Nastily, I hoped it was all fragile and highly breakable.

"You again!"

Uh-oh. Martha had spotted Isolde lurking behind Mick and the unidentifiable pile of stuff he was carrying.

"Dear —" I put a gentle hand on her arm, trying to hold her back from something impetuous.

"All of you!" She shook off my hand. Sure enough, all three of the gruesome Graces

245

were gathered behind him, advancing en masse like a tornado or some other unstoppable force of nature.

"Please —" a small voice pleaded at the back of the crowd. "Let me through . . . please . . ."

Reluctantly, some of them shifted and Jocasta stumbled free, tenderly cradling a small pile of tatty notebooks.

"Jocasta! Did you — !" Martha began.

"Right! Cool it!" Mick dropped his burden and strode forward. "This deal is done and dusted," he informed Martha. "You have nothing to say about it."

"That's what you —"

"Tom and Isolde are doing the photographs here in the kitchen. The others are working on the notebooks in the living room. I'll be going back and forth between the two groups. So will Jocasta. The sooner you shut up and let us get on with it, the sooner you'll be rid of us. If you don't like it, you can get out!"

"Oh!" Martha hadn't been told off like that since her early days in grade school. She opened her mouth and shut it several times. I ignored Evangeline, who was trying not to laugh.

"I can see you're a very good troubleshooter," I told Mick.

"Women!" he said bitterly. "Nothing but trouble, all of them! They don't know what they want and when they get it, they try to change it. Give me the frozen wastes every time!" He picked up his clobber again and headed for the living room.

Looking triumphant, Edytha and Valeria followed him. Isolde advanced to the kitchen table and began arranging some of her pottery.

Martha stood there fuming. She was going to recover in a few moments and return to the fray. I knew. I dreaded it.

"Trixie!" Evangeline said. "Have you forgotten? We have to go to the police station today and sign our statements."

"So we have." Suddenly, the day seemed a lot brighter. We had a perfectly legitimate reason for getting out of here and leaving the others to fight it out amongst themselves.

After the formalities, which were over surprisingly quickly — could they have been anxious to get rid of us? — Evangeline and I found ourselves back on the pavement with the rest of the day in front of us.

"It looks like rain." Even as I spoke, the first drops splattered down at our feet.

"What a surprise." Neither of us had

brought an umbrella.

"When do you think it will be safe to go back?"

"About mid-April." Evangeline cherished no false hopes.

Glumly, I looked around for a shop where we could buy umbrellas. It was going to be a long day.

"Boots!" Evangeline had been keeping an eye out, too. "Over there. They always have umbrellas."

"You mean we haven't run them out of stock yet?" No two ways about it, we really had to learn to carry umbrellas with us when we went out. We couldn't go on accumulating them like this . . .

"Offhand, I can't say that was the worst film I'd ever seen, but it's certainly well up there in the running." At least, it had stopped raining when we emerged from the cinema.

"So bad it was almost good," Evangeline agreed.

"It reminded me of that famous letter the boy wrote home from boarding school: 'The senior class put on *Hamlet* for the school play . . .' " I began.

" 'Some of the parents had already seen it, but they laughed anyway.' " Evangeline finished the quotation.

248

We briefly released the giggles we had been stifling through the dire film, then Evangeline grew serious again.

"Should we risk going back to the flat, do you think? I doubt that Jocasta has done any cooking, but perhaps we could pull something out of the freezer and thaw it. Or should we try for a table at the Harpo?"

I liked that *we*. As though she ever did any cooking — or thawing — herself. I knew who'd end up doing all the work. "The Harpo, by all means."

And there he was. Robin-Toby-Jake. Strange, the way once you become aware of something — or someone — they seem to show up everywhere. Of course, he worked here, we had just never been properly aware of him before.

"Ladies!" He greeted us with delight. "Of course, there's a table for you. Always. One of mine has just been readied. This way please." We followed him to a table.

"*Everyone's* here tonight," he confided. "But don't worry. There'll always be room for you." He produced our menus with a flourish, then darted off in response to a plaintive bleat from a neighbouring table. They seemed to have been waving at him for quite some time.

"Don't look now!" Evangeline warned sharply, just as I began to look around to see who comprised "everyone" in Robin's opinion. I settled back in my chair, raising a questioning eyebrow.

"Directly behind you," Evangeline said. "No — don't turn. See if you can catch a glimpse in the mirror over there."

By squirming around a bit and tilting my chair as though I were adjusting it, I managed to get a glimpse of the reflection in the mirror.

"Good heavens — it's Frella!"

"And she's with Jem," Evangeline said grimly. "I didn't know he was up in town again."

"Well, of course," I tried to be reasonable, "he doesn't have to tell you everything he does."

Abruptly, disconcertingly, Frella seemed to look straight into my eyes in the mirror. We both froze.

Too late, I remembered the bit of information that had hitherto stood me in good stead in a lifetime of crowded dressing rooms: if you can see someone else's eyes in a mirror, they can see you.

We both looked away hurriedly, pretending the momentary contact hadn't happened, but it had and we both knew it.

"Something wrong?" Evangeline wanted to know.

"She's spotted me."

"Bad luck. You should have been more careful." She returned her attention to the menu.

I continued to look around the room, paying more attention to the placement of the mirrors. The place was filling up with the pre-theatre crowd, cheerful and laughing and anticipating a pleasant evening ahead.

One laugh sounded above the others: Frella's — and with a defiant ring to it. Almost a challenge. If it was aimed at me, I wasn't going to pick it up. I'd already figured that she wasn't going into deepest mourning over Teddy. Although I'd be interested to know what she'd been doing prowling about our dock after the sad event. Returning to the scene of the crime? But had she been responsible? If so, how had she known where Teddy could be found in the first place?

Unless . . . When had Teddy actually purchased that revolting harness for Cho-Cho? If Frella knew about it, she'd know Teddy would be visiting us. Perhaps he'd even mentioned it to her on one of what seemed to be the increasingly infrequent occasions when they met. She could have

251

been lying in wait for him.

Perhaps . . . A cold chill slid down my spine. Perhaps she'd even hoped to kill both Teddy and Cho-Cho at the same time. Teddy, to get rid of him. Cho-Cho out of sheer spite.

Something flickered at the corner of my vision. I blinked and it flickered again. I turned to bring it into focus.

"Isn't that Nigel?" Evangeline's attention had been attracted, too.

"What's he doing here?"

Not waving, but drowning, it looked like. A very elderly gentleman was sitting at the table with him. They bore a vague resemblance to each other. I suspected this was the aged relative Nigel occasionally mentioned. Nigel was now semaphoring wildly, like a castaway on a desert island trying to signal to a passing ship. It looked as though he had been experiencing heavy weather entertaining his companion.

We smiled at Nigel and waved back with enthusiasm. It was so good to see someone who was not only not ignoring us, but actually seemed to want to talk to us.

Nigel rose and said something to his companion. It looked to be along the lines of "I'll be back in a minute." He might as well have saved his breath. As he started towards us, I accidentally made eye contact with his relative while I was still waving and beaming invitingly.

The old boy jolted upright as though a bolt of electricity had shot through him. He lurched to his feet and followed Nigel. It seemed as though he'd been having heavy weather himself. Perhaps Nigel had been trying to sell him a flock of ostriches.

Nigel reached our table, a hopeful smile on his face. I noticed that Evangeline had one eye over his shoulder as she caught him by the collar, pulled him down, and kissed him soundly on both cheeks before swinging him over to me. I can take a cue. I did the same. He reeled backwards slightly as I released him.

"So these lovely ladies are your friends?"

Nigel leaped a mile. He thought he'd left the aged relative waiting safely at the nearby table.

"Egad, boy! I didn't know you had such good taste. I trust you're going to introduce us."

"Ah! . . . Ah! . . ." Nigel was still reeling. "Uncle, this is Evangeline Si—"

"Not that way round, boy! I know who they are. Introduce *me* to *them!*"

"Ah, yes. Sorry. Of course. Evangeline, Trixie, this is my Uncle Humbug-Humbert!

Humbert — Humbert!"

"Don't be a fool, boy! I know what the family calls me behind my back. They wouldn't dare, to my face!"

"Ah, yes. Sorry, sorry," Nigel babbled. "It was just —"

There was something going on here that we weren't clued in to. Behind Evangeline, Jem had snapped to attention and was watching us intently.

"You're joining the ladies." It wasn't a question, it was a fact. Robin dashed up, carrying the chair from their table. Another waiter was right behind him with the second chair.

"Delighted! If I may?" There was little question in his voice, either. "Champagne —" he called, as the waiters brought the place settings from their former table. "Champagne for the beautiful ladies! The best!" He fell into his chair, beaming at us. "Call me Bertie."

We did the only thing possible: we fluttered our eyelashes as him and cooed appreciatively. We'd both been here before, it was like old times. It *was* old times.

Nigel slid into his seat, looking inordinately pleased with himself. He gave us both an approving nod. Of course, it was a relief to have someone else around to share the burden when dealing with a difficult relative — they're always on their best behaviour when they're in the company of strangers. We'd all been there.

Then Evangeline gave me an entirely different nod and I followed the sideways dart of her eyes towards the mirror where Frella could be seen standing up and leaning forward to say something to Jem.

Then Frella straightened and started across the room. She left her shawl draped over the back of her chair, so she was obviously heading for the powder room and would return.

Jem did not seem displeased to see her go. As soon as she turned the corner, he pushed back his chair and came over to us. After the preliminary flutter of greeting kisses, he turned to Uncle Humbert almost obsequiously.

"Good evening, sir. It's good to see you out on the town again. Quite like old times."

"By gad — it's young Jem! The child star in Evangeline's big hit so long ago . . . too long ago. And you still keep up with each other — wonderful! Wonderful . . ." A wistful look flickered across his face and he sighed.

"Ah, well . . . Bring your chair over here, my boy, and join the party — you and your lady friend."

"How very kind of you." Jem needed no further urging and Robin was already moving his chair. "But I'm not sure about the lady —"

"Before the revelry starts" — Evangeline flashed Uncle Humbert her *you devil you* most flirtatious glance — "Trixie and I must powder our noses."

"Of course, of course, although nothing could improve them." The old boy was blossoming by the minute. He even tried to stand up as we rose and followed in Frella's wake. We had a few questions for that woman.

But the powder room was empty!

"She's gone." I stated the obvious. "She left her shawl so that we'd think she was coming back, but she skipped out."

"Precisely." Evangeline nodded grimly. "Why am I not surprised?"

CHAPTER TWENTY

By the end of the evening, Nigel could have entered a purring competition against Cho-Cho — and won. Basking in what was obviously a glow of unfamiliar approval from his elderly uncle, he was one happy kitten.

Of course, Evangeline and I were in top form, if I do say so myself. And Jem revealed an unsuspected musical talent with a couple of spoons and an array of water glasses filled to varying levels.

Somehow, it all got a bit blurred, but very merry from then onwards. Robin, our waiter, turned out to have a passable baritone. Evangeline did a merciless parody of "Father, Dear Father, Come Home with Me Now" and several other Victorian tearjerkers. And I contributed my full share. We both managed to stay off the tabletops this time, despite voices from some nearby tables urging us on.

For the other tables were joining in the

fun with friendly banter, turns of their own, and much applause. It had turned into a room-wide party.

"Three tables have cancelled their theatre reservations," Robin confided happily, topping up our champagne. "They say the show is better here."

At some point, I was conscious of camera flashes and those ghastly phones that take pictures being waved about, but I was having too good a time to care.

It began just after Evangeline had done the Charleston and I was riposting with my version of "I Wish I Could Shimmy Like My Sister Kate," which is just a couple of grinds short of a full-fledged burlesque routine.

We were both harmonising "Diamonds Are a Girl's Best Friend" when I noticed that Uncle Bertie was fading. Nigel noticed it at the same time. He leaned towards his uncle and said something.

"No, no, I'm all right. It's just —" Bertie dabbed at his eyes with his napkin and gave a deep sigh. "If I had known that it could be like this, I'd have opened the Jewel Box."

"No, really —" I demurred politely. "That isn't necess—" Evangeline's venomous look stopped me cold. If anyone was in the mood to start tossing baubles in our direction, I was not to dare to discourage them.

I nodded agreement in principle, but I would hate Bertie to think we'd been hinting at him with that last song. On the other hand, we didn't even know whether he was worth hinting at.

"It's not too late, Uncle — Bertie," Nigel said, then shrank back at his own temerity, not sure that the invitation to such intimacy had included him.

"Too late, my boy. Too late . . ."

Oh, dear. Bertie had drunk himself into the lachrymose stage.

He mopped at the increasing moisture. "Too late . . ."

"Ah . . . yes . . . late." Nigel rose. "I'll see you home . . . Bertie."

"No, you won't!" Bertie snapped. "Don't forget your manners, boy! You'll see these lovely ladies home. I'll be all right."

"But —" Nigel was stricken. He didn't want to offend his uncle. But if anything happened to their uncle Humbug while he was in Nigel's care, poor Nigel would face a lifetime of recriminations and blame from his other relatives.

"We'll be perfectly all right on our own," I said. "We always have been."

"I could —" Jem began to offer.

"Nonsense!" Evangeline settled the matter. "Another bottle of champagne — to take away," she ordered. "And we'll *all* see Bertie home! And *then* Nigel can take us home."

Unfortunately, morning had to come. I awoke late and stretched luxuriously. Beside me, Cho-Cho stirred and did some stretching of her own before snuggling up against my rib cage and going back to sleep.

It wasn't a bad idea and I let my eyes close again. Just a few more minutes . . .

There was a tap at the door and Jocasta came in with a tray and a harassed look.

"Sorry, I'm so sorry," she apologised. "But can I ask you two to please, please have your meals in your rooms today? It's chaos in the kitchen —" Her voice broke. "It's chaos everywhere!"

"Oh dear!" I jumped out of bed and took the tray from her before she dropped it. I'd been afraid of this. They were all driving her to the verge of a nervous breakdown. "Sit down for a minute. Did you have anything to eat yourself? Did you get any sleep last night?"

"No . . . yes . . . not much . . ." It was an all-purpose answer to all of my questions. "I can't sit. Isolde wants me to rearrange everything in the kitchen and — at the same time — Banquo needs me in the living room . . . he needs me . . ." Despite herself, she sank into an armchair and covered her face with her hands.

"Good morning. What have we here?" Ignoring Jocasta, Evangeline went over to examine the breakfast tray. Cho-Cho joined her. Neither of them seemed very pleased with what they found.

"Muesli." Evangeline sniffed. "And —" She picked up a small tin and squinted at the label. "Yummykins Gourmet Gala Fish Feast." She set it down in front of Cho-Cho. "I hope that's for you."

Cho-Cho circled it, checking it from all angles, then sniffed almost as disparagingly as Evangeline and turned away, sweeping us with an accusing look. She had learned to expect better than tinned cat food in this establishment.

"I've got to go." Jocasta struggled to her feet.

"Be sure to eat something," I called as the door closed behind her. "I worry about that girl," I told Evangeline. "She isn't going to let up until she collapses."

"Sometimes that's the only way they learn." Evangeline absently popped the ring and pulled back the lid of Cho-Cho's Fish

261

Feast before setting it back on the floor.

Cho-Cho sniffed at it again, her indifference fading. Fish was fish, after all — and her people were faring a lot worse with the food offered them. But . . . She looked up at me imploringly.

"Not like that, Evangeline." I caught up a saucer and scooped the contents of the tin into it and returned it to Cho-Cho.

"Mother! How could you?" The door burst open and Martha was with us. "*Now* look what you've done! How *could* you?"

I looked. Cho-Cho had begun eating placidly. What was wrong with that?

"Not there, Mother — here!" She slammed down a pile of tabloids in front of me. "This terrible story! Those awful pictures!"

Bracing myself for the worst, I picked up the top paper and gasped with delight. "What do you mean, awful? That's the best picture that's been taken of me in years. And you, too, Evangeline." I held out the paper to her.

There we were: leaning our heads together as we sang, a glass of champagne in one hand, the other arm draped across Jem's shoulders. His head below ours with the line of glasses in front of him, formed the base of a festive triangle. We were all beaming

262

and obviously having a wonderful time.

"We must order a dozen copies of the print at once," Evangeline agreed.

"And wouldn't it make a great Christmas card? We could have a line from a carol over our heads and —"

"And we could run it as a Christmas greeting to all our friends in *Variety* and *The Stage* —"

" 'Hilarity at the Harpo,' " I read out the headline on page three of the next tabloid, which was featuring the same picture. " 'Those golden stars of Broadway and Hollywood — and now London's own — gave an impromptu performance to the lucky diners at the Harpo last night. Someone should give these glorious gals their own show immediately, so that we can all enjoy —' "

"It's disgraceful!" Martha wailed. "Making an exhibition of yourselves like that!"

It never ceases to amaze me, the way my darling daughter manages to blank out the realisation that I have earned my living — and hers — by doing what she calls "making an exhibition" of myself across a lifetime. What does she imagine paid the mortgage, put the food on the table, and paid for her education?

"That's the best, but they're all good

pictures." Single-mindedly, Evangeline was oblivious to all minor distractions as she rooted through the rest of the papers. "We were really cooking with gas last night."

"Cooking — ooh!" Martha was reminded of another source of anguish, just as a muffled cry was heard on the other side of the wall. Either Jocasta had dropped something or Isolde had rapped her across the knuckles with a wooden spoon. Possibly both.

A strident voice was raised in angry words that were indistinct, but clearly furious.

"Poor Jocasta," I murmured.

"That awful woman! That ghastly, terrible creature!" Martha raged. "I could *kill* her!"

"Martha!" A cold chill swept over me. "I wouldn't say things like that around here, if I were you, dear."

CHAPTER TWENTY-ONE

The voice brayed out again, this time clearly calling for Martha.

Cho-Cho flicked her delicate ears and uttered a bitter complaint to the management.

"Sorry about that," I told her. "We don't like it any better than you do." There were just a few flakes of the Fish Feast left, so she abandoned it and came over to sit at my feet and continue her list of grievances. I'd already figured that she'd had a rotten day yesterday because it had taken me twenty minutes to coax her out from under the bed when we got home last night. It now appeared that I didn't know the half of it.

Martha was still fuming quietly, but she wasn't verbalising it, which was a step in the right direction. Martha was too impulsive, too fond of dramatic statements — and had been a suspect in a murder case a couple of years ago. The police were only too aware of that and weren't going to forget it for one minute. If anything happened to Isolde . . .

But that was just wishful thinking.

"Martha —" The door burst open and Isolde charged into the room. "There you are! You've got to come at once! Bring the stupid cat with you. I think it's unsanitary myself, but Tom insists it will make a good picture."

"Cat . . . ?" Martha looked around vaguely, but Cho-Cho had darted into hiding the instant Isolde had appeared.

"Hurry up!" Isolde ordered. "Tom's waiting. We . . . we need your help." It obviously pained her to admit it.

"Can't Jocasta . . . ?" Martha wasn't in a cooperative mood, either.

"Useless, that girl! Young people have no backbone nowadays. A few words of constructive criticism and the silly chit runs off snivelling!"

Personally, I thought Jocasta had done well to put up with Isolde as long as she had. And to simply run away, rather than trying to break the iron frying pan over Isolde's head.

"Where's Jocasta?" The door bounced open again and, all scarves flying like the flags on a battleship, Edytha was in the room. "Banquo requires her urgently. There

266

are two whole pages he can't decipher."

"We need her here, too." Isolde was ready to do battle, then remembered. "But it's no use. She's gone."

"Gone? What do you mean, gone?" Edytha was incredulous. "We have far too much work to do. When will she be back?"

"Who knows?" Isolde shrugged. "Most unreliable, that girl. Most unsatisfactory."

"Gone?" The echo came from behind Edytha. "Where did she go?" Mick, in full troubleshooter mode. He looked ready to pick up poor Jocasta and carry her off bodily from wherever she was.

"She didn't say." Isolde sniffed disparagingly. "She just . . . ran off . . . suddenly . . ."

"Oh, Isolde!" Edytha sighed. "You should try to be more tactful, dear. I've explained to you just how sensitive these creative types can be."

"Like that, was it?" Mick understood immediately, too. He looked at Isolde with open disgust. Edytha sighed again. It was obvious that neither of them had any faith in Isolde's ability to make friends and influence people.

"And Banquo was *so* depending on her," Edytha said.

"You'll just have to tell him she isn't available."

267

"He won't like it," Edytha said. "Oh, dear. I'm afraid that will count as a black mark against her."

"I'm afraid so." Isolde exchanged a swift glance with Edytha. They weren't afraid at all — they were delighted. They nodded emphatically to each other and left the room, forgetting about their original errand — and forgetting about Martha in their haste to get to Banquo and vilify Jocasta.

Martha slumped into a chair, folded her arms forbiddingly across her chest, and closed her eyes. The message was clear: *do not disturb.*

"All right." Mick had stayed behind. "Where did she go?" He exuded menace, but it was wasted on anyone who had worked with certain Hollywood directors. They could have eaten him for breakfast.

"How should I know?" And, if I could make a pretty good guess, I certainly wasn't going to share it with him. "The first I knew about anything was when Isolde barged in here baying for Martha." I widened my eyes, giving him my most innocent look.

"You're sure about that?" He was still narrow-eyed and suspicious. Evidently my innocent look wasn't what it used to be. Ah, well, the passage of the years will do that to one.

"We shall have to get a bolt for that door," Evangeline said. "I won't have those frightful creatures charging in whenever they feel like it."

"They must be nearly finished here." I tried to soothe her. "They can't be around much longer."

"Another ten minutes is too long! And I wouldn't put it past that Edytha to be able to slither in through the keyhole."

"She's a slippery one, all right," Mick unexpectedly agreed. Was this the beginning of a rift in the lute? I thought they were all supposed to be such a great team.

"Nothing any of them would do would surprise me," I said. "As things turned out, it was certainly convenient that Edytha was in Glastonbury about that burglary that night Melisande died."

"Convenient in more ways than one." Mick was being unusually indiscreet. "She did well out of the whole thing. The insurance company paid out on the most . . . imaginative . . . inventory I've ever seen."

"You mean . . . ?" Evangeline's eyes were as wide as if she had never confused a zircon and a diamond when she was making out her own list of losses after a Hollywood burglary. "You mean she falsified her claim?"

269

"They could have disallowed three-quarters of it and she'd still have made a killing." He stopped abruptly as it seemed to occur to him that his choice of words was rather unfortunate. "I mean —"

"We know what you mean," Evangeline said. "You mean she swindled the insurance company."

"Why should she be any different?" With a shrug, he abandoned any attempt at tact. "It's a way of life with those . . . ladies."

"Really?" Evangeline was all agog.

"You mean, they haven't tried anything with you yet?"

"No. What do they try?" I was agog now. "I thought Edytha had a shop in Glastonbury, Isolde played around with food, and Valeria . . . I'm not really sure what Valeria does," I realised.

"Valeria runs the show," he said. "Edytha's shop is just a useful sideline. It pulls in the vaguely interested and then she works on them. The real loot comes from the courses they run. Edytha fronts the operation, but they're all in it. I'm surprised they haven't tried it on with you before now. You'd be a real feather in their caps."

"What courses?" It didn't take Mick's sardonic tone and twisted smile to make Evangeline suspicious. We'd always had our doubts about those creatures.

"You, too, Are a Secret Goddess," Mick intoned portentously. "Just start with the opening course, *Discover the Goddess within You* — I believe the search costs a thousand pounds. Then you move on to *Cultivate the Goddess within You* — that's about fifteen hundred pounds. Follow up with *Utilise the Goddess within You* — that's a bit pricier —"

"Enough!" Evangeline held up her hand. "I've just discovered the Cheapskate within Me!"

"Lucky you," Mick said. "Most of them go on until they discover the Bankrupt within Them."

"But how do they get away with it?" I protested. "Doesn't anyone complain to the authorities?"

"Complain about what? That they still don't feel like a goddess? That nobody has started worshipping them? How would you like to go to the cops with a complaint like that?"

Evangeline shuddered and so did I. The police could be difficult enough when you simply reported a murder. The reception they might give to anyone rash enough to go to them with a complaint like that didn't bear thinking about.

271

What I did find myself thinking was that Mick was being unusually forthcoming. I hadn't heard him talk this much since we first met. The immortal line that occurred in practically every B movie I'd ever been in and definitely in every episode of Evangeline's *Happy Couple* series drifted into my mind and wouldn't go away:

"But why are you telling me all this?"

"They were furious when they realised they weren't going to get their hands on Melisande's money that way. They had to regroup and work towards getting it through Banquo after the marriage. I think they really needed some money at that point. That's why the burglary was so . . . . providential."

Did he realise he had just given us a motive for the Graces to dispose of Melisande? Did he care? Definitely, Mick was on the turn. I wondered if he was growing as fed up with Banquo as he was with Banquo's retinue.

"Were they aware that Melisande was allergic to nuts?" Evangeline was in full *Happy Couple* mode now, nose down on the trail Mick was so obligingly laying out for her.

"After the hysterics she threw when Isolde waved that plate of Brazil nut crisps at her" — Mick gave a short bitter laugh — "everyone in a five mile radius knew about it."

I was startled by a sudden knock at the door and I noticed that Evangeline jumped, too. We had grown unaccustomed to such minor courtesies around this place lately.

The door opened and Tom poked his head around it. "Excuse me, but has anyone seen Martha? I could use a bit of help. Is she here?"

She was, but only just. Perhaps learning from Cho-Cho, she had faded so far into the background she was nearly invisible.

"Oh, there you are." He'd spotted her. "Could you come and give me a hand, please? Banquo has commandeered Isolde and I'm on my own here. I'd appreciate some help."

Now it was Martha's turn to be startled and I didn't blame her. Words like "please" and "appreciate" had been in short supply around here ever since the Graces had taken over.

"Oh, Tom . . . I . . . I suppose so," Martha said reluctantly.

"Perhaps I can do something, too," I volunteered. If only he could keep Isolde out of the way permanently, he'd have as much help as he needed.

Evangeline wasn't going to be left behind and Mick trailed after us, obviously in no

273

mood to rejoin Banquo and his harpies in the living room.

The kitchen was more cluttered than ever. Strange crockery and utensils crowded together on the draining board, unidentifiable objects were soaking in murky water in the sink, a strange smell was leaking from the oven. Evidence of Jocasta's absence was everywhere. Martha looked around with distaste.

"What's all this?" She advanced on a pile of jumbled papers, photos, maps, charts, and notebooks teetering precariously at one end of the kitchen table.

"Part of the problem," Tom said wearily. "Edytha came in a while ago and dumped it all here. Said they were surplus to requirements and, worse, distracting Banquo. So now they're distracting me. Shift them somewhere else, would you? I need that space to set up for the next shot."

"Where can I put them?" Martha caught up the jumbled heap and looked around for a vacant spot. The unevenly balanced stack quivered and shifted. Martha gave a small shriek as most of it slithered out of her grasp and tumbled to the floor. She never should have tried to move it all in one go.

I kept that observation to myself as I stooped to help her gather up the mess.

Unfortunately, there was nowhere else to put them except back on the table. They needed to be sorted out by bulk, weight, and size before we could find a better spot for them.

Evangeline strolled over to assist, confining her efforts to the material we had replaced on the table. Automatically, she began making separate piles for photos, maps and charts, papers and notebooks.

The heap began to look almost manageable. Martha and I retrieved the last of them from the floor and added them to their proper categories.

Tom continued fiddling with his cameras and lighting equipment while Mick looked on sardonically, not offering to help.

Most of the photos were marked with a small X in one corner signifying that they had not been chosen for inclusion in the book illustrations. As with the others I had seen earlier, in most cases the reason was clear, but . . .

"But these are charming, delightful —" I picked up the three rejected photos. "Why aren't you using them?"

"Not suitable," Tom said shortly.

Mick snickered, then tried to cover it. "I think they're great, too. They belong in the book. Adds human interest —" He intercepted and registered Tom's furious glare. "Very interesting to animal lovers," he amended.

They would be. They added a whole fresh dimension to the story of the expedition. The first showed the sled dogs just strapped into their harnesses at the beginning of the trip, revealing that one of them was noticeably pregnant. The second shot showed her proudly suckling a newly born litter of pups. The last was taken a few weeks later, the puppies were older, plump and frolicsome, already showing signs of burgeoning personalities.

"The readers would love them," I said. At my elbow, Evangeline studied the shots and nodded agreement. "Everyone would want to know about them."

"That's the trouble," Tom said. "They'd take all the attention away from Banquo."

"We couldn't have that." Mick snickered again.

Yes, Banquo wanted the limelight all to himself. He wouldn't take kindly to being upstaged by a group of lovable little rogues. Actors notoriously hate working with children and animals — why should Banquo be any different? It was the same principle.

But . . . reluctantly, I added the photos to the others, tilting them slightly askew on

276

the pile so that I could retrieve them later.

Surely, Jocasta should have the final say as to what illustrations were used. And, if her choice were vetoed, perhaps she would begin to notice that Banquo's ego was really more than any reasonable woman would want to waste her life coping with.

Chapter Twenty-Two

After such a beginning, what else could the day do but disintegrate completely?

Smouldering and ready to erupt, Martha grudgingly followed Tom's instructions as he, oblivious, continued setting up his cameras and lighting. We could hear increasingly acrimonious voices being raised in the front room. Cho-Cho was under the bed and made it clear that she was staying there.

Evangeline and I consulted silently and, with the flick of an eyebrow, agreed. This was no place to hang around. We sidled towards the exit.

"Shouldn't we get our coats?" Evangeline glanced at the windows. "It's going to rain again."

"Not necessary," I said. "I think we should go downstairs and drop in on Nigel."

"Nigel? Now? Why?"

"Because."

"Just because?"

"Just because," I said firmly, heading for the lift.

"What have you got up your sleeve?" Intrigued, as I knew she would be, Evangeline followed.

"Nothing," I admitted. "But I think Nigel's sleeves are getting more interesting every day."

"Can't we have lunch first?" Evangeline grumbled, getting into the lift. "I'm hungry and we can use our emergency supplies."

"I suspect Nigel has lunch all organised," I told her. "If we're lucky, maybe we can get in on it."

It took an inordinately long time before the door swung open slowly — and not very far.

"I'm not coming back!" Jocasta peered around the opening. "You can't make me!"

"We wouldn't dream of it," I assured her. "We've come for sanctuary. We're refugees ourselves."

"It's chaos up there," Evangeline said piteously. "Utter chaos!" Her eyes widened pleadingly, her shoulders slumped, the picture of despair. She was the orphan waif on the ice floe, drifting down the freezing river. "We had to get away."

"I know the feeling." The door swung wide

and we were allowed to enter.

"Come in, come in." This welcome was warmer, but it did not come from Nigel, who was beaming at us from behind the speaker.

"Jem!" Evangeline exclaimed. "What are you doing here? And so early."

"Simple explanation," he said. "I never left. It was so late when we got here last night — this morning — the trains would have stopped running. I would have been stranded for hours, except that Nigel kindly offered me his sofa. I'm deeply indebted to him."

"Not at all, not at all." Nigel beamed. "My pleasure. Besides, we had a most productive conversation."

Oh, dear. Nigel was looking entirely too pleased with himself. What harebrained financial scheme was he hatching now? Surely, Jem was too smart to be taken in by it.

"Ah, yes, the sofa." There was nothing like the sofa for losing Evangeline's interest. She was far more intent on the delicious aromas wafting through the flat. She raised her head and sniffed pointedly.

"You must stay for lunch." Nigel was getting to be a dab hand at picking up a cue. "There's always plenty when Jocasta cooks."

His smile at her was definitely growing proprietorial, but she didn't even notice. My heart sank. If it weren't for that blasted Banquo . . .

Why is it always the wrong person who gets murdered?

"It's just chilli con carne, I'm afraid," Jocasta apologised, "but it seemed like a good idea on a day like this."

"Quite right!" Evangeline glanced at the first icy raindrops starting to hit the windows and shivered.

"That will be perfect," I agreed, closing my mind against the question of where she had found all the ingredients in Nigel's kitchen. He was not the sort to keep a well-stocked pantry — or any pantry at all. Oh, well, if she had borrowed anything of ours, she was entitled. After all, we were going to be eating the lunch now, too.

"Actually," Jocasta said, "I think it's just about ready. I'll just put two more plates on the table."

It tasted as good as it smelled and we were doing it full justice when the doorbell rang.

"I'll go —" Nigel raised a hand to forestall Jocasta's automatic leap to her feet. It was his flat, after all.

Unfortunately, it was my daughter.

"Mother —" Martha surged into the

281

room. "I thought I might find you here. You didn't take your coat, so I knew you couldn't have gone outside. Oh!" She had spotted Jocasta. "You're here. So this is where you've disappeared to."

"It's no use, tell them it's no use." Jocasta had begun wringing her hands. "I'm not going back! You can't —" She broke off, noticing Martha's suddenly wistful expression and the way she was inhaling the fragrance of the cooking, just as Evangeline had done.

"Have you had lunch?" She changed tack abruptly.

"Not a bite. I couldn't eat with those terrible women around." Martha shuddered. "It would have choked me."

"Oh, my poor darling." I started for the stove, but Jocasta beat me to it. She ladled out a bowl of chilli and I settled for pulling out another chair. Martha sank into it gratefully.

"You've got to get rid of them, Mother! I can't stand much more. I — I'll do something desperate!"

"Eat first, then talk," I advised, suppressing a pang of anxiety. Of course she wouldn't do anything really desperate — at least, not to herself. She had too much to live for. The worry was that she might do something not quite law-abiding and punishable by imprisonment to someone else.

"Think of Hugh and the children," I reminded her, just in case. "You can go home to them at the end of the day. But we live here — we're stuck."

"That's just it — you shouldn't be." The words were somewhat indistinct, due to the large mouthful of chilli. She swallowed too quickly and coughed.

"Your mother is right," Jocasta said. "Eat first, then we can discuss it comfortably." It was the wrong thing to say. With Martha in this mood, anything would be the wrong thing.

"You!" Martha exploded. "It's all your fault! They're here because you're here! They barged their way in because they wanted to get to you. And you let them!"

"Darling —" I warned. She had a point, but getting upset about it wouldn't do any good.

"It's true —" Martha insisted. "She only came here because she was hiding from them. Now that they've found her, she has no reason to stay. She can go — and take them with her!"

"Martha!" She was being unpardonably rude. I thought I had brought her up better than that.

"I don't think you could get rid of them

that easily," Evangeline said. "They like it here and they're well dug in. It would take dynamite to dislodge them now. Jocasta's leaving wouldn't make any difference."

Except that we would no longer be comfortably supplied with a housekeeper and cook, but she didn't mention that.

"Also," Jocasta pointed out, "the cooker still hasn't been fixed at home. We wouldn't be able to test any more recipes for your book."

"*My* book —" Martha said bitterly. "*Mine?* They've started sneaking in their own stupid useless recipes — pemmican and all sorts of impossible things no touring actor would have on hand. They're hijacking my book — and you're letting them! You and that ghastly Banquo of yours!"

"Banquo is *not* ghastly!" Jocasta flared. "And" — her voice broke — "he is *not* mine."

But, ooh, how she wished that he was! Evangeline and I exchanged glances, then looked at Nigel. He hadn't missed the implication, either. His shoulders drooped dejectedly. Jem moved closer and put an encouraging arm around those shoulders and gave him a brace-up-old-boy shake.

Jem. Come to think of it, Jem was being unusually quiet. Apart from welcoming us to a flat that wasn't his, he had faded into the background. Was it just a hangover, or was there another reason?

I raised an eyebrow at Evangeline. She gave a small shrug in reply.

"I never dreamed this project could get so out of hand," Jocasta admitted. "But I've been thinking about the problem. Perhaps we could divide it into two separate books."

"Back the way they should be." Martha was only slightly mollified.

"I'll speak to my —"

The doorbell cut across Jocasta.

"No!" She quivered, shrinking back into her earlier terrors. "I'm not going back there! I'm not!"

"It's all right," Nigel soothed, starting for the door. "You don't have to. I'll see to that!" Grimly, he squared his shoulders, clenched his jaw, and threw open the door, prepared for battle.

A large man stood there, carrying a case of bottles.

"Delivery," he said, setting the case down at Nigel's feet. "Sign here, please." He thrust a small electronic device at Nigel and indicated a space on it.

"What — ?" Nigel stared incredulously at the bottles. "I haven't ordered —"

"Gift card right there," the man said.

"Dozen bottles of the best Scotch. I've just delivered a case of chilled champagne to the ladies in the penthouse. They were proper grateful —" His tone suggested Nigel was not. "Opened the first bottle before I'd even left."

"Ladies? Penthouse? Champagne? Let me see that!" Evangeline tweaked the gift card from Nigel's hand and scanned it while Nigel absently signed the device the delivery man was holding out.

"Bertie! I knew it!" Evangeline glared at the delivery man. "Did those harpies actually have the nerve to sign for *our* gift of champagne?"

"Yeah . . ." The man began backing away nervously, obviously unwilling to turn his back on her. "I couldn't have left it, otherwise."

"Forgery!" Evangeline trumpeted. "And they began opening *our* bottles?"

"Look — how do I know the right people are — I mean, they were at the address. They came to the door." He was moving rapidly towards the lift. He didn't want to get involved. "I didn't see them open anything. I just heard a cork pop —"

"Fraud! Theft!" Evangeline was triumphant. "We've got them dead to rights! Trixie! Martha! Forward! We'll catch them red-handed."

I was relieved to see Jem and Nigel also responding to her call for action. Even Jocasta joined us reluctantly, whether because she wanted to help or didn't want to be left alone, I neither knew nor cared. The more reinforcements the better, as far as I was concerned.

The retreating deliveryman had beaten us to the lift, no doubt already rehearsing his excuses if we complained to his employer, so we had to wait until it returned to us and we crowded into it.

It was a tight squeeze and we were in direct contravention of the permitted number of passengers. I held my breath until the lift slowly, but eventually surely, reached our floor and decanted us.

"Now!" Evangeline led the charge and swung her pointing finger at the door, clearly expecting them to throw themselves against it and break it open.

"Steady on —" Jem held out a restraining hand. "We're not at the barricades, you know. One of you must have a key."

Of course we had, but — we exchanged guilty glances — not one of us had the key with us.

"That does it!" Evangeline started forward again, fists upraised, ready to hurl herself against the door alone.

"Hold it!" Jem caught her again, thank heavens. All we needed was a broken door and Jasper really would be furious enough to evict us immediately.

"Let's try it the civilised way first." Jem tapped the doorbell. Nothing happened.

"You see? You can't be civilised with people like that. They don't know the meaning of the word!" Evangeline wasn't going to give up easily.

"Wait . . ." Jem stepped between her and the door and tried the knob. The door swung open easily. "It's unlocked."

"Typical." Evangeline sniffed. "Too careless to lock the door properly after the deliveryman. Too anxious to get at the champagne!"

There were distinct sounds of revelry ahead of us. Grimly, Evangeline marched towards them, moving so fast we almost had to run to keep up with her.

They had made themselves at home — even more at home — in the living room. One bottle of champagne had been emptied already and Isolde was pouring from another one.

"Put that down!" Evangeline thundered. "How dare you steal our champagne?"

"Don't be silly," Isolde said coldly. "It's

288

our champagne. But you may have a glass, if you like," she added graciously.

Uh oh. Red rag to a bull. Evangeline even snorted like one as she tried to snatch the bottle away.

"There ought to be a gift card." Jem was trying to be peacemaker again. "That should settle the question."

"Here it is —" Nigel saw it on the coffee table and swooped on it before any of them could get there first and tear it up. Then he hesitated.

"Go on, read it!" Evangeline snapped. "Prove it!"

"Ah . . ." Nigel said unhappily and read out: " 'For the beautiful ladies in the penthouse.' "

"You see," Edytha said triumphantly. "We told you it was ours!"

CHAPTER TWENTY-THREE

The harpies stood there, ranged in front of us, smug and smirking. Defying anyone to suggest that they were not beautiful.

"The signature!" Evangeline snapped. "Who signed that card?"

"There was no signature," Isolode said.

"It's from an unknown admirer," Edytha said complacently.

"We have many, too shy to sign their names, but wishing to honour us."

Nigel turned the card over. "Bertie, of course."

For an instant, there was a blank look of incomprehension on their faces before it was quickly masked.

"He may be unknown to you," Evangeline said triumphantly, "but not to us. Bertie is a dear friend."

"I'm sure we know him," Valeria said. "Although perhaps not by that name."

"All your friends have aliases?" Evangeline's tone insinuated that she was not a bit surprised.

"The acolytes of the goddess often choose another name," Edytha intoned solemnly. "One more in harmony with their inner spirit."

"Goddess?" Bewildered, Nigel looked around as though expecting to find that a deity had joined us. The only newcomer he saw was Cho-Cho, who, hearing our voices, had come to investigate and was sniffing at the case of champagne with great interest.

"Oh!" Isolde had noticed. "Stop that! Get away!" She stamped her foot, then raised it threateningly, aimed at Cho-Cho.

"Don't you dare!" I moved forward protectively.

"Then make her get away from our champagne! Get that horrid, unsanitary beast out of here!"

"Cho-Cho *lives* here," I said pointedly. "*She's* one of the beautiful ladies." Well, she would be, once Bertie had met her.

"Nasty, useless thing!" Isolde shuddered in revulsion. "Get her out of here!"

"As I said — *she* lives here." My control slipped. "*You're* the ones who should get out!"

"Cool it! Cool it!" The order came from Mick, who seemed to have belatedly decided

291

that his troubleshooting expertise was called for.

It had not escaped my notice that he had been lurking in the background — nor that he had snared one of the bottles all for himself and been quietly depleting it. I must admit I'd blinked. I hadn't thought of the troubleshooter as someone with an alcohol problem. Or was it just the result of being cooped up with Banquo's relatives for so long? At that point, he had suddenly realised he was being watched and had raised his glass to me in an ironic salute before draining the contents and swiftly refilling it.

"The cat isn't doing any harm." Now he had decided that it was time he intervened. "It's only a cat, not a dog. It isn't going to lift its leg against the bottles."

"Oh!" Isolde reeled back, clutching dramatically at her heart. "How coarse!"

"Vulgar!" Valeria agreed.

"Common." On a higher plane, Edytha dismissed it with a *what else can one expect* shrug, but there was a faint frown line between her eyebrows.

"Are you going to stand there — ?" Isolde turned to Banquo, who was oblivious and quietly guzzling his champagne. "Just stand there and allow language like that in front of ladies?"

"It's all right," Evangeline said. "We don't mind."

"I wasn't referring to *you!*" Isolde snarled.

Definitely, Mick must be drinking because of them. Who could blame him? I reached for a glass myself. Tom stepped forward and filled it for me.

"Let's keep the party polite." He spoke without any real hope as he then did the same for the others.

I agreed silently, although I picked up Cho-Cho just to be on the safe side. She relaxed, purring in my arms. All was well with her world. I wished I could say the same.

"Ah . . ." Nigel spoke into the uneasy silence. "Don't you want to hear the message from Bertie? It's rather important."

"Of course we do." Evangeline was barely controlling her impatience. "Spit it out, man!"

"Vulgar . . ." The source of the murmur was indeterminate, but the harpies were all nodding agreement to each other. Perhaps if we could just summon up enough vulgarity, we might drive them away to more refined regions.

I searched my memory for some of the more colourful phrases I had encountered in a long lifetime in the theatre, but the trouble was that most of them were not so much colourful as monotonous. The same word, used as verb, noun, gerund, adjective, adverb, and all points north, south, east, and west soon loses all meaning and just becomes a tiresome noise in the background.

"Collect you . . . limousine . . . tomorrow . . ." I became aware that Nigel was reading out the message on the card and began to pay attention. "The Jewel Box!" he finished, with a triumphant flourish. He and Jem looked at each other and seemed to just restrain from giving themselves the high-five.

"Jewel box . . ." Evangeline breathed rapturously, stretching out her hands as though deciding whether she would rather have another ring or would prefer a bracelet.

"Now that should settle the question," Jem said smoothly. "We'll just wait and see for whom the limousine calls tomorrow."

"We shall see, indeed," Isolde said frostily, but I could tell they were all shaken. Perhaps none of their followers had a limousine. "Right now, we should get back to work." She glared pointedly at Jocasta. "You've wasted most of the day."

"Quite right," Edytha said. "We're coming up to one of the most poignant moments in the book, when poor Banquo, cold, hungry, lonely, and desolate, sits beside a flickering candle, gazing at a photo of dear Melisande, and dreams of the happy moment when he will be reunited with his lovely bride, never suspecting that she is already —"

"I'm sorry," Jocasta said tightly. "I'm not feeling well. I can't do anything more to-day."

"More?" Valeria exploded. "You haven't done anything yet!"

Apart from cooking lunch for six people, but I decided it wouldn't be wise to mention that.

"You must try," Edytha said softly. "Banquo needs a sympathetic helper to bare his soul to, to give voice to his deepest emotions. Banquo needs you. Tell her so in your own words, Banquo."

"Hic!" he said. Nice try, but Banquo was blotto.

Mick wasn't very far behind him. Having been thwarted in his brief spurt of trying to deal with the situation, he had retreated. Swaying now, as he tipped the last of his bottle into his glass, he raised that glass to us again in the same ironic salute.

Tom was watching him warily. Of them all, he seemed to be the one who had imbibed the least of their pilfered champagne. Because he didn't trust himself? Or because he didn't trust them?

"Listen everyone —" He seemed to have come to a decision. "I think we've all done enough for the day." He glanced hopefully towards Mick, whose job this ought to be, but Mick was ignoring him, ignoring everyone.

"The light is going and the weather is closing in again. I suggest we leave before the worst of the storm hits. We wouldn't want to be marooned here."

He was right. The swift-falling darkness and rising wind threatened more than mere rain. I saw the others scan the sky and come to the same conclusion. Apart from which, he was offering them the most graceful way out they were likely to get.

"Come, Banquo." Edytha put an arm around his shoulders and turned him gently towards the door, quite as though he was going to contest their departure.

"Very well." Isolde looked at her male teammates and ordered, "Tom and Mick, help me with our champagne."

"Oh, no, you don't!" Evangeline started forward and I was right behind her. But Martha was ahead of us all.

She stepped in front of the case, then sat down firmly on top of it, folding her arms and daring anyone to touch her.

Even though it must have been uncomfortable sitting on those bottles, not to mention chilly, her intention was clear. She would stay there all night, if necessary. They would have to drag her off by force — and she wouldn't go easily. Furthermore, she had us for reinforcements.

The harpies exchanged glances. They, too, had reinforcements, but theirs weren't in very good shape. Apart from Tom — and he didn't have the right fighting spirit.

"That's it," he said, proving it. "Game, set, and match. Time to call it a day and cut your losses. Right, men?"

Mick raised his bottle in salute, then seemed to notice it was empty. He blinked muzzily at Martha, but obviously decided it wasn't worth the effort. He retreated a step, distancing himself from the proceedings. This was one trouble he couldn't shoot.

"Hic!" Banquo was swaying. "Hic! Hic!"

"Poor Banquo is distraught with grief!" As though that were a signal, they clustered around him. Edytha lowered her arm for a discreet grasp around his waist.

"Recalling his lost happiness has been too much for him." Isolde laid a consoling hand on his shoulder.

"Poor boy." Valeria was the tallest of them.

She stroked his hair. "You must be brave."

"Hic!" They'd be getting no sense from him now, if there had ever been any there to begin with. They urged him firmly along. Supporting him, comforting him — imprisoning him?

He leaned on them and they chose to see him as a heartbroken hero. To me, he looked more like a hollow man, his life dictated by the nearest person overbearing enough to take command. Surely, Jocasta could see it?

It appeared not. Her eyes brimmed with wistful tears as she watched him leave. It was only too apparent that she wished to be the one with her arm around his waist, stroking his hair . . .

Oh, dear. Nigel was watching her and he recognised it, too.

"Ah . . ." He cleared his throat diffidently. "Perhaps I ought to get back to my flat. There might be a message for me on the back of my card. We, um, left so suddenly, I didn't get a chance to examine it properly." How tactful of him to gloss over the fact that Evangeline had snatched it before he'd had a chance to look at it.

"Good idea." Jem was helping Martha to her feet. "Bertie may have a couple of chores for you to do before tomorrow."

"Ah . . ." Nigel turned to Jocasta. "You'll

be all right here?"

"I will . . . now." Jocasta rallied enough to give him an absent smile. "They've gone."

"We'll take good care of her," I promised him. It wasn't exactly what he wanted to hear. He wanted to be the one to look after her, but she wasn't even noticing.

With a regretful sigh, he helped Jem carry the champagne into the kitchen, where we could hear Martha loading it into the fridge.

"I hate to admit this, but I'm baffled," Evangeline complained. "Utterly, completely baffled — why Melisande?"

"We can't win them all," I said. "It happened so long before we came on the scene — there was nothing we could do. Even the police thought it was an accident. The coroner ruled misadventure."

"That's not the question bothering me." Evangeline brushed it aside. "What I can't understand is why anyone would want to kill a harmless innocent like Melisande when those ghastly women keep getting underfoot and just asking for it!"

CHAPTER TWENTY-FOUR

"I've been asked to convey their apologies." Tom was the only one who showed up in the morning. "Banquo is not feeling well today and the ladies are looking after him. In short, everyone is indisposed."

"Indisposed?" Evangeline snorted. "You mean hung-over."

"There's that, too," Tom admitted.

"Especially with Mick." There was no delicate way to approach this, so I plunged straight in. "Does he have an alcohol problem?"

"Mick?" Tom grimaced and shook his head. "Not really. Mick has a civilisation problem. He can't stand too much of it — and he's just about reached his limit."

"Yes, we've noticed he's becoming . . . restive." That was a prize understatement after the way he'd talked about the Graces.

"He hates cities. Sometimes he hates people, too. He can't wait to get back into

300

the wild again."

"And you?"

"Me?" Tom shrugged. "This was my second expedition with the Great Banquo and His Travelling Circus. He doesn't know it yet, but it was also my last. It's been an interesting career step, but I don't plan to spend the rest of my life dancing attendance on him. I happen to like civilisation — and I'm not leaving it again."

The Great Banquo, eh? Mick may have been on the turn, but Tom was doing the complete about-face.

Why, oh, why, couldn't Jocasta resign from the fan club, too?

Perhaps because she hadn't yet had enough of a steady diet of Banquo. She would see even less of him when he departed on his next expedition. I had the unhappy feeling that she was one of those *absence makes the heart grow fonder* romantics. Give me the *out of sight, out of mind* types every time. There was less strain involved.

"I like everything about civilisation," Tom went on. "All the noise, the crowds, the buzz of excitement, the food — especially the food. It's all ambrosia — after the messes Banquo had us eating out in the wild."

"I must admit he never struck me as

one of the world's great gourmets," I agreed. "How did he and Melisande ever get together? I'd think she was wasted on him."

"You don't know the half of it," Tom said grimly. "Not any of it. Poor Mellie. She was a romantic and he was —"

"I think we all know what he is," Evangeline cut in sharply.

"Yes, well . . ." He paused, staring into space at some vision only he could see. The might-have-been, perhaps.

"Yes, well . . ." he repeated, then gave himself a little shake, coming back to the real world — however unwillingly. As he turned abruptly, he dislodged one of Isolde's ersatz cupcakes from the peak of a carefully arranged stack. It bounced as it hit the floor and continued bouncing across the room like a rubber ball.

With a happy chirrup, Cho-Cho bounded after it. This was more like it — there hadn't been many games around here lately.

"Don't try to eat that," Tom warned as she captured it. "Although," he added grimly, "it would be a lot more palatable than most of the stuff Banquo served up." He shuddered reminiscently, then brightened. "At least I'll never have to face that again. They can go to their Antarctica and freeze to death. I'll stay here in the comparative tropics of dear old London."

"Antarctica . . ." Evangeline mused. "I'd have thought he'd had enough of all that ice."

"Glutton for punishment — if not for food. And all the discomfort and rotten food were just a trial run before the big one. That's when he's really going to pull out all the stops and try some kind of crazy heroics. And those crazy cousins of his are egging him on all the way. It's a wonder they haven't killed him instead of —" He broke off abruptly.

Instead of Melisande, he nearly said. Another vote from a member of the expedition. I wondered if he and Mick had discussed their suspicions or come to them separately.

"Never mind," I soothed, covering his gaffe. "You're not going to be there. You'll be well out of it by then."

"If not sooner." He brightened. "I'll never have to eat any more freeze-dried goo! And —" He shuddered, the gloom returning. "I never want to see anything boiled in a bag again!"

In that case, there were quite a few restaurants he'd do well to avoid, but I decided not to mention that. Let his dream of civili-

303

sation remain untarnished for a while longer. He'd find out soon enough.

"You just hang on to that thought," Evangeline told him. She gave me a *we'll discuss this later* look and I knew she hadn't missed his gaffe, either.

I nodded agreement but, before we could do anything else, a key scraped in the lock and footsteps sounded along the hall. I wasn't the only one who flinched and braced myself.

But it was only Jocasta, and Nigel right behind her.

"Your car is here," she said. Was there more than a trace of wistfulness in her voice? I wondered how long it had been since she'd had a day out. She no longer had to hide from Banquo's awful cousins — they had found her, moved themselves in, and, with Banquo, kept her poor little nose so steadily to the grindstone that it was a wonder she had any nose left at all. She needed some time off — and they weren't around to thwart her today.

"Why don't you come along with us?" I invited her impulsively. "You've been working so hard, you need some time off."

"That's right," Nigel seconded, beaming. "Do come."

"But . . ." She wanted to, it was there in

her eyes. But she was a properly brought-up young lady. "I wasn't really invited. Your uncle —"

"He'll be delighted. He's the most generous man in the world. Ah, providing he's in the right mood."

There was a small humming noise, almost a purr, from Evangeline. If there was anything she was an expert at, it was putting generous men in the right mood.

But — the look she shot at me should have encased me in ice — she wasn't good at sharing the wealth. If Bertie opened his jewel box, she didn't want competition for any booty around.

"Go on," Tom urged. "I can manage perfectly well by myself today. In fact, I'd welcome the chance to catch up with lots of fiddly little jobs without anyone else underfoot."

I'll bet he would. After trailing across the frozen wastes with Banquo and Mick for company and then finding himself stuck with them back here — and with Banquo's ghastly cousins, as well — it was no wonder he'd welcome a chance to work alone with no one else to keep interfering.

"Well . . ." Jocasta was increasingly willing to be persuaded. "If you're sure . . ."

"That's settled then," I said firmly. "Get

305

your coat and let's not keep everyone waiting."

Jem was already sitting in the limo when we got downstairs.

" 'Hail, hail, the gang's all here,' " Evangeline greeted, not altogether pleased to see him. "I thought you'd be back in Brighton now."

"Things got more complicated than I expected." Jem moved his large attaché case to make more room as we got in. "I see you talked Jocasta into it," he said to Nigel. "Good."

"Are we dropping you at the station?" I asked. That was a very big attaché case, the sort that can double as an overnight case, perhaps even a weekend case.

"Not quite yet." Jem looked amused, but slightly nervous. "There are still a few things I have to see to."

"Hmm . . ." Evangeline had caught that trace of nervousness, too, and she knew Jem better than I did. Her swift glance told me she knew he was up to something. She suspected the worst: another rival for the promised jewels. At least, he was unlikely to pounce on any of the female fripperies so close to her heart. Jocasta would be her main rival there — and, of course, me.

306

Nigel got in last and shut the door behind him. The limo glided off. We were on our way . . .

The journey seemed to go on forever. Even Evangeline got restive enough to stop studying her hands and deciding what kind of rings she'd like and looked out of the windows impatiently.

"Where *are* we going?" she demanded, not without cause. We were threading our way through narrow streets somewhere between the river and a lot of railway yards. Not the most salubrious area in town. Although, to be fair, it seemed to be fighting to improve. In fact, if gentrification set in around here, convenient to town as it was, it might become highly sought after.

We turned a corner and the narrow one-way street gave way into a wider, more pleasant thoroughfare with a few trees, definitely an improvement. Judging from the scaffolding surrounding what seemed to have been warehouses, the improvement was set to continue. I began to relax — until the car pulled up in front of one of the scaffolded buildings and stopped.

"This is it?" Evangeline glared at the scaffolding shrouding the building as Nigel got out and held the door for us. "This is where we're going?"

"Dear ladies —" There was now no doubt about it. A small door opened at the foot of the precarious structure and Bertie stood there with a welcoming smile, flanked by two men who were surely security staff. Of course, some of these buildings must house storage vaults for valuables. I could see Evangeline relax, but I wasn't so sure. Somehow, although it seemed generically familiar, it did not seem like security vaults.

"Come in, come in — and forgive me for not going to collect you personally. I wanted to see that things were ready for your arrival here. And —" He broke off as he saw Nigel tenderly assisting Jocasta out of the limo, with a care he had not extended to us.

"And — who is this new lovely lady?" Behind Nigel's back, his eyebrows semaphored a question to me.

I shrugged slightly and, with what I hoped was an enigmatic smile, held up my crossed fingers. He got the message.

"Welcome, my dear!" He surged forward and captured one of Jocasta's hands, tucking it into his arm. "Ah, Nigel, Nigel." He waggled a playful finger. "Yet another beauty. You *are* a dark horse."

"More a chip off the old block, I'd say." Evangeline was still here pitching, although not quite so confidently as usual.

"Possibly, possibly," Bertie preened, still keeping Jocasta firmly by his side. "Come inside and let me show you our wares."

Evangeline brightened, this was more like it. I wasn't so sure. There was something hauntingly familiar about this place, yet I knew I'd never been here before. I'd never been in any English security vaults before, either.

There was scaffolding inside the building, too, and the smell of fresh paint. Ladders were propped against walls, dim shapes were shrouded in canvas.

"This way." Bertie swerved and led us through a door I had not noticed. "Sorry for the mess," he apologised, "but I'm trying to get things back into order. Hope no one is allergic to the smell of paint."

Allergies again! I winced and looked at Evangeline to see if the reference bothered her, but she was too busy agreeing with the others that paint didn't bother her at all.

"Good, good. It's not so bad back here, they haven't started working on it yet."

I'll say they hadn't. The smell of dust almost won out over the paint. Tatters of barely disturbed cobwebs dangled in corners of the ceiling. There had obviously been a hasty but not very comprehensive tidying-up before we arrived. Patches of old paint, cleaner than the grime-streaked rest of the wall, told of pictures removed.

I had to stop myself from looking around for Miss Havisham. Evangeline's nose was twitching and it wasn't because of the dust — or perhaps it was. She was growing increasingly suspicious. This wasn't the sort of place she expected to find a casket of precious gems stored. My suspicions were getting pretty well confirmed the farther into the building we ventured. But then Evangeline probably hadn't played in as many rundown fleapits as I had in the early days of my career.

"In here." Bertie opened another door and led us into an office. I could see Evangeline's hopes rise momentarily and then crash as she got a good look at the place.

She had never before been in a security vault whose walls were lined with theatrical posters — and that meant she was not in one now. She gripped my elbow so fiercely that I winced.

"Trixie," she muttered, "we are betrayed!"

Maybe she thought she was, but I knew I wasn't. I never expect anything until it is firmly in my hands and then I am duly grateful. Evangeline expects everything and, when she gets it, she has it appraised.

I twitched my arm in a gentle hint and

she relaxed her grip slightly. Not good enough. I pulled away firmly, ignoring her hiss of annoyance, and went over to study the posters more clearly. Even I recognised that there were legendary names and shows among them, although some were well before my time. Here and there lighter patches of wallpaper hinted at shows that had not been so successful. Or possibly the original posters had disintegrated, some of them looked ancient enough.

There was not a safety deposit box in sight, nor even a safe. But Evangeline was the only one bothered about that.

Nigel was looking extremely pleased with himself and so was Bertie. Jem still looked uneasy — perhaps he had noticed that Evangeline was quietly seething. Those deep breaths she was taking were not meant to calm, but to build up a head of steam. At any moment, the explosion might come. I moved closer to Jem, who seemed the least likely target of her wrath.

At the same time, I tried to signal her to be quiet. I had the feeling that something interesting was going on and I didn't want her to spoil it. She ignored me.

"Where — ?" she demanded in a danger-ously quiet voice, "where is the jewel box you promised?"

"Yes, yes." Bertie beamed, not taking offense. "Right along this way." He led us along a narrow corridor, so quickly that I lost count of the closed doors we passed. I had the impression that a couple had stars on them.

"Through here . . ." We stepped out of the wings onto what was definitely a stage. Furniture in the Art Deco style was arranged as a drawing room, with a white grand piano upstage of a sofa. There was a further sofa opposite it in the shadows.

A beautiful piano; I wondered if it was still in tune. As I gravitated towards it, Bertie pushed a button and the curtains parted, revealing the auditorium. We all stared, transfixed.

"Hugh!" Evangeline spotted him first, leaning back in the second seat from the aisle in the third row. "What are you doing here?"

"What?" he said.

"I said, 'What are you doing here?' "

"Hugh, is Martha with you?" I called.

"Good." Hugh stood and began to make his way up to the stage. "The acoustics are perfect."

Before he could reach us, something uncurled from the corner of the farther sofa and darted into the wings. I gasped, but it wasn't a rat, it was a sleek grey cat.

"The theatre cat?" I smiled.

"Mothball!" Bertie cried. He clutched at his chest and staggered. Nigel caught him before he fell.

CHAPTER TWENTY-FIVE

"Steady on, Bertie." Nigel half-carried him over to the matching sofa, which was nearer, and stretched him out on it. He drew a small flask from his pocket and held it to Bertie's lips. "Drink this . . . slowly . . . it's brandy."

Evangeline looked on enviously.

I hoped Jocasta, who hovered behind Bertie, was paying attention. This was a side of Nigel we hadn't seen before. Kind and caring and genuinely fond of his great-uncle. Or perhaps she had seen it — or sensed it — since she had flown to Nigel for refuge. Which he had been delighted to provide. Now she just had to realise what she had, so unlike the selfish ego-on-legs that was Banquo. If only she could see that monster clearly and get over her fatal infatuation.

"Mothball!" Bertie drank, choked, gasped. "Mothball — it can't be!"

314

"Ah . . . it isn't . . . not actually." Nigel seemed unsure whether the news might upset his uncle Humbert even more. "That's Mothball the Fifth . . . or perhaps the Sixth. We've all lost count."

"Of course, of course." Bertie was getting himself under control, breathing more easily. "I knew it couldn't be the real Mothball. He was just a kitten when we . . . we . . . found him, wrapped in an old sweater that smelled of mothballs. That's where he got his name. *She* named him and we made him our theatre cat . . . but that was thirty-odd years ago. It was just that . . . for a moment . . ."

"More like forty-odd, Bertie," Nigel reminded him gently. "You've . . . been asleep . . . a long time."

"Aye." An ancient man came out of the shadowed wings. "And now we have Mothball the Fifth. Direct descendant — as you've just seen. A fitting name for a cat guarding a mothballed playhouse. More's the pity . . . more's the crime . . ."

"Good Lord! It's young Sam!" Bertie gasped. "Are you still here?"

I nearly gasped myself as the old boy came over to us. If that was young Sam, then I was baby Trixie.

"Aye. Like the Fifth, another generation is

315

keeping safe watch over your theatre, Bertie. My son is young Sam now, though he's getting a bit long in the tooth, too, these days."

"So long ago . . ." Bertie sighed. "So long . . ."

"But you're waking up now," Nigel prodded.

"Am I? I suppose so." Bertie sighed again. "I feel like Rip van Winkle — if anyone remembers him . . . or me."

"You were never forgotten, Bertie." Hugh strode to the fore. "You're a legend. Everyone speaks of you with admiration and —"

"They think I'm dead," Bertie interrupted. "I've heard the rumours, I've seen the stories in the papers, I've —"

"Ah!" Nigel said hastily. "Um, that is . . ."

I've heard better attempts at trying to change the subject, but at least he was trying.

"They're all going to find out differently when you burst on the scene again and reclaim your rightful place in theatre land." Hugh could be depended on to know the right thing to say.

But what exactly was he saying? There was a subtext there that I couldn't quite fathom.

Before I had time to consider it, another shadow stirred on the far sofa, leaped to the floor, and stretched luxuriously. I realised

Mothball had been curled up with this cat — and who could blame him? She — it had to be she — was a little beauty. Also grey, but with slightly longer fur, silver-tipped at the ends.

"Ah," Nigel said. "Here's Dustbunny. She's Mothball's . . . ah . . . mate." As a diversion, this was more successful. Hearing her name, Dustbunny strolled across to us and greeted Nigel as an old friend.

"She knows you," I said inanely.

"And you seem to know a lot about the cats —" Bertie shot a keen glance at his nephew. "Their names, their relationship, their place in this theatre . . . ?" Pointedly, he waited for an explanation.

"Ah . . ." Nigel was caught out. "Well . . . you gave us — the family — a passkey to the theatre and asked us to look in once in a while and make sure that everything was all right. I . . . I like to do that . . . more than the others do. I come here quite a bit, actually. It's so peaceful and there's such a pleasant atmosphere. I just like to sit here . . . even with everything under wraps, it feels safe and happy, like . . . like coming home after a hard day. I . . . I didn't think you'd mind."

"Mind?" Bertie beamed. "Mind? Dear boy, I never dreamed . . . no one else in the family ever cared a toss about the theatre. Oh, they've pretended they do to humour me, but I know if they ever get their hands on it, they'll have the developers in bidding for the freehold to tear it down and put up a tower block before the flowers have wilted on my grave."

"Tear it down? They'd have to fight me!" Nigel clenched his fists. "It . . . it would be sacrilege!"

"Sounds like your DNA is coming through, Bertie." Hugh smiled.

Dustbunny had wandered over to sniff at Evangeline's ankles before rubbing against them. I tried not to be jealous, perhaps I reeked too much of Cho-Cho.

"This one is more friendly," Evangeline said approvingly, picking her up.

"And beautiful." Bertie also approved. "A fitting ornament to reside in my Jewel Box."

Jewel Box! And we all were in it. It was the name of the theatre itself. I heard Evangeline's explosive release of breath as Bertie's words registered with her. Dustbunny squeaked a reproof at the arms that had suddenly tightened around her.

No diamond bracelets, no emerald rings, no glittering jewels, no heavy gold trinkets at all.

But . . . perhaps something even better.

Instinctively, I moved towards the white piano to test whether it was still in tune. But something stopped me even before I caught Nigel's warning shake of the head.

I changed direction, almost as though someone had turned me, and found myself downstage facing the footlights, looking out over the auditorium. Now that I could see it properly, from the stage, I caught my breath with delight. No wonder it had been named the Jewel Box.

The place was small, but exquisite. Two shallow tiers above the rows of seats sent out gleams of fresh gold paint from behind their scaffolding. The first few rows of seats in the auditorium had been uncovered and their new red plush glowed dully. The whole theatre was hushed and seemed to be waiting for the show to begin.

I was drawn forward inexorably, picturing an audience in those seats — the sort of audience Dame Cecile commanded — rustling expectantly.

I couldn't help it. I took a deep breath and let out a rivulet of notes, running the scale, testing the acoustics. As Hugh had said, they were perfect.

"Sing out, Trixie," Hugh called. I'd been in enough straw hat circuits with *Gypsy* to recognise that cue.

"Curtain up . . . light the lights . . ."

The footlights sprang to life. Someone else could recognise a cue.

"We've got nothing to hit but the heights . . ." Evangeline was not going to be left out of it. She was beside me. We harmonised and finished as a duet.

"This *is* a Jewel Box!" I exclaimed as the last echo died away.

"Yes! Yes!" Evangeline was equally enthusiastic. So there weren't any actual jewels, what did that matter? We already had plenty.

Even Dustbunny gave an approving chirrup, looking around. Probably she had never seen the seats uncovered and the footlights shining before.

"It's all yours," Bertie said. "If you want it."

"*If* we want it!" I could hardly speak. "Oh Bertie! Bertie!"

"A theatre — at last!" Evangeline breathed.

"Three hundred seats. The refurbishment should be complete in a couple of months." Incredibly, it sounded like Bertie was trying to sell us on the idea. He needn't bother, we were already sold.

"You could begin rehearsing then, while we see to all the finishing touches working around you, and have the grand opening in

320

the autumn. Hugh will produce. I'll be presenter . . . again."

"Wonderful!" After a moment of delirium, I came down to earth with a thud. "Now all we need is a play."

"Still no news from that playwright you commissioned to write one for you?" Jem was elaborately casual. "The one who took off on a world tour — with your advance payment."

"Not even a postcard," Evangeline said bitterly. "If we only knew where he was, we could sue him for fraud, extortion, taking money under false pretences —"

"And having dirty fingernails," I cut in. "I think we can safely write him off and look around for a better prospect."

Was it instinct that drew my gaze to Jem — or was it because he was clutching his attaché case so tightly and fidgeting nervously?

"Oh?" Evangeline caught something in my tone and turned to look at Jem, as well.

He looked away.

"We'll have to start putting it out on the grapevine," I suggested.

Jem twitched.

"Or put an advert in *The Stage*." Evangeline joined in the tease.

Jem grew red, twitched again, and

clutched the attaché case closer. Bertie beamed at us complacently. So did Nigel. Hugh folded his arms and watched with amusement. Jocasta was perplexed, but game.

"My sister knows someone who self-published his own book of poetry once," she volunteered.

"I don't think we need to look that far," Hugh intervened. "I've had a couple of preliminary discussions since it began to look as though you were going to be let down."

"Really?" Evangeline widened her eyes innocently. "With anyone we know?"

Hugh quirked an eyebrow at Jem. "You might as well tell them."

"We . . . um . . . I, er —" he started.

"Oh, spit it out!" Evangeline's patience snapped.

"Yes, right." She might not be the most tactful person in the world, but they were old friends and she obviously knew how to handle him.

"Right!" Jem went from red to ashen, but he straightened his back, marched over to the coffee table, set his attaché case down, unlocked it — and took out a sheaf of paper.

I knew it! A lot of incidents fell into place, from the way Jem had hastily hidden a notebook the day I dropped in on him unexpectedly in his attic apartment at the theatre in Brighton, to the quiet satisfaction he had oozed the day he took us to the London theatre and solicitously enquired about our missing playwright. Not schadenfreude at all, but checking up that the way was still clear for him.

"Here —" Jem handed each of us a script. "See what you think . . ." His voice faltered, then firmed. "Of this. I started writing it just for you as soon as I saw you in action last year."

"Jem," Evangeline purred. "Darling Jem!"

"You — you might not like it," he warned. "Don't be afraid to tell me . . ."

Hugh's snort of amusement let us know that he'd read the script and had no doubts about our reactions. Hadn't he already committed himself to producing it?

We were in business!

CHAPTER TWENTY-SIX

I know the truism has it that *If something seems too good to be true, it is.* But not this time. Bertie took us back to his office and whipped out contracts, all prepared and just awaiting our signatures. Hugh gave us the nod, we signed on the dotted line, and then went off to the Harpo to celebrate.

On the other hand, this was the morning after. My aching head reminded me of that other truism, the one that says *Things are too good to last.* Loud noises from the other side of the wall warned me this one was true.

Although I wanted to remain in bed, savouring our triumph and playing with Cho-Cho, those dominating voices meant the harpies were back in force. There would be no peace now, I might as well get up. Also, Martha and Jocasta might need reinforcements.

"We lost a full day yesterday —" Isolde

pulled her head out of the fridge and glared at me accusingly. "We've got to work doubly hard today to make up for it."

"I hope you're feeling better." I smiled smugly at her. I knew what she'd been looking for, but we were way ahead of her. Evangeline and I had transferred the champagne to our private fridges where no one could get at it. There wasn't much room for anything else in the fridges now, but it was the principle that mattered. I made a mental note to lock our doors. Theoretically, our rooms were out of bounds to the crew, but who could trust them?

"I've settled the poor dear on the sofa —" Valeria brayed her report, returning from the front room. "We must concentrate on him today."

Three pairs of eyes converged on Jocasta, quailing behind Tom. "The cookbook isn't important."

"But the cookbook deadline is coming up first," Jocasta protested feebly.

"Poor, dear Banquo is really suffering —" Expertly, Edytha manipulated Jocasta. "Illness now — on top of heartbreak. He needs sympathy, help, the tenderness of a woman who isn't one of his relatives —"

An eligible woman who can replace Melisande, was clearly implied. Preferably one the harpies could dominate. I cleared my throat warningly, but it was too late. Jocasta was hooked.

"Oooh, poor Banquo." She dashed towards the living room. The others followed more slowly, pausing to exchange complacent nods.

"Jocasta can't take much more of being torn apart like this," I complained. "They might give her a break — other than nervous, that is."

"You don't get it, do you?" For once, Mick didn't sound sardonic. "Nothing matters but Banquo. Nothing — and no one." He wheeled around and went after the others.

"Nothing matters except their meal ticket." Tom was increasingly bitter. "Banquo — the showpiece, the mouthpiece — the meal ticket."

"At least you're getting away from it." I watched his fists slowly unclench as I reminded him. "If they trap Jocasta —" It didn't bear thinking about: a lifetime in that nightmare.

And, if Jocasta finally woke from her deluded fantasy and began to assert herself? If she stopped being so malleable . . . would she go the way of Melisande? That was even worse to think about.

"Have they gone?" Evangeline's head

poked around the door.

"For the moment," Tom said. "But they'll be back."

"How comforting." Nothing was going to disturb her this morning. *She* was all right, Jem's play was brilliant, the theatre was secured, and Hugh was looking after our interests. There was nothing to worry about.

Ah, well. Leave her in her fool's paradise a while longer. I could worry enough for both of us.

"Have they gone far?" Evangeline was ever hopeful.

"Only as far as the living room." I dashed those hopes.

"Do we have to burn the place down to get them out?"

"It's an idea, but we'd be out, too."

"It would be worth it."

"Just the same, let's try for a bit less drastic solution."

"Less drastic than what?" Martha asked sharply from behind me. I hadn't heard her arrive, but she was here and she was on the warpath, as she so often was these days. Not surprisingly.

"Good morning, darling." I repressed a sigh.

"Is it? I hadn't noticed." She glared around, noticing everything else. "Where's

327

Jocasta? Has she wimped off again?"

"It's not her fault," I defended. "Those ghastly females practically frog-marched her away to work with Banquo today."

"Him again! That man has got to go!"

"My sentiments exactly," Evangeline chimed in.

"Then *do* something!"

They both turned to look at me.

"Now wait a minute —" I began.

"There's no use expecting her to do anything," Evangeline said. "She's useless!"

"Thank you, Evangeline. It's so nice to be appreciated."

"Can you keep it quiet in here?" Mick was back. "Banquo can't concentrate with all this noise."

"Oh, really?" Martha's tone was dangerously sweet. "Do forgive us." I braced myself.

"That's all right," Mick said generously. "Just watch it."

I noticed Tom backing unobtrusively towards the far corner. He might not know Martha well, but unlike Mick, he could recognise an explosive situation when he saw it.

"Don't worry, we will." Martha's voice oozed syrup. Even Evangeline began to look uneasy. "We wouldn't dream of upsetting your precious boy. Is there anything else we can do? Anything else at all that he might want?"

"Uh, yeah, now that you mention it." Mick was still recklessly oblivious. "He wants a pot of hot coffee and a lot of sandwiches. Oh, and Jocasta wants a glass of cold milk and a couple of aspirins."

Martha froze, nostrils flaring dangerously.

"Don't bother saying 'please'," Evangeline said. "We serfs don't expect such niceties."

"Yeah, yeah, sure," Mick said impatiently. "Please, thank you, you're welcome — and all that stuff. Just get a move on, will you? Before the lord and master sets the bitches on you."

The lord and master wasn't the one we had to worry about right now.

To my relief, Martha moved to the fridge first, although she flipped on the coffee-maker as she passed, and began pouring cold milk into our largest glass. I retreated to the bathroom to get Jocasta's aspirins — and a towel.

The outraged bellow sent me scurrying back to the action, just in time to hear Martha say: "Your hot coffee will be ready in a moment."

Oh, no, it wouldn't. I switched off the cof-feemaker and rushed to toss the towel over

Mick. Cold liquid was one thing, boiling hot could do serious damage. And Martha was too furious to care.

"What's going on here?" Valeria stormed into the room at hurricane force. "We send you out here to keep them quiet — and now you're making more noise than any of them!"

She tried unsuccessfully to snatch the towel from Mick's head. "What are you playing at?"

A muffled snarl came from the folds as he backed away from her. It was indistinct, but definitely uncomplimentary.

"What?" She caught the gist of it. "What did you say to me?" This time she succeeded in wrenching the towel from him.

"Crazies —" He dabbed at a runnel of milk dripping off his chin with the sleeve of his shirt and tried to grab the towel back. "You're all crazies!"

"It takes one to know one," Evangeline observed sagely.

I took an involuntary step backwards. The sudden fury that blazed in Mick's eyes before he masked them again with the towel was wild enough to make me think for a moment that Evangeline had unwittingly stumbled on a truth.

"What's keeping you?" Now Isolde was in

the room, which seemed to shrink and grow airless. "Banquo is waiting!"

"They're being obstructive," Valeria snapped. "As usual."

"They are, are they?" Isolde glared at us, her eyes glittering with the unholy light of someone about to fire some unsatisfactory employee — just before she remembered that we didn't work for her.

"What's that?" She changed course abruptly, snatching at the packet I was holding. "Aspirins! Just what our poor boy needs. I fear he's getting a headache with all this commotion. He's not used to it."

"Who is?" Mick was undoubtedly longing for the peace and silence of the wide open spaces.

"They're for Jocasta," I said. "She already has a headache. And they're the last in the packet."

"All the more reason for Banquo to have them!" She added dismissively, "Jocasta won't mind."

That was the awful thing: she probably wouldn't — or not very much. No sacrifice was too great for her hero. Sometimes I despaired.

As I did now. Isolde had possession of the last of the aspirins. What use was there in trying to fight for Jocasta when she wouldn't lift a finger to help herself? She didn't even realise how much she needed help.

With a triumphant toss of their heads, they went back to their precious Banquo. Immediately there was more air and space in the kitchen.

"Are you still here?" Evangeline rounded on Mick, who was taking a few breaths of freedom.

"He's waiting for the coffee," Martha said dangerously.

"Forget it!" He flung down the towel and stalked away. "Let them get their own coffee," he snarled over his shoulder. "I'm going out!"

The slam of the front door echoed down the hallway.

"He's cracking up," Evangeline observed with relish.

"He was never a ladies' man to begin with." Tom emerged from his corner. "And these particular ladies have been the last straw."

"Oh, dear." For once, I wasn't sure which ladies he meant. Certainly Martha had done her part. "Really, Martha —" I began.

"Don't worry," Tom said. "He'll just walk around for a while until he cools down. He'll be back."

"I'm not so sure."

"I am." Tom shrugged. "He has nowhere else to go."

CHAPTER TWENTY-SEVEN

Tom knew his colleague, although even he seemed surprised when Mick returned bearing a towering stack of pizzas. Nigel followed behind him with a shorter stack and the bemused expression of one who has unexpectedly been pressed into service. Setting his boxes down beside Mick's he looked around hopefully for Jocasta.

"I'm not sure who'd like what —" We didn't see Mick's ingratiating smile often. "So I got the small size with half-and-half toppings. I thought, that way, there was bound to be something for everybody."

"I think Banquo prefers pepperoni," Tom said, sorting through them.

"I'm not bothered about him." Mick sent Tom a meaningful look, undecipherable to the rest of us, but vaguely unpleasant. "He'll eat anything."

"Meeorreow?" Suddenly, Cho-Cho was at my feet, lured by the unfamiliar smells seep-

ing from the cardboard boxes. Another one who was ready to eat anything.

"This looks fine." I pounced on a half-meat, half-seafood feast and quickly flipped a small meatball to Cho-Cho, who disposed of it in two bites and continued looking at me hopefully. I obliged with a chunk of tuna and an anchovy.

"Let her have it all." Mick was magnanimous. "I got plenty for everybody. She can use it," he added, assessing her critically, "not much meat on *her*."

Until that point, I hadn't realised that he'd been drinking while he was out.

"Shut up, you fool!" Tom snapped, more conscious of our — my — sensibilities where Cho-Cho was concerned.

I quickly set the entire pizza down in front of Cho-Cho and snagged another one for myself. Evangeline had already claimed one of the prized pepperoni, although the other half seemed to have corn, spinach, and several chunks of mince hidden beneath a double-cheese blanket. She and Cho-Cho were now completely lost in their food, equally heedless of the strands of mozzarella and dribbles of tomato sauce trailing down their respective chins.

"Aha! Provisions!" Banquo led the way as the others surged into the kitchen, Jocasta

335

trailing behind them with a woebegone look. "Good man, good man." He nodded to Mick. "Don't know what I'd do without you."

"You won't have to," Mick said. "I'll always be there, backing you up."

I didn't like the look that swirled across the harpies' faces. It could be interpreted as: *we'll see about that.*

With a sudden cold chill, I saw that Mick had registered it, too. He frowned, as well he might. They had rid themselves of Melisande — were they now planning to dispose of anyone else who might have too much influence over Banquo?

"Jocasta isn't looking well," Nigel murmured in my ear. He had his own priorities to worry about. "They'll drive her into a nervous breakdown, working her so hard."

"That's what I'm afraid of." No point in telling him she was a willing victim. He didn't want to know, even though he was bitterly aware of it.

Tom, I noticed, had retreated to the far end of the table with his untouched pizza and was watching us all with a wary expression. Somehow, that increased my uneasiness. The mood in the room seemed to darken.

The sky was darkening, too, I realised.

More rain? How could there be any more left up there? But the wind was also brisker, blowing in a fresh supply from somewhere in the stratosphere. I began to shudder and it took a sheer effort of will to stop.

Only Banquo seemed immune to the atmosphere. He reached for his second pizza and tore into it with gusto, then swallowed and looked up.

"Anything to go with this?" he asked hopefully. "Beer? Chianti? Scotch?"

"Champagne?" a female voice suggested nastily.

"Try water!" Evangeline snapped. If anyone thought they could shame her into sharing what remained of our cache, they could think again.

"Try this —" Nigel was coaxing Jocasta. "You must eat."

"I'm not hungry . . . there's no time . . . there's so much to do." It was a muted wail. "I can't waste time . . ."

"Quite right," Isolde approved. "Time is short. Our deadline looms."

"So does mine!" Martha snapped.

"Yours —" An expressive shrug gave Isolde's opinion of anyone else's unimportant problems.

"Don't you dare shrug off —" Lunging forward in her fury, Martha stumbled against a discarded pile of photographs and sent them tumbling to the floor.

"Oh, dear!" Jocasta darted to help Martha gather up the photographs.

"Don't —" Tom tried to block her way. "I mean, I'll do it. I know the way they were sorted —" Too late.

"So do I." Jocasta riffled through them. "But — these are the rejects. We needn't bother — Oh, what's this? I haven't seen it before. I wouldn't have put it in the reject pile."

Sure enough, she was holding a contact sheet of the puppies and their mother. Her reaction was the same as mine.

"These are charming."

There was a nasty snicker from Mick and a dangerous light in his eyes when I turned to look at him.

"Leave it!" Tom warned, glaring at Mick.

"What is it?" Banquo's attention was caught. He glanced over and seemed to recognise what Jocasta was holding, despite Tom's effort to take it. "Oh, those —" He turned away dismissively, identifying competition, so cute they might divert attention from him. "They're not important."

"That's what I mean." Tom reached for the sheet again and captured a corner of it. "And besides, the focus isn't right. They

338

won't reproduce well."

Mick snickered again.

"You needn't worry about that." Jocasta wasn't letting go. "They can do so much with computer enhancement these days."

"Not *that* much." Tom had a firm grip on the contact sheet. "Isolde scribbled all over them." He tugged at the sheet again but Jocasta wouldn't let go.

That nasty snicker of Mick's was getting on my nerves. It hinted at things we didn't know — things we didn't want to know. Couldn't others see it?

It appeared not. The harpies had gone back to placidly stuffing themselves with pizza. Banquo was busy demolishing yet another — could it be his fourth? Martha was too caught up in her own annoyance. Evangeline didn't care.

Only Cho-Cho met my eyes with an expression that betrayed her own growing unease. She sensed there was something wrong, too. But neither of us knew what it was, or what we could do about it.

There was a sharp ripping sound. Jocasta and Tom stumbled back from each other, each clutching half of the contested contact sheet.

"Now look what you've done!" Mick jeered.

Cho-Cho abandoned her pizza — she'd licked the base clean anyway — and moved over to lean against my ankles. I bent and picked her up.

"It's all right." Jocasta glanced with satisfaction at the portion of contact sheet she retained. "Tom will have the negatives."

"I destroyed them," Tom said.

"It's all right." Evangeline had been looking through the rest of the pile of discards and found the three glossy prints I had originally discovered. "These are just perfect to use."

"Those are mine." Tom moved towards her. "I'm keeping them to remind me in case anyone ever tries to get me onto some loony expedition again."

"Which ones have you got?" Mick closed in on her other side and looked over her shoulder. "Ah, yes, they were fattening up nicely at that stage."

"Shut up!" Tom snarled.

Cho-Cho gave a convulsive shudder and shrank back against me. They say cats can pick up the images in one's mind and react to them. She was watching Mick in horror, still shivering.

Never mind cats, I was beginning to get a pretty nasty intuitive flash of my own. It couldn't be . . .

"Oh, stop all this nonsense!" Martha had her own priorities. "You've wasted enough time with these people, Jocasta. You promised me we'd test those cheese nibbles recipes today to decide which one we want to use — and we were going to test whether Rice Krispies were a good alternative to plain potato crisps."

All three Grace women seemed to explode in snorts and whinnies of contempt and derision. They sounded like a stableful of spooked old nags about to stampede. Mick gave his revolting snicker again.

I toyed with the idea of turning the coffeemaker back on and letting Martha do her worst.

"Banquo needs Jocasta far more than you do!" Isolde stopped whinnying and spoke for them all.

Jocasta seemed to shrivel within herself. She looked from Martha to Banquo and there was no doubt which one was going to win, even though it seemed to be against her sense of fair play.

"Tomorrow —" she began, clearly guilt-stricken.

"We'll need you tomorrow, too." Isolde was implacable; the others nodded their heads in agreement. "We must finish this as soon as possible. Time is getting short."

"Too right," Mick endorsed. "We've got to start getting our supplies lined up for the expedition."

Again that strangely eloquent silent communication seemed to sweep from cousin to cousin. Banquo excepted, of course.

"We'll want more spices this time, old boy." The presence of food all around him concentrated Banquo on the subject closer to his heart. "Lots more. We didn't have nearly enough for the little boys' stew this time."

"Little boys' stew?" Martha frowned at Jocasta, who frowned back, shaking her head. "I've never heard of that one. It must be something new — ?"

"Oldest in the world," Mick corrected, sneering. "You know: *What are little boys made of? Snips and snails and puppy dogs' tails —*"

"Mick!" Tom tried to call him to order, but Mick was enjoying this, he wasn't to be stopped.

"We weren't sure what snips were, and we couldn't count on finding snails where we were. But we had plenty of —"

"Puppy dogs' tails . . ." Jocasta finished faintly, staring down in horror at the photos in her hand.

Nigel urged her gently into a chair and

342

stood behind her, patting her shoulder.

"Of course, many people dock a dog's tail —" Edytha said dreamily. "And things mustn't go to waste in the . . ." She faltered to a stop under our accusing eyes.

"Good try," Evangeline said briskly, "but not good enough to save this situation."

"What's the matter?" Banquo couldn't understand what all the fuss was about.

"Of all those photos we sorted through, choosing the illustrations —" Jocasta's voice was still faint, but gaining strength. "I didn't see any of the adult dogs without tails. "Unless" — she looked hopefully to Tom — "you still have some I haven't seen?"

"Anything you haven't seen," he said grimly, "you wouldn't want to see."

"We should have had lots more dried onion flakes." Banquo was lost in thoughtful reminiscence. "And perhaps some oregano, or do I mean sage?" He sighed deeply. "Melisande would have known."

"Melisande wouldn't have told you, even if she did know," Mick reminded him brutally. "She didn't want you out on the ice. She wanted you by her side every minute. She didn't understand a free spirit. She didn't care that you'd be bored, stagnating . . . nothing mattered to her except keeping you tied to her apron strings."

"It wasn't that bad," Banquo said. "You don't understand —"

"Don't I?" Mick's face was ugly. "I know she was planning to pull the plug on your funding to keep you in line."

"Just what *did* happen to those puppies?" Jocasta interrupted in a chill remote voice. "Apart from their tails, that is."

"Roasted, grilled, fried." Mick's unpleasant grin was the sort that invited you to take what he said as a joke. Except that it wasn't. "Boiled in a bag."

Someone retched audibly. I thought it was Nigel, then realised it was Tom. I remembered his hatred of boiled-in-the-bag meals. He had good reason.

"That's disgusting!" Martha was looking rather queasy herself.

"You don't want the recipes?" Mick jeered. "They'd spice up your dull old cookbook no end."

"What's the matter?" Banquo was still baffled. He looked from Jocasta's ashen face to Isolde's warning frown.

"Not now, dear," Edytha said. "We'll talk about it later."

"But —"

"Forget it," Mick advised. "We've got more important things to think about."

"What happened to the mother dog?" I

wanted to know. I had the nasty feeling that I hadn't seen her in any of the other pictures.

No one spoke for a moment. That said more than anything.

"She . . . took exception to . . . to what was happening to her puppies." Tom's voice was tight, as though he were fighting nausea. "They — She —"

"We had to take care of her." Mick grimaced. "Her meat was as tough as she was."

But not as tough as he was. Tough, callous, icily calculating — and single-minded. What had he said? Something about nothing counts except Banquo. The meal ticket, while he was the hanger-on. We'd seen a lot of them in show biz: the yes-men, the enablers, the entourage.

Tom made an indistinct noise in his throat, clutching his camera as though it were a life-support system. Perhaps, for him, it was. I felt a renewed sympathy for him. There he'd been, the lone adult, out on the ice with the boys' adventure team acting out their male fantasies, growing wilder and more extravagant with every sortie. No wonder he was getting out.

"How could you?" Jocasta choked. "How could you?"

Nigel bent to put his arm around her

345

shoulders, while he backed her sentiments with a censorious head shaking.

"What's the matter with everybody?" Aggrieved, Banquo appealed to his cousins. "All I did was follow in the tradition of the great explorers — the great survivors. They did it and they were heroes. I do it and you all treat me like some kind of . . . of criminal."

"Try monster," Evangeline suggested helpfully.

"Ignore them," Mick said. "Who cares what they think?"

"We foretell public opinion on this," Evangeline pointed out, mildly for her. "If this gets out."

A shadow crossed Edytha's face.

"That's all very well" — Isolde was ready to dismiss the subject — "but all that's for the next book. This little . . . episode . . . was only a trial run for the real thing."

They were all monsters! Inhuman! That "little episode" was the destruction of beautiful innocent creatures who had been coldly included in the expedition for that express purpose. And they were planning to do it again. Just to satisfy the grotesque fantasies of a mad ego.

"Next time," Isolde encouraged, "you'll be able to get public sympathy on your side by describing the desperation, the peril, that forced you to such desperate measures —"

"With tears in his eyes, no doubt," Evangeline prodded.

"As a matter of fact, yes!" Isolde snapped.

"What else?" The mockery was from Mick. Tom's teeth were clenched. Even though he was soon to be free of them all, he was pale with the memory of the senseless slaughter.

"It will be most touching," Valeria trumpeted. "In the next book. Melisande's death was quite enough tragedy for one expedition."

"Dearest Melisande," Banquo brooded. "There'll never be anyone else for me."

Jocasta heard this impassively, I was pleased to note.

"Now that's settled," Isolde said briskly. "Let's get back to work. Come along, Jocasta, there's a difficult chapter to untangle. Poor Banquo's fingers were nearly frozen writing it and the handwriting shows it. Perhaps we could include a photo of the original pages among the illustrations —"

"I'm not coming." Jocasta stood and faced them, squaring her shoulders. "I resign."

CHAPTER TWENTY-EIGHT

I had all I could do not to cheer.

"My cookbook —" Martha protested.

"Oh, I'll work with *you*," Jocasta assured her. "But not with them! Never again!"

"How dare you!" Isolde snarled. "I am not without influence. You'll come with us right now and see this book through to its conclusion or I'll make it my personal business to see that you never get a job again!"

"You'll have your work cut out for you, then," Evangeline said. "It's a big world with lots of jobs in it. And influence can only reach so far — even for a goddess."

"Ah. Very true," Nigel said. "In fact, we're going to need a good assistant at the Jewel Box — and Bertie likes you already."

"Now, now," Edytha cooed, fluttering her draperies like an anxious dove ruffling its feathers. "Let's not be hasty. We're all a bit tense right now. We must take deep breaths and calm ourselves. Surely we can come to some agreement with so much at stake."

"Don't worry," Jocasta said coldly. "I'll see that you get a replacement for me right away. She'll be here in the morning."

"That's not good enough!" Isolde was not to be placated.

"No, no," Edytha cried. "That's not the right attitude. Everything has been going so well. We must sleep on it and I'm sure we'll be able to reach a compromise in the morning."

"You may be right." Obviously against her better judgement, Valeria decided they had better retreat for the moment. "Poor Jocasta is just overtired. Perhaps a day or two of rest will help her reconsider . . ."

They were going to try sweetness and light as a tactic. It was a gruesome sight.

"She's been doing so well," Edytha said, giving Isolde the sort of look that meant it was her turn to say something nice.

"Yes . . . brilliantly . . . really impressive." Isolde joined the toadying. She did it rather well, for her; you could barely hear her teeth grinding. "It would be a shame to abandon it all now, when we're so near the end."

"Quite so." Valeria bared her teeth, unfortunately projecting something more like *the better to eat you with* than sympathetic understanding. "And I'm sure we might even manage —"

"You can manage without me." Jocasta turned away. "Where shall I tell the editorial department to send my replacement?"

"Why, here, of course." Edytha seemed surprised at the question.

"No!" Evangeline set her straight. "Not here. You're leaving here now. All of you. If Jocasta isn't working with you, there's no reason for you to be here in the morning. You can start clearing your things out now." She hunched forward, thrust her hands into her jacket pockets, and glowered at them, managing to look incredibly menacing.

"But we can't!" Edytha was aghast. "We're at the most delicate stage of Banquo's story. He can't have all that disruption. We can't do without Jocasta. We can't —"

"Try," Evangeline advised. "You'd be surprised at what you can do, if you try."

"But we have no transport —" Edytha was going down fighting. "We'd need a van. These things take time to arrange."

"I'll order a van for you." Evangeline began to remove one hand from her pocket, then seemed to think better of it. Perhaps she realised she might throttle one of them if her hands were free.

"But it's going to rain —" Edytha gestured to the window as though she were playing a trump card. "There's going to be another dreadful storm. You can't send us out into that."

"Face it, ladies." Mick was openly gloating over their consternation. "The welcome mat is being pulled out from under you."

"What welcome mat?" Martha snapped. "There never was one. They . . . they foisted themselves on us. And why you ever allowed it, Mother —"

"Now that's too much!" I protested. "It wasn't my doing —"

"It's *my* fault," Jocasta admitted. "If my cooker hadn't broken down, if there hadn't been all that trouble with the gas supply just when we needed to start testing the recipes —"

And if she hadn't been on the run from these harpies to begin with — but she seemed to have forgotten that. I wasn't going to remind her, she was guilt-stricken enough.

"The point is —" Isolde wrested us back to reality. "Time is running out."

"That's another thing." Martha looked at me uneasily. "Ours is running out even faster. Mother, I meant to tell you —"

"Don't all rush to take the blame, girls —" Mick called out. "There's enough to go around."

351

"We have a crisis pending at the childrens' school," Martha said. "The board of governors are having a meeting about it today, but everyone is pretty certain what the result will be."

"We have to get this to the printer immediately," Isolde interrupted. "The book must be out in time for the tour in the autumn."

"What tour?" Mick abruptly stopped enjoying himself. He looked at them suspiciously. "We're on our way back to the ice in the autumn."

"Yes, yes —" Valeria brushed him aside. "But next year — not this year. This year Banquo is touring America with this marvellous lecture bureau we've signed up with. He'll be in the Midwest all winter and the East Coast in the spring talking about his expeditions. The bureau believes he'll pull in the crowd with his talk: *So You Think This Is Cold?* Or possibly *You Call This Cold?* We haven't decided on the title yet, but we must have books available to sell at the close of each lecture. They should sell like hotcakes."

"But-but," Mick stuttered. "But he doesn't need the money. He's got bags of it from Melisande's estate."

"It's not all that much." Isolde pursed her lips; nothing would ever be enough for her.

"And it will take time to come through probate. Then there are the lawyers' fees and costs. And there's some stupid sort of ancient entailment, so that the lands involved have to go to a male blood relation. If Melisande had had a son, there'd be no problem. As it is, there's a search on for some distant male relative supposed to be living in the Antipodes, or perhaps the South Seas. We'll fight it, of course, but —" She shrugged.

"A son," Banquo mourned. "We hadn't time enough. There was the expedition to mount and . . . and . . ."

"There, there, dear." Edytha patted his shoulder. "Be brave. We must look to the future. This lecture tour will be a fresh start . . . away from memories . . . away from empty ice fields where you have too much time to think . . . to brood . . ."

"Wait a minute —" Mick was growing increasingly restive. "What about our plans? We were due to leave in the autumn —"

"Yes, yes, but we told you, not this autumn." Valeria was dismissive. "Next year, perhaps. Banquo needs a complete change of scene to recover himself. Lots of people around to distract him. Fine restaurants . . . exciting shopping . . . lovely luxury hotels . . ." She was practically drooling. "Oh, we'll have a marvellous time."

So they were planning to accompany him. How could I have doubted it? They were going to have themselves a marvellous time all right. For poor Mick, it would be hell on earth. Unless . . .

"I feel —" Edytha looked raptly into the distance. "I feel that Melisande would have truly wanted you to do this, dear. She always thought you should have another string to your bow — that was why she was so keen to have you do more cooking with her. I can feel her smiling down on us . . . What a tragedy that she can't be here to come with us . . ." There was genuine regret in her voice. "You would have made such an inspiring couple. And, with us to guide you both —"

I felt my preconvictions shifting. There was even a trace of anger as Edytha's far-off gaze turned accusatory. "If only she hadn't had that fatal weakness. We could have built a wonderful . . ." She trailed off, perhaps undecided as to whether to say "business" or "empire."

Perhaps they hadn't wanted Melisande dead, after all. She'd have been more use to them alive, her fortune readily accessible, her culinary career on the rise. And, in the suggestible states, she'd have drawn prospective goddess fodder into their net as they assisted her — and advertised themselves.

"You're not really going to do this, are you?" Mick appealed directly to Banquo, who would not meet his eyes.

"It will be much the best thing for him," Edytha said. "He needs time to heal . . . to restore himself . . . to —"

"To make a lot of money," Isolde cut in. "It's going to be very lucrative, we can't afford to miss the opportunity."

"And the lecture bureau is sure that there'll be television opportunities, too." Edytha was lost in dreams. "Chat shows, at first, and then perhaps, even his own —"

"That sounds," Mick spoke in slow measured tones, "like we may be gone for some time."

Banquo blinked uncertainly, not sure whether that was a quotation or just accidentally phrased.

Any nuances in the conversation left the harpies blissfully oblivious. They had their own concerns and pointed glances flew among them.

"Actually —" It seemed to have been decided that Valeria should act as spokeswoman. "Actually, *we* —" She emphasised the word, leaving no doubt as to whom it included. "*We* may quite possibly be gone for an indefinite period. It all depends on how things work out."

"We'll call you as soon as we get back," Edytha cooed soothingly. "Don't worry."

And don't call us — we'll call you. Even Mick knew how that one went.

"I see." Mick barely inclined his head. "That's just about what I was figuring."

An unpleasant silence hung in the room. The harpies moved closer together and I found that Evangeline, Martha, and I had edged nearer to Nigel and Jocasta. The groups were polarising and it was not up to us to intrude on this little confrontation. In fact, I wished we weren't there at all.

Tom stood alone in the corner with his camera. I began to lose any faint hope that he might intervene as peacemaker.

"What about you?" Mick turned to challenge Tom. "They're taking you with them, I suppose, to get their precious pictures."

"I'm not going anywhere. This is the first I've heard about this scheme." Tom drew a deep breath. "But I've made other plans, anyway. I'm staying in London."

"Oh, but we told the lecture bureau we had our own photographer," Edytha protested.

"No, thanks." For a moment, Tom's smile

was as unpleasant as Mick's. "I have better plans already in place."

"You — you can't *do* this!" Isolde was outraged. All the crew were jumping ship. Except the one she really wanted to get rid of — he seemed determined to put up a fight.

"*You* knew!" Mick accused Banquo.

"No. No . . ." Banquo squirmed, still unwilling to meet his eyes. "It . . . it was just . . . a vague idea . . . of Melisande's. I didn't think it would come to anything. It was all up in the air. Melisande wanted —"

"Damn Melisande!" Mick snarled. "She was nothing but trouble from the beginning. The bitch got what she deserved! I'm glad —" He broke off, but too late.

I'm glad I killed her! hung in the air, as distinctly as though it had been said. Even Banquo got it.

"*You!* You killed Melisande!" Banquo launched himself forward, propelled by fury. "I'll kill *you!*"

"Hold it right there!" How long had Mick been carrying that gun? We stared at it disbelievingly.

"Where did you get that gun?" Evangeline trumpeted in a voice that reverberated from the high ceiling.

If she had been trying to startle him into

357

dropping it, she nearly succeeded.

"Don't move — any of you!" He had twitched, but recovered himself, gripping the gun tighter than ever.

"I suppose you killed Teddy, too," the voice of doom announced. I wish he'd included mouths in that command not to move. Evangeline couldn't keep hers shut.

"Shut up!" *Now* he said it. The gun veered towards her dangerously.

"Why?" She got the word out just ahead of his order.

"He had it coming," Mick snapped. "He got on my nerves."

"Also," Tom spoke slowly and thoughtfully, as though some things were just beginning to make sense to him, "Mick drank more than his share of that wine you sent down to us when we were stuck in the lift. It was a long night. He began talking too much . . . rambling . . . ranting. I dozed off. I'd heard it all before — or thought I had. When I woke, he was still talking . . . hinting at I don't know what. I dozed again. I guess Teddy kept listening — and he wasn't as dumb as Mick thought he was."

"You can shut up, too!" The gun moved to point at Tom. "None of you move. None of you talk." He muttered, almost to himself: "I've got to think."

358

CHAPTER TWENTY-NINE

He had a lot to think about. And so did we.

One mad sociopath who'd finally snapped, holding ten civilised people at bay.

He'd clearly killed twice already — he had nothing to lose.

It looked as though we were destined to be tomorrow morning's headlines. London's own massacre. Another crazed gunman mowing down everyone in sight.

Evangeline and I exchanged looks. We'd been in this situation — or one similar to it — often enough before, in practically every B picture we'd ever made. But we'd always had a script behind us and a director waiting to call: "Cut!"

This time we were on our own.

Except that there were all these other people around. If we banded together . . . if they weren't too traumatised . . . how many would be taken out before —

"I should have known —" Isolde had been

thinking along her own lines. "*You* were in charge of supplies, you were always in and out of the storeroom where Melisande kept her demonstration equipment." She glared at Mick. "You contaminated her supplies."

"Ground almonds in the flour and walnut oil in the olive oil," Evangeline clarified helpfully — and loudly.

"Beast!" Isolde was equally loud. "Monster!" She looked as though she might rush him.

"Shut up!" Mick turned the gun on her. "All of you!"

I became aware of a stealthy movement from Tom's corner and my hopes rose. Until I heard the telltale *click*.

Oh, great! We might all be slaughtered, but there'd be some prizewinning photos left behind recording the event. Too bad Tom wasn't going to live to claim the credit — and all the syndication payments for them.

Another stealthy movement beside us. Nigel had unobtrusively stepped in front of Jocasta to try to shield her.

I wished I didn't know that one bullet could take out two people standing that close to each other.

Meanwhile, Banquo was trying to shuffle behind Valeria, the largest of his cousins.

My hero!

"Stop! Stop right there!" Mick shouted hysterically. "You're moving! Nobody move!"

Click. The sound was covered by Mick's ragged breathing. He stared around wildly, beginning to realise the situation he'd got himself into.

He was as trapped as the rest of us.

Stalemate.

"You'll never get away with this." Isolde ignored the no-talking ban. "Give up and go away!"

"You'd like that, wouldn't you? That was what you all wanted — me to go away."

"Really, dear." Edytha seemed determined to be the voice of sweet reason — or else she had a death wish. "You're being very silly, you know. You're hugely outnumbered and —" She inched forward.

"Get out of the way! Yes, you!" This time the *click* was from the gun and it sounded ominous. He waved Valeria aside, leaving Banquo exposed.

"The first one who moves, I'll shoot Banquo!"

The cousins froze.

"You wouldn't —" The threat stunned Banquo. "Mick, you couldn't —"

"Oh, couldn't I?" With a victim so blatantly terrorised, Mick felt more in control. "Try me!"

No one took him up on his offer. Nervously, I saw that Martha was scanning the kitchen for likely objects to hurl at him the moment an opportunity arose. I tried to sidle in front of Martha and, at that moment, I realised I was still clasping Cho-Cho to my bosom. This wouldn't do. No point in an innocent cat intercepting a bullet. She was the least real danger to Mick of us all. *She* couldn't testify.

Bidding her a silent sad farewell, I relaxed my hold and let her slip to the floor. All other doors closed, she scampered in the direction of the drawing room.

"Where's that cat going?" Mick demanded.

"To call the police, of course!" Evangeline snapped.

For a split second, he almost believed her. Then his face darkened, but not as much as the sky. Rain was close now. If only we could have a full-fledged thunderstorm with lots of lightning and thunderclaps, perhaps Mick might be distracted —

Too much to hope for. His suspicious gaze kept sweeping over us. That was when he noticed that Martha was inches away from a large pottery casserole with a heavy lid.

"That does it!" He'd already experienced her throwing arm. "Move in closer together. All of you —" He waved the gun at us. It looked awfully businesslike and not like any I had seen before. I wondered if it was one of those semiautomatic ones, where you could forget about counting six shots and know they'd run out of ammunition. This looked like the sort that just kept spraying bursts of bullets until no one was left standing.

"Turn around —" Mick ordered. "We're moving into the front room." Where there weren't so many small heavy objects that could be used as weapons.

"You three —" He gestured with his gun at the harpies. "Lead the way. Tom, behind them. Then you . . . and you . . ."

Martha, Jocasta, and Nigel fell into line. Evangeline and I brought up the rear, where he could keep a mistrustful eye on her.

At first, I thought it was my heart thudding, then saw that the rain had started. Not the hoped-for thunderstorm, but a steady tropical downpour without pyrotechnics, just flooding.

"What about me!" Banquo obviously had visions of being left behind — slumped on the floor.

"You're my insurance policy. You walk

with me. Remember," he warned us, "any funny business and Banquo gets the first bullet."

There was a flutter of consternation from his cousins. The rest of us took the news stolidly. I swear Evangeline was biting back a smile at the thought.

"Okay — move! *Mush!*" Mick gave a grotesque laugh as he shouted out the command traditionally given to sled dogs to start them running. *"Mush, you bitches! Mush!"*

With much stumbling and backwards glances, the harpies moved forward slowly, reluctantly leading our parade. The rain had settled down to a steady drumming. I tried not to think of funeral marches.

Evangeline and I locked glances. I knew that, like me, she must be frantically reviewing every film she had ever starred in to find some clue as to how to get out of this situation.

Unfortunately, most of our scripts had involved seducing the gunman who, naturally, had cherished a mad passion for us from the first reel. These days, even more unfortunately, we were a decade or three beyond the seducing ploy. Apart from which, I somehow doubted that Mick had ever fallen for such a trick.

The enormous floor-to-ceiling windows in the drawing room usually provided a glorious panorama of the Thames. Right now, however, all they revealed was gloom beyond the blinding sheet of rain curtaining the windows.

"Right." Mick looked around with satisfaction: no small objects that could be thrown. Only piles of paper — no threat there. "Now sit." He waved the gun towards the twin sofas.

"Sit!" We weren't obeying fast enough to suit him. His temper was fraying again.

"Not you!" Banquo was starting forward hopefully. "You stay with me. The rest of you — SIT!"

The rest of us moved to the sofas and lowered ourselves gingerly to sit on the edge. Nigel steered Jocasta to a corner seat, then perched on the armrest by her side. He was obviously planning to throw himself across her to shield her when the shooting started. Jocasta smiled tremulously and reached for his hand, clasping it tightly.

"You, too —" Mick snarled at Nigel. "On the seat. Everybody sit back — all the way back. Lean against the back of it." His mouth twisted in a terrible mirthless rictus. "Make yourselves comfortable."

He might be mad — but he wasn't stupid.

Packed in like sardines and as far back as we could go, there was no way any of us could launch a sudden attack now. We'd be shot down before we could even struggle to our feet.

Click. I sent Tom a sour look. Too bad he wouldn't be around to caption the resulting photo. Something like: *Last few minutes of their lives,* perhaps. The police photographer would get the aftermath, showing all the blood and sprawled bodies.

On the sofa opposite, Isolde moved her feet uneasily.

"Don't try anything!" Mick aimed at her, then swung the gun back as Banquo twitched and froze.

From where I sat I could see the reason for Isolde's sudden unwise movement. A pair of small bright eyes looked back at me from behind her ankles. That cold wet inquisitive nose thrust against her ankles had been the reason for her convulsive movement.

Go back . . . I implored Cho-Cho with all the concentration I could muster. *Don't let him see you. He doesn't like you anyway. He'll hurt you . . . kill you . . .*

The little head moved back and disappeared. Had she received my message? Did she understand?

After that, the silence seemed to go on forever. Evangeline began sneaking impatient peeks at her watch. That made me even more nervous. If she ran true to form, at any moment she would snap out *"Oh, hurry up!"* or *"Get on with it!"* or something equally fatal. I tried to concentrate on willing her to keep her mouth shut.

"Mick, old boy . . ." But it was Banquo who broke the threatening silence. "Be reasonable, old chap. Put that gun away and we'll forget all this and never mention it again."

Some hope! Mick's harsh bark of laughter said he didn't believe it, either. How could he? Now that all of us knew that he'd committed two murders. No one was going to keep quiet about that if he was fool enough to let us go.

"Liar! You were going to let them dump me!" In a sudden explosive burst of rage, Mick raised the gun and struck Banquo a savage blow in the face. Banquo staggered back, but not fast enough to escape a second blow. Blood spurted from what might have been a broken nose or tooth. What difference did it make? Now that Mick had been provoked into once shedding blood, we were all doomed.

There was a sharp *ping,* as of a spring giving way under the accumulated weight on the other sofa. Perhaps one of the harpies had shifted as a prelude to rushing to Banquo's aid. If so, the look on Mick's face would have changed her mind. It was not the moment for anyone to draw attention to themselves.

Curiosity killed the cat. Oh, no, no, not that! Drawn by the atmosphere in the room, and perhaps the smell of blood, Cho-Cho had crept out from under the sofa to come and see what was going on.

She was directly behind Mick now, sniffing at his heels. My only consolation was the thought that he couldn't shoot her without shooting himself in the foot. And he wasn't quite that crazy. I hoped. *But he was crazy* — and now bloodlust had set in. He stared at the blood running down Banquo's face as though mesmerised. A cold vicious smile curved his lips.

"Yes . . ." He aimed the gun at Banquo. "Yes . . ." He had reached the point where he was hyped-up enough to begin shooting. He took a step backwards for a better shot.

"MRREEOW!" He'd stepped on Cho-Cho and stumbled. Furious at this treatment, she wrapped herself around one ankle, digging in claws and teeth. I watched transfixed as my cuddly little geisha cat turned into a

battling Samurai warrior.

On one leg and trying to shake her off the other, Mick swayed, perilously. The gun, already cocked, let off a fusillade of shots.

Deafened by the gun, I barely heard the crash of breaking glass. Banquo dived to the floor and began crawling towards the door.

Between the recoil from the gun and the attacking Cho-Cho, Mick had tumbled to the ground, still trying to escape those deadly little teeth and claws. They turned into the least of his troubles when the Avenging Furies swept down on him. Try to kill their precious Banquo, would he?

Valeria sent a vicious kick to his head, Isolde jumped on his stomach.

"Are you all right, dear?" Edytha ran to Banquo, still on his hands and knees, halfway to the door. "You weren't shot?" She inspected him closely. "The flying glass didn't cut you? Speak to me —"

"I was just going to get help." He mumbled his alibi feebly.

"Don't bother," Evangeline said. "I've got Ron on speed dial —"

She pulled the cell phone from her pocket. "We've been broadcasting since Mick pulled the gun —"

"That was why you were shouting so." Now it made sense.

"He should be here any minute," she said smugly.

"Let me up . . ." Mick groaned. "Get these nuts off me . . ."

"Nuts . . ." Valeria moved to kick him again, this time in the spot he had carelessly reminded her about.

He howled and doubled up — as much as he was able to with Isolde kneeling on his stomach.

Click — click . . . click . . . Tom's camera was going to be red-hot at this pace.

"Wait! Wait!" Banquo scrambled to his feet and rushed over to elbow Valeria aside.

"Get this, Tom!" he shouted, placing one foot on Mick's head and adopting the traditional Great White Hunter pose.

"The blood — all that blood —" Edytha protested, trying to mop at it. "You must look your best."

"Leave it!" He pushed her away. "Get down, Isolde. Out of camera shot!" She obligingly flattened herself across Mick's body, keeping him pinned down.

Click . . . click . . . click. "Great!" Tom called enthusiastically. "Now look down at him —" *Click.* "Now, chin up and look at me —" *Click.* "Smile — just a little — job well done, smile —" *Click.*

They were all mad. Outside, a police siren

wailed closer, then stopped abruptly, as though someone had realised that the sound might set off the massacre they were trying to prevent.

"Got enough?" Banquo asked. Mick was beginning to stir, moving his head too much under the not-so-firm foot.

"I think so, but I need to reload. You can relax in a minute. We've got some great stuff."

"Yes." Banquo was complacent. "I thought so. It should make a great frontispiece. Probably the cover." He looked to Jocasta. "What do you think?"

Jocasta turned away in revulsion, clinging to Nigel and burrowing her head into his shoulder. Nigel's arms tightened around her and across his face spread the amazed and gratified look of a man who has achieved his greatest ambition against all the odds.

"Urrgg . . ." A deep groan from Mick signalled that he was regaining conscious-ness. "Take them away . . . make them leave me alone . . . I want to get up . . ."

"You stay where you are." Evangeline looked at him coldly.

"So we were wrong to think Frella might have killed Teddy because she came back to the scene of the crime," I said.

"Unlikely as it seems, the woman has a

371

sentimental streak," Evangeline said. "She was just saying good-bye to him."

I shivered, not just in sympathy. I was cold. In fact, we were all cold — and increasingly damp. I looked across to the few shards of glass still clinging in the window frames, no impediment to the wind and rain at all.

"Oh, heavens — Jasper!" I gasped.

"I hope his insurance is up to date," Evangeline said.

"He's going to be furious, anyway." I stated the obvious.

"So he is." We gazed at each other thoughtfully. "You know, Trixie, I think we owe ourselves a little vacation after all this. Get away for a bit while the repairs are being done. Warmth, sun, blue skies . . . I have some business I really should see to in California —"

"I'm not sure I want to go that far —" I began. California was another world, another life, away from everything I cherished now. Cho-Cho finished cleaning and grooming herself and strolled over to reclaim her place in my arms.

"Mother, there was something I wanted to tell you before all this —" Martha cast a disparaging gaze over the confusion as Ron and his colleagues began hammering at the door. Jocasta fled to answer it, Nigel so close they might have been glued together. My mind began turning towards wedding presents . . .

"Mother, are you listening?" Martha called me to order. "This is important. They're going to close the children's school for two weeks. So many teachers are down with the flu that it's easier to close than to try to carry on. I've booked a holiday for them in Croatia, where the au pair comes from, but I'm afraid she may have too many distractions in her hometown to look after the children properly. And I can't get away right now —"

"I'd love to!" I could see where she was heading and I cut to the chase. "It sounds wonderful. Wouldn't you rather come along, Evangeline, than go to California?"

Evangeline sniffed and went to greet Ron as he entered with his team, all looking around uneasily.

"It's all right," Evangeline told them. "We have the situation under control now."

"So I see." Ron surveyed the scene glumly. "Can't you ever control a situation without resorting to mayhem?" He stared at Mick's bloodied face.

"It wasn't us, Ron," Evangeline protested. "It was them." She swept out a hand indicating the Graces. "I swear it was."

"I believe you." He leaped suddenly to pry Valeria's fingers from Mick's throat, where her thumbs were digging into his windpipe with deadly intent.

"Please, Madam." He lifted her to her feet. "Not in front of us. We'd have to charge you with grievous bodily harm."

"He was going to kill us — all of us!" Valeria blustered "It's self-defence!"

"He's in no condition to harm anyone right now." Ron nodded to one of his men, who advanced to handcuff the semi-conscious Mick. "Get him to the station and have the medics ready to check him out."

"Where are the press?" Banquo demanded, striding over to us. "That man killed my wife! He admitted it. I want to make a statement to the media!"

"We're not the army. We don't have journalists embedded in our units." Ron's assessing gaze correctly pinpointed Banquo as a first-class publicity hound. "No doubt they'll be along . . . eventually."

"Eventually!" That wasn't good enough for Banquo. "But I'm ready now!"

"In that case, we'll take your statement now . . . sir." Ron nodded to his team again and another man moved forward, notebook in hand.

"I have nothing to say to *you*." Banquo drew himself up stiffly. "I speak to the *world!*"

"Banquo, dear —" Edytha advanced on him, scarves fluttering in the icy wind blowing in through the broken window. "You're overwrought. Traumatised. This has been such an ordeal. To discover such treachery, such disloyalty — and in people you trusted with your life." Her glance swept from the doorway through which Mick had been assisted to encompass Jocasta, obviously including her among the traitors.

"We must take you home, where you can rest properly." Edytha patted his arm consolingly. "We can call a press conference for tomorrow."

"Yes . . . yes," Banquo murmured, taking his cue. "Then I can tell them how I single-handedly rescued my friends and family from the clutches of a crazed gunman and avenged my precious wife."

With a long-suffering look, Ron blocked their path as they started for the door.

"I wouldn't advise telling anyone that nonsense," Evangeline said crisply. "Try it and we'll hold a press conference of our own and tell the 'world' what really happened."

"Never mind the world," Ron said. "Suppose you start with me."

"You know what happened," Isolde said. "Banquo just told you." The three Graces had surrounded Banquo, protecting him, imprisoning him. "Now let us pass."

"People tell me a lot of things," Ron said wearily. "But I haven't heard from everyone yet."

"You can't expect to hear any truth from *them!*" Valeria sneered at us. "They hate poor Banquo."

"No," Jocasta corrected her. "We just despise him."

"Oh!" Edytha clutched at her heart. "How can you, of all people, say such a dreadful thing."

"She speaks for all of us," Martha said. "And Tom was busy with his camera all through this nightmare. So we have a photographic record to prove what actually happened."

"No!" Isolde screamed in denial.

"Sneak!" Valeria exploded at Tom. "They're all sneaks! Not one of them can be trusted!"

"Monstrous!" Edytha was clutching at her heart even more dramatically. She was going to find bruises in the morning.

A piercing whistle cut through the uproar — Ron was calling us to order.

376

"Right!" he said. "We're all going back to the station. You will be kept apart and interviewed one at a time."

The Graces burst into a torrent of protests.

"Sounds all right to me," Evangeline said cheerfully.

"At last we'll be warm again." I held Cho-Cho closer. "And those pictures will give Cho-Cho the proper credit for distracting Mick at the crucial time."

"Come along . . ." Ron's team were herding the others into line.

Chillingly, I saw that they were automatically lining up in the order Mick had assigned to them. His influence had been stronger than anyone had realised.

Click. And, even now, Tom was still recording everything. He deserved the success that was waiting for him.

ABOUT THE AUTHOR

Marian Babson was born in Salem, Massachusetts, but has lived in London for the greater part of her life. She is the author of more than 30 mysteries.

The employees of Thorndike Press hope you have enjoyed this Large Print book. All our Thorndike, Wheeler, and Kennebec Large Print titles are designed for easy reading, and all our books are made to last. Other Thorndike Press Large Print books are available at your library, through selected bookstores, or directly from us.

For information about titles, please call:
 (800) 223-1244

or visit our Web site at:
 http://gale.cengage.com/thorndike

To share your comments, please write:
 Publisher
 Thorndike Press
 10 Water St., Suite 310
 Waterville, ME 04901